SO LITTLE TO GO ON

SO LITTLE TO GO ON

D M Dickinson

Matador
9 Priory Business Park,
Wistow Road, Kibworth Beauchamp,
Leicestershire. LE8 0RX
Tel: 0116 279 2299
Email: books@troubador.co.uk
Web: www.troubador.co.uk/matador
Twitter: @matadorbooks

ISBN 978 1800462 533

British Library Cataloguing in Publication Data.
A catalogue record for this book is available from the British Library.

Printed and bound in Great Britain by 4edge Limited
Typeset in 12pt Adobe Garamond Pro by Troubador Publishing Ltd, Leicester, UK

Matador is an imprint of Troubador Publishing Ltd

To Hilary, Johnny, Kate and Joe with love.

The Travellers

Dieter – economist/development consultant
Frieda – entomologist
Jalal – civil engineer
Leandro – journalist and poet
Magome – administrator/civil servant
Mama Ulemu – peasant farmer
Mathew – priest
Nita – volunteer biology teacher (the narrator)
Nyezi – palaeoecologist
Radhika – architect.
Reece – (does not offer details of his work)
Sven – doctor/epidemiologist
Tom – primary school teacher
Vernon – archaeologist
Zak – businessman (involved in extraction)
Zehra – heterodox economist/civil servant

1

Departure

Since the bus hit the mine a few weeks back I had been haunted by images of horror. They kept invading my mind, clear and repetitive like memories, even though the blast happened ten miles away and I had seen nothing but a few pictures of the wreck. Fortunately, no one I knew had been on that bus but I did not need anyone to describe to me what the journey would have been like. I had travelled that route myself several times, squashed in with an excess load of passengers, encroached on by children and by knobbly bundles from which chickens hung. So far I had always been given a bit of seat and would sit there trying to shrink myself and longing for the consolation of arrival, the moment of jumping down and breathing freely. It troubled me that the travellers in the blown up bus had been denied that consolation and instead were repaid for hours of moderate misery by sudden pain and terror. Where the blast was strongest bodies must have mingled indistinguishably one with another and survivors at the back would have seen this.

'Stop it,' I said to myself, aware that this was not a healthy train of thought to follow while travelling the same potentially mined road. This time I was riding in relative comfort, the only passenger in a jeep. But that did not reduce my fear. I tried exerting some philosophical distance by asking myself why the thought of being blown to bits is worse than that of being killed tidily. I could not find a rational answer but all the same felt certain that my mother would mind whether she received a whole dead daughter or box of unrecognisable remains. It then occurred to me that in reality, if I died in the present circumstances, my parents would be unlikely to receive anything except a phone call or perhaps a visit of some kind. Who would have the task of telling them? I wondered.

'Stop it,' I said to myself again as I stared out though the dusty windscreen. My fear had evolved into a superstitious ritual whereby I had to glare at the road ahead, willing it to cover no mine, and then switch my gaze to the approaching trees, commanding them to conceal no ambush. I'd been up early to leave at dawn and, as the day warmed, I had to fight a tendency to slip back into my interrupted sleep. If my concentration lapsed, death could burst upon us. I ridiculed the idea but continued to be ruled by it so that as soon as I dozed, lulled by the jeep's vibration and the monotony of passing forest, I would jerk awake in guilty fear to return to my self-imposed vigil.

There are few distinctive landmarks on the way to the provincial capital, Mufalenge. The road is mostly straight, a strip of disintegrating tarmac cutting through unchanging forest, which now and then gives way to cultivated plots beyond which the grass roofs of a village may be seen, and by the roadside there will be a tea stall or two, men chatting and women sitting on mats selling things. We were travelling much faster than the bus and I was unsure how far we had gone until the jeep suddenly turned off the road onto a gritty and slightly rutted track where we bounced about, kicking up a thick trail of dust as we passed some small houses half hidden by banana trees. I recognised the short cut to the airstrip, which would bring us out directly by the terminal. The sight of this shabby little building brought such an immediate sense of relief that it was as if a switch had been flicked in my body extinguishing the fear and tension of the last few hours. By the time we had pulled up and John, the driver, was getting out my case, thoughts of violent death had almost entirely been replaced by minor anxieties about the likely state of the toilet and whether the snack bar would be open.

The small waiting area was crowded and it was clear from the bundles of luggage that no one had yet checked in. The number of prospective passengers was disconcerting, as it seemed unlikely they would all fit into a tiny plane like the one that had brought me here. I looked around hoping to see someone I knew. Mufalenge is a small town and in two brief visits I had met all the British and most of the other foreigners attached to NGOs or aid programmes. Assuming that most of the foreigners were also being withdrawn, I was surprised and disappointed to see no one I recognised. The strangers also did not promise at first sight to be very enticing companions. A hasty impression was of fat local bureaucrats and ageing European 'experts'. John had disappeared to find out about the plane and I hovered awkwardly, reluctant to settle down until he left. I felt guilty that I was leaving while he was not. It was striking that here, in the middle of Africa, nearly half the people waiting for the plane were white.

John returned with the information that the daily flight was suspended but replaced by a shuttle to cope with the rush of departures. The shuttle plane had already made one trip that morning and would return in an hour or so. He offered to stay to make sure that I got on its next flight but I encouraged him to go. I was aware that he had been driving for hours and must have left in the small hours to collect me so early from Batawe. I also looked forward to being freed from the effort of finding topics of conversation that John's English could handle and that stood a chance of not leading too soon to God. Until coming to Africa I had hardly met anyone who identified conspicuously as Christian, but here I found that almost everyone does and people were always asking me what church I belong to. At first I tried to be truthful but the answer 'none' seemed so puzzling or upsetting that I decided to go with 'Methodist' in line with my father's family. Fortunately a label proved sufficient and I was not forced into awkward theological definitions.

I would be fine, I reassured John, and of course I would call the Mufalenge office of our NGO if I had a problem. Gordon, who was in charge there, was going to stay on unless the situation became critical and he would certainly make sure his volunteers were safe. After enough reassurances John agreed to go and, although relieved, I felt a chill of regret as he turned away. John is employed as a driver but also acts as helper, guide and fixer for the young volunteers. He was the first person I had met on arrival. He had collected me at this airstrip, driven me around in Mufalenge, delivered me to Batawe, and yesterday came to collect me with many kindly reassurances. I stood for a moment watching the jeep getting smaller and half enjoying the heat all round me, radiating up from the ground as well as burning down from the sky. It was the cool season, as far as there is one and the morning temperature was not unpleasant. As the sound of the engine died away the place became very quiet, uncomfortably quiet, reminding me of a supermarket car park during the few hours that the shop is closed.

Back in the concrete shed of the terminal there was only one waiting area where all the unknown passengers were assembled. It was not so quiet here. The whir of a big ceiling fan mingled with subdued chatter and louder exclamations from a group gathered round a board game which I now think of as 'bao' although I first came across it as 'wara', being played by a bus stand where holes in the dusty ground served as a board. There are many variants but the general principle is that two contestants distribute little pebbles in holes around their side of a board, aiming to drop the last pebble in the right place to capture pebbles from their opponent's side. It goes on until the winner ends up with all the pebbles. In this case one player was a young, fair-haired white man and the other with his back to me I thought probably African. They appeared to be the focus of a sociable scene that suggested these strangers all knew each other, an impression that underlined my discomfort at finding no one to greet.

There were a few unoccupied seats and I picked one hurriedly to avoid the embarrassment of being seen to choose my neighbours. As I approached I saw that my unchosen neighbours were both white, on one side an elderly woman who reminded me of a stick insect, thin but far from frail, with iron grey hair; on the other a large balding man of indeterminate age, with pinkish skin. The woman was reading and seemed enclosed by the world of her book. The man was chatting to his immediate neighbour, a young African woman wearing a grand dress in vivid green and yellow and with her hair neatly plaited. As I sat down the large, pinkish man turned towards me and said in a Germanic accent, 'Welcome to the late shift.'

I probably looked inquiring because he explained, 'Most people came yesterday. We came only in the evening but we were told that in the morning, before the first flight went, it was chaos. Of course, you may have wanted to miss that er…' and he searched for a word, 'that cattle market. Or did you not want to leave?'

'Leave!' That sounded extreme. When our field officer, Gordon, rang from Mufalenge he told me only that I was recalled to the capital temporarily because there was some danger of unrest following an attempted coup. Assuming I would soon return, I had left most of my things in Batawe where I was volunteering as a biology teacher. Now I thought of my little room there, of the rectangles of bright cloth I had spread on the bed and pinned up over the peeling paint on the wall and which I had chosen in the market with care, riffling through piles of crisp cotton, unfolding too many pieces in my indecision. After three months the place felt enough like home for me to mind the idea of abandoning it for good, although growing familiarity had come with a slight sense of boredom. Batawe is very small, only qualifying as a town because of its concrete buildings: shops, government offices, a clinic, two schools and a few blocks of middle class housing. Social life is limited and ruled by codes of propriety which I had by then realised would make it unwise for me, as teacher, single woman and foreigner to be too friendly with men, a discovery which was not particularly disappointing but contributed to a feeling that life had settled into a routine which would chug on bringing few surprises. But I fully expected, and wanted, to return. The teaching, at first a bit of a struggle, was getting easier; the girls were well behaved; the teachers were kindly, if a little distant and I was just beginning to get closer to one of the younger ones, Anisa, who was from the area. A breakthrough came when she invited me to her grandparents' village which seemed to belong to a world quite different from the neat suburbia of Batawe. It was just a weekend and

I felt a clumsy outsider, unable to understand what people were saying or to remember who I'd been introduced to and how they were related to Anisa, but I was hoping for subsequent visits when things might become clearer. I enjoyed the unfamiliarity of the mud and thatch houses, the smell of straw and wood smoke, the sense of being far from a main road.

Instead of answering my neighbour's unsettling question I asked if he'd seen an update on yesterday's news.

'I saw a bit this morning,' he said, 'It was the same – all the time the same. The terrorists contained – the army in control...'

'So, do you think there's really no need to leave?'

'That is the television saying this and television here is not perfect in objectivity.'

'What about the internet? I couldn't find much last night. Have you looked since then?'

He hadn't, he said sourly, because in the morning he'd not had time to do anything but switch on the TV as he was rushing to catch the first flight, which had, of course, been late and full. Since then there had been no chance as there was, it seemed, no Wi-Fi in the terminal.

Just then the brightly-dressed woman on the far side of the man I was talking to lent across to say reassuringly that she'd phoned friends in the capital and they confirmed that the fighting appeared to be over and the situation calm.

Soon we were introducing ourselves. I discovered without surprise that the man I'd been talking to was

German, an economist and development consultant called Dieter. The woman, Zehra, was Tanzanian. I'd half thought she might be the wife of the African bao player but it turned out I was wrong. She was another economist, a heterodox economist, she said with a smile and I suspected she stressed the word 'heterodox' to distance herself from Dieter. She was a civil servant and worked in planning. She introduced the thin woman reading on my other side as Frieda, an entomologist and expert on termites in the built environment.

'Or "house pests" as they are sometimes unfortunately called,' said Frieda looking up from her book a little reluctantly. She spoke in a crisp voice coloured by the residue of a faint accent which, because of her name, I took to be German. I couldn't help smiling about her profession, given my first impression of a stick insect.

Frieda, who had missed the first introductions, turned to me inquiringly.

'I'm sorry,' said Zehra, 'I forgot to say, this is Nita, from England.'

'And Nita, just now I suppose you have not come from England but from somewhere a little nearer?' Frieda asked, prompting me to explain about the NGO and the school in Batawe.

'Is this a gap year?' asked Dieter, and added with a hint of condescension, 'I hear this gap year has become an industry in Britain.'

'That's different,' I said, annoyed that he had taken me for a school leaver. 'The "gap year" ', I went on huffily, 'is between school and university and you're right in that there's a bit of a racket with companies making people pay to do token jobs. The programme I'm on is for graduates or professionals taking a career break. We're expected to do a real job and we get expenses.'

'That makes sense,' said Zehra, 'especially if you're teaching science. There's often a shortage of science teachers.'

Frieda closed up her book and began to press me about why I'd chosen to come here and what I was planning to do later on. There was none of the veiled criticism I sensed in Dieter's remarks, but I was unwilling to relate the unflattering truth that I'd finished a biology degree wondering if I'd chosen the wrong subject, unwilling to chase graduate jobs and afraid that going for postgraduate study would lead me further into a cul-de-sac. I just wanted to get away and there was nothing in my personal life to hold me back. The last of a few superficial love affairs – or more accurately, sex affairs – had petered out. Any destination would do. I didn't chose Batawe, or teaching, but just applied for anything I was qualified for and took the first acceptance. What I said after a moment's pause was: 'I wasn't quite sure about doing a higher degree and as I hadn't taken a gap year, I thought it would be sensible to have a break.' This seemed to be well received but to deflect further questions, I hurriedly asked what had happened about the flights the day before.

As Dieter had begun to tell me, there had been a big exodus when the little plane made several flights back and forth. Women had been given priority, Zehra said.

'And, of course, Government Big Men,' Dieter added.

It turned out that my three neighbours had arrived too late for whatever priorities were applied and had only heard about the morning chaos. Along with several of the others now waiting they had been at an international conference on sustainable building. This group was there because they had opted to stay on for a trip to a far away village where experimental building methods were in use. It was only on their return that they heard about the attempted coup and rushed to the airstrip, where they had waited until nightfall and then returned to Mufalenge to spend the night in a not very satisfactory hotel.

'And then back here for more waiting,' said Dieter. 'They had said, "seven o'clock" but, of course, at seven o'clock – no plane. It appeared at nine but only one of us got on. And what is it doing now? It should be here. The flight's only an hour.' He got up with a gesture of irritation, pulled out a packet of cigarettes and headed for the door.

I asked Zehra if most of the people waiting were from the conference and she pointed out to me the ones who were: the two bao players, a neatly turned out Indian-looking man in the small group watching the game and, sitting a few seats away from us, absorbed in her laptop, a full-figured woman, also Indian-looking and wearing a splendid tunic and trouser outfit of crisp blue and white cotton batik. Again I wrongly assumed the last two were a couple. Zehra corrected me with quiet surprise indicating that to her it was clear they were from different worlds. She added that the woman in blue, Radhika, was from India, a rather well known architect and one of the keynote speakers; the man, Jalal, she thought was Kenyan, probably Ismaili, an engineer with no particular expertise in sustainability but sent by his employer, a big contractor, to give the company a presence. Furnished with this extra information I saw that Jalal was a bit young to be married to Radhika.

There were about half a dozen other would-be passengers, mostly men, and I was about to ask if she knew anything about them when my attention was distracted by a small commotion in the group around the bao board.

'Cheat! He cheated. You must have seen it!' exclaimed the fair-haired player as he jumped up and turned for support to the group watching. His opponent, whom I saw now as a rather good-looking, youngish man with golden skin and unruly Afro hair – from North Africa, I wondered, or the Arabised East Coast perhaps – was laughing mischievously.

'It's the game,' he said. 'That's how you play. And I've been making it bit by bit more obvious each move, waiting for you to notice. But you didn't and again you didn't…'

'You've been cheating all the time?' The fair man looked scandalised.

The bystanders laughed. One of them was a grey-haired, scholarly-looking man. When he spoke it was in restrained Oxford English, which perfectly matched his appearance, although was slightly at odds with what he said.

'I'm afraid I must confirm that cheating – or let's say "rule evasion" – is an element in the strategy and quite acceptable, indeed expected – at least as it's played in this region. I can't speak for all versions but we should follow local custom, don't you think?' He turned to the indignant player. 'Now, this time, because you caught him – he let you catch him – he has to give you back those last pebbles he took from you and the ones that came from his side as well, but you can't go back beyond that last move.'

'So, what's the point if you can cheat as much as you like?'

'Ah no,' the grey-haired man corrected, 'only as much as you can get away with.'

Zehra smiled and turned to me. 'Do you know the game?'

I told her I had played once or twice and asked about the two players.

The fair-haired indignant one, she said, was Sven, an epidemiologist from a Swedish NGO who had given a paper on improving health outcomes in urban slums. His opponent with the golden skin, she said, was a journalist. He seemed to know a lot of people at the conference and she'd heard the name before, Leandro Ramires, but was not sure where he was from or why he was there. I tried to get a better look at him but he was turned away from me.

The game resumed and Frieda returned to her book. Dieter wandered back to his seat trailing with him a smell of cigarette. He began grumbling that the village trip took much longer than they'd been told and added nothing to the written material about the project. Zehra disagreed, saying that words and figures give you one kind of information but going to a place and talking to people nearly always adds a lot.

'Of course,' Dieter responded wearily, 'why would I have gone if I thought the trip was necessarily pointless? But in this case it is clear to me that we learned nothing worth the long drive.' He said this with a tone of finality before exclaiming, 'God, is this plane ever coming?'

Zehra seemed willing to let him have the last word and began telling me that she was anxious about her husband, left in charge of their two young children and expecting her back that morning. She brought out her phone with a picture of two cherubic girls staring solemnly at the camera, their hair plaited into tight bobbles like a set of spokes around their faces.

I wondered how old she was and guessed less than ten years older than me and here she was with a serious job, two children and a husband who, unlike the stereotype of African husbands, apparently shares the childcare. I felt a flicker of envy.

Dieter continued to fret about the plane. 'What can be going on? It's an hour's flight. Can't they at the least provide information?'

His agitation spread to me so that at the first moment I heard the sound of a distant engine I said excitedly, 'Is that the plane at last?'

Zehra listened and said regretfully, 'It's just a car, I'm afraid.' By this time the sound was so clearly not from a plane that I felt foolish.

'It's a car, ' confirmed Dieter and got up to have a better look or just to stretch his legs again. The car arrived and disgorged a thick-set, middle-aged white man who took his luggage, paid the driver and lit a cigarette before approaching the building, where he stopped in a patch of shade outside to finish smoking. I remembered my own arrival and brief hesitation, but in his case the signs were that he was only pausing to smoke.

'One more passenger,' said Dieter without enthusiasm.

When he stubbed out his cigarette and entered the building, the man looked round as I had done, noted the deserted check-in desk and then surveyed the waiting passengers. Unlike me, he spotted an acquaintance and headed for the bao group where, slightly to my surprise, he greeted Leandro. The two men were evidently not expecting to meet and it was difficult to tell whether Leandro was pleased or not but they talked animatedly, mainly, as far as I could tell from their gestures, about the absent plane. Then the new arrival dumped his luggage by a nearby chair and sat down.

It was a measure of our boredom that this non-event had caused heads to turn and conversations to pause. Now that it was apparent that the car had only brought another passenger, everyone returned to laptops, books, chatter or stupor. The ceiling fan clicked round insistently but did no more than feebly stir the warm air. I decided to get a coffee from the little snack bar and offered to bring something for my neighbours too. Dieter declined and I returned with plastic cups of sticky caffeinated liquid for Frieda, Zehra and myself. We sipped cautiously and agreed that it was better than nothing but Frieda made it taste worse by reminiscing about the smell of grinding beans. Zehra trumped this by mentioning that her family home is in a coffee-growing area and talked of picking the beans and roasting them at home, still green. When I remarked that I'd never seen coffee growing she gave me the kind of look you give a foreigner in England who says they've never seen a bluebell wood and began to describe a hillside, planted thinly with majestic hardwood trees under which the coffee bushes grow with dark shiny leaves and, in the right season, covered with white flowers. Tiny birds and butterflies flit between the bushes and the treetops.

'It sounds great,' I said.

'Does it?' she laughed, 'Try working there... And I'm talking about old plantations. They don't all have trees like that now.'

As we chatted, I half noticed that almost everyone else had drifted over to where the bao players were sitting, although the game seemed to be discontinued and, instead, some kind of general discussion was under way.

Suddenly someone said in a raised voice, 'Oh no! Definitely not that.'

We looked round as did the one or two other people not in the group. It must have been the scholarly Englishman who had spoken because everyone was staring at him. There was a moment's silence and then he laughed and said more quietly, 'Well, all I mean is I'm not keen myself.'

'Do you know him?' I asked my companions.

It was Frieda who answered, 'Vernon Craig, archaeologist, works in Uganda mainly and a bit in Tanzania. Well known in his field and, I gather, a bit of a television pundit. He's from your country originally. I thought you might have heard of him.'

She spoke hurriedly as she was also listening for whatever would be said next and when no one said anything of much interest she walked over and asked in a tone of mild amusement, 'Vernon, what are you so decisively not in favour of?'

'Oh, nothing,' he said hurriedly.

'Enough to make you shout,' countered Leandro, the golden player, who then turned to Frieda. 'We were just talking about ways to pass the time and a story-telling competition was suggested…'

Vernon interrupted him. 'It's trivial. It's just that I have some not very happy associations with that sort of game. I didn't mean to shout.'

'Ah, and what kind of thing could spoil so very badly such an innocent entertainment?' Frieda wondered aloud. 'What happened?'

'Yes,' said the golden one seizing everyone's attention. 'You had better tell, Vernon, otherwise we will imagine something quite disgraceful!'

'If only it was that interesting!'

'Let them decide.' Leandro waved vaguely at those listening and a few people muttered encouragement. 'You see, we're all waiting.' As he spoke he pushed a chair forward for Vernon and shifted a couple of others discretely to make the beginnings of a circle. 'I think you have no choice now. You'd better confess.'

'Leandro's such a manipulator,' Vernon sighed.

From how they spoke I assumed he and Leandro must be old friends.

'So, what do you know about this Leandro?' I asked Dieter, who said he knew no more than Zehra but added that Leandro was probably the kind of journalist who writes opinion pieces and feature articles. The way he put it suggested he had not entirely taken to the man.

Almost everyone by then had drawn near, hungry for the mild entertainment that a little argument might offer. Vernon took in the expectant stares, shrugged and sat down, resigned to satisfy our curiosity.

Of course these are not his exact words but only the gist, as far as I remember it, of what he and other people said.

2

Vernon's Story

'It was such a trivial thing,' he began. 'You will wonder that the memory could still affect me a lifetime later. But...' He paused.

I took a chair on the edge of the circle and waited for him to go on.

'As a boy I went to one of those old, tradition-ridden schools called "Public" which, of course, in Britain, perversely, means private. My parents weren't that well off but I had a partial scholarship and went as a dayboy although it was essentially a boarding school, which meant we attended for an extended week of compulsory activities. On Monday afternoons we were cadets and had to dress up in military uniforms and play at soldiers. I hated it and my parents didn't approve as they thought the army was being misused in remnants of the British Empire and on top of that my mother was a Quaker.

'At a certain time I decided I should conscientiously

object but before I got round to staging a possibly damaging confrontation my classics master, who sympathised, stepped in. Dr Oakshot – "Okkers" or "Old Okkers" to us – was a kindly polymath who probably thought our training in heel clicking, blancoing and presenting arms was a waste of good reading time. He liked me, not only because I was good at Latin but also because I paid extra attention whenever he abandoned the set text for one of his tangential leaps into philosophy, linguistics, Tuscan gods or Roman rubbish dumps. It happened he had an archaeologist friend in the university who was having difficulty finding time to deal with an antiquarian's collection of Roman objects recently bequeathed to the university. By good fortune the archaeologist didn't teach on Monday afternoons and somehow Okkers convinced him that he needed a volunteer assistant and persuaded the Head that "services to archaeology" would be a respectable alternative to cadet training. So, relieved of the opportunity to be a martyr, I pottered off every Monday to sort bits of broken pottery and write labels. I turned out to be reasonably useful and not long after I started, the archaeologist mentioned that a colleague was looking for volunteers to help at weekends with a dig in the nearby Mendip Hills. He wondered if I'd like to go. The snag was that on Saturdays we had compulsory sport, but again the resourceful Okkers found a way to get me released. It probably helped that I was no sportsman.'

By now Vernon seemed quite at ease having entirely forgotten his reluctance to speak.

'Although I knew enough not to call it "treasure hunting", my idea of archaeology was coloured by accounts of uncovering Pompeii, opening Tutankhamen's tomb or unearthing the golden ornaments at Sutton Hoo. Our Mendip dig turned out to be in a quite different league. It was a Palaeolithic site, and by the time I joined the small team working there the most exciting finds had been a couple of flint knives and a piece of worked bone that might, or might not, have been part of a comb. After a brief moment of readjustment, I found I didn't mind. To be on the trail of such an incredibly distant age held another kind of romance for me, fully compensating for the near certainty that there would be no spectacular discoveries. I very quickly came to love the process, the scratching and sieving and meticulous mapping and labelling – not that there was a great density of things to label but there was a permanent feeling of suspense about what *might* turn up. I was beginning to wonder if I'd at last found an answer to that favourite adult conversation starter, "What do you want to do when you grow up?"

'There was a feeling of solidarity among the volunteers partly due to the archaeologist in charge – Marion, as she liked us to call her – who fostered our sense of shared purpose, treating us all as potential colleagues, discussing theories with us regardless of our level of understanding and never talking down, even to me. Naturally, I liked this and began to feel quite adult. I gathered that Marion was prominent in her profession and slightly known beyond. I thought of her as quite old but, given that I was sixteen, this probably meant she was forty-something.

'When I started going to the dig it only happened at weekends. I came and went with everybody else and some of us camped in a field above the site on the Saturday night. Among the volunteers were three postgraduate archaeology students who turned up with complete regularity. The rest of us included a couple of undergraduates who faded away when exams approached, myself, and an assortment of amateur enthusiasts. I have a hazy picture of an apple grower, a woman from a local church and an ex-military type who'd fallen for the lure of ancient ruins when serving in the Middle East.

'The pattern of work changed when lectures at the university stopped for the summer exams and Marion and her students stayed at the site during the week. Before, I'd usually got a lift, but now I made the journey on my own by bus, a big green double-decker that I took from the bus station. I'd secure my favourite seat on the top deck at the front and sit there full of anticipation for the moment when the vehicle would lurch as the driver climbed in and shudder into life as he started the big engine. The bus dropped me at one of the main tourist attractions of the area, a famous limestone cave which had turned the nearby hamlet into a busy resort full of cars, cafès and souvenir shops. From there I would head up a narrow road, leaving behind the noise and activity until, after about half a mile, I'd turn off onto a footpath which led across rough pasture into a steep wooded valley which soon became a small gorge.

To find our site you had to branch off the path to climb up a faintly-marked track through undergrowth, and over patches of scree to a ledge near the top. On the ledge was the entrance to a cave that had been blocked by earth, which we were carefully clearing away. Above this point the path was better marked as it led on up to the camp and so served as the main access route.

'The weather around the particular weekend, that I would rather not have been forced to recall, was changeable. When the bus dropped me it was raining gently. As always, I felt my excitement mount at each significant point on my route: when I turned onto the path, when I reached the shadow of the trees and, most of all when I entered the narrow gorge and breathed in the faint smell of limestone. (If you think rocks have no smell you have never been in a rocky place and paid attention.) On that still, damp morning the odour was so distinct that I would have known in the dark where I was. In the gorge I felt a fanciful closeness to the people whose traces we were searching for. I imagined my bare feet treading the stony ground, my senses alert for food and danger, and liked to think that this long dead youth whose sensations I was trying to conjure would have seen the same hilltops I could see. Although I knew quite well that the vegetation was different then, I couldn't help seeing the twisted yews of the present, the dark box and grey ash saplings, as a primeval forest.

'As I approached the cave I listened for voices but heard none. When I found the ledge deserted I could have gone on up to the camp to find out what was going on but part of me was pleased to find myself alone, for once, in solitary possession of "our cave". So, I sat there trying to enter the mind of a hunter-gatherer while the soft rain kissed the earth, as it must have done on cloudy days all those thousands of years ago.

'My reverie was broken by the sound of slithering earth on the path and in a few moments Marion appeared.

'"I thought you must have arrived by now," she said, "and would be wondering why no work is happening. The shirking is my fault, indirectly. Some of my students discovered it is my birthday today and decided we must celebrate. The fact that I never celebrate my birthday was dismissed as irrelevant. So, we've been having a slow breakfast and now they have gone to buy provisions for a party tonight."

'"So, Happy Birthday!" I said and couldn't think of anything to add. Marion would be aware that card or flowers could hardly be expected.

'"Meanwhile, shall we get on?"' She said, handing me an implement and indicating the place where work had presumably left off the day before.

'After a while some of the other outsider volunteers came and we all dug and sifted steadily, finding nothing, until shortly before lunchtime when the three PhD students turned up and announced there would be a feast that evening in the top meadow. Marion suggested we might curtail the lunch break if we were planning to stop early but as it turned out we took a rather extended break. Perhaps it had something to do with the rain which came down more heavily and made us huddle together in the sheltered area of the cave.'

Vernon paused, pulled off his glasses and rubbed his face, perhaps trying to remember or to organise his thoughts before returning to the story.

'I had better admit now,' he continued 'that it wasn't only the work I'd fallen in love with.

'I mentioned there were three postgraduates. One was Bryn, a restless, opinionated man with a tendency to play up his Welshness. Then there was Colin, quiet with mildly upper-class mannerisms. It was the third, Maya, who was the object of my fantasies. She was Indian, here with some Commonwealth scholarship, and I fear it was probably her exotic presence as well as her beauty that captivated me. At that time, you have to remember, Indian students were something of a rarity, and Maya was not like the modern jeans-wearing young Indian girls you see now. She wore a sari which at first attracted some mild teasing from Bryn and others who complained that it was a perversely impractical way to dress for a dig. She defended herself, pointing out that in India women in saris manage much rougher work, transplanting rice or labouring on building sites. She didn't object in principle to trousers, she said, but it would be a major investment to switch over to wearing them. Apart from the trousers she'd need the things that go with them, all to be bought in English money. Why go to that expense when she could round up from her family plenty of age-worn saris to do duty as work clothes?

'So, there she'd be, scrambling up and down the rough path or squatting on the bare earth wielding trowel or sieve, dressed in flowing drapery, like a

Greek nymph, I sometimes thought, which seems an unnecessarily remote analogy except that we'd done Greek mythology at school and not touched on Indian. Now when I think of that time, an image comes to mind of someone glittering with jewellery like a Bollywood goddess, but when I force my mind back properly I see there was nothing showy about her beyond natural beauty.

'Going to an all boys' school I'd not had much contact with girls; I wasn't particularly keen on the cinema and certainly wasn't drawn to its heavily made-up stars. Of course I'd heard boys "talking dirty" and had come across a good deal of passion in literature but had reacted to all that rather as part of life to come, as not quite relevant in the present. So, I was at first faintly surprised when I noticed the way I looked forward to seeing Maya and detected waves of jealousy towards Colin and Bryn. Of course you shouldn't imagine I was thinking rationally. If I'd done that I should have seen how improbable it was that a suave postgraduate would even think of a sixteen-year-old schoolboy in the context of romance. All I was consciously thinking about was how to get her attention, how to impress her and mostly my thinking was pretty ineffective because by the time I honed a brilliant remark the conversation would have moved on.

'This damp lunch break I was, as usual, missing my cues while the others conducted a desultory argument kicked off by Colin.

'"What a grim life it must have been! Imagine sitting in this cave with the rain dripping down and knowing that there's nothing out there but rain soaked hills and swamps stretching away to the sea."

'"No sneaking off to a warm pub, you mean?" said Bryn.

'"Oh yes," someone else put in, "a world without pubs is a sad thought."

'"No need to mock," said Colin, "Poor sods. Just because they had nothing to compare it with doesn't mean they'd enjoy shivering in a cave."

'"You're looking at them too much from the vantage point of the Rose and Crown."

'"Yes," chipped in Maya, "Stop judging their lives. We don't really know if ours are better."

'One of the outsider volunteers was shocked by that thought and it looked as if an abstract argument about progress was burgeoning when Bryn cut in to remind us it was Marion's birthday and to ask her what, if the cave would grant her a special find that day, she would wish for.

'Marion laughed and said, "What a question! But if we're going to talk fantasy then I'll tell you what I dream of sometimes. It's that one day – for instance when we finally open the way into the next chamber and shine our torch into the darkness – that the beam will reveal something like the Hall of Bulls at Lascaux."

'We all looked involuntarily towards the opening at the back of the cave.

'Lascaux! It was a word that had only entered my consciousness since my recent conversion to archaeology but now evoked a complex tangle of adventure, mystery and indignation. In case some of you have missed this modern legend, Lascaux is a cave in France, covered with extraordinary animal paintings, which was discovered in 1940 by young boys looking for a dog. The paintings, probably the most famous and most reproduced of Palaeolithic art, date to around 15,000 BC, and their discovery changed art and archaeology forever. Sadly, it also brought about the paintings' ruin. The landowner hurried to capitalise on his cave's tourist potential and within a few years the stream of visitors passing through had altered the chemistry of the underground space and caused the paintings to deteriorate. The French government stepped in eventually, in 1963, and had the cave closed. So, I could only read about this extraordinary place, which, not surprisingly, had acquired the added attraction of the forbidden.

'There was a short silence broken by Bryn saying, "You all look as if you expect a procession of spectral bulls to ooze from the hole and flatten themselves across the cave wall."

'We smiled embarrassedly and adjusted the direction of our gaze.

'"But that is almost how they seem," said Marion, "as if a living creature had pressed itself into the rock."

'"You are lucky to have seen them," said Colin. "I suppose there's dispensation for professionals."

'"Yes," said Marion, "I probably could have access now, if I had a good reason, but I visited before the caves were closed. In fact before they were even open."

'"How did you manage that?" one of the older volunteers asked. "Surely you can't have been qualified then?"

'"No, and I hadn't even discovered archaeology yet, but I was generally interested in the past even as a child."

'She explained that when she was a student, although not yet of archaeology, she heard about the painted cave and decided she must see it. So, in the spring holidays, she set off with her bike and travelled partly by train and partly by bike all the way through France on her own only to discover that the caves were not yet open to the public. Nor surprisingly she was devastated but, while she was sitting glumly by the closed entrance, some archaeologists working in the cave showed up and she managed to talk them into letting her go in with them.

'"You can imagine," she said. "I felt like leaping in the air and hugging all three of them.

'"I was unbelievably lucky. The walkways and lights were already in place, but I was able to be there almost alone. I find it hard to describe the extraordinary affect that the place had on me.

'"We went into a cool underground space which felt, as all caves do, strange and distinctive but, at first, that was all. Then the passageway opened out to reveal a pale vault across which cavorted a parade of black, red and brown beasts, including graceful long-horned cattle and little, frisky brown horses with tightly arched necks and bristly manes. Nothing had prepared me for the size and extent and richness of this mural, which glowed with its warm colours and heaved with latent motion. It was frightening in its intensity. When Bryn joked just now about ghostly creatures emerging from and blending back into the rock it brought back something of the sense of danger and threat I felt. My first reaction was to the beasts as beasts, and it was only when the first shock receded that I remembered that I was looking at representations. With that there came a new sense of wonder about the artists, invisible themselves and yet present in their work.

'"From there the cave narrows and branches in different directions, each with its surprises. In a distant place there is perhaps the strangest group of images, the only one to include a representation of a human. The man, if that is what he is, is depicted lying on his back underneath a huge bison but if the bison has killed him then it is strange that the man seems to have an erection."

'At that time,' Vernon interrupted himself, 'you wouldn't expect a middle-aged teacher to use that kind of word without embarrassment but it was typical of Marion that she said this in a completely normal way.'

No one commented and Vernon went on. 'When Marion finished her story there was a thoughtful silence until Maya asked, "I suppose there's no way we can ever find out why those paintings were done?"

'"There was a time," replied Marion a little briskly, "that we thought we'd never know why the days lengthen and shorten." She got up as she spoke. "And now look at us, because of my story we've taken a long break after all and, certainly, if we spend all our time sitting around, we won't find out anything."

'"Don't knock stories," said Bryn. "If we hadn't started by thinking up stories about why the days change, maybe we'd never have found our way to astronomy. Which has just given me an idea for tonight." He looked round to be sure he had everyone's attention. "Maya was saying earlier, wouldn't it be fun to tell stories round the fire, and now we have a theme. Let's all tell a story about those paintings, who did them and why."

'"Oh yes," said Maya, "a great idea!"

'I cursed myself for not being the one to suggest it!

'"It can be a competition for the most plausible idea," said the military type.

'"And Marion can be the judge," suggested the apple grower.

'"Yes, and no," said Marion. "Story telling could be fun but I'm not going to judge. It's not a beauty contest and there'll be no prizes."

'So, it was agreed. We'd have the time until dinner to think up our stories and we'd draw lots for the order of telling.

'I didn't find this a particularly daunting prospect as I was rather good in English, especially at imaginative composition. It occurred to me that this could be my chance to make Maya notice me. So, I directed my thoughts towards ideas that might impress her and after a while I hit on one I considered startlingly original, which was that the paintings were the work of women. I'd noticed she was a bit of a feminist, although that's not a word I'd have used then. So, I was sure she'd take notice if, in my story, the bison painters were women. I struggled a bit as everything I'd read or seen about the old Stone Age was about men and it had never before occurred to me that women might have done anything other than sit in the background holding a baby. But it wasn't long before I came up with what I thought was a reasonably convincing idea and started to weave around it a storyline. Meanwhile, the rain petered out, the clouds thinned, and by the time we started our party it was a perfect June evening. Maya had changed into the best of her "old, worn out" saris, a rich maroon and green shot silk with a thick maroon border that was, admittedly, tattered in places. I thought she looked like the goddess of the woods as she sat under a tree in the afterglow of the setting sun.

'As well as beer, they'd acquired from a nearby farm a barrel of excellent home-brewed cider, not remotely like the sweet stuff from bottles but also not as harsh as the rough cider served in pubs. I wasn't very familiar with pubs as I'd only recently begun to look old enough to pass for eighteen, but on the few occasions I'd ventured in I'd drunk cider because of its extreme cheapness. I'd not enjoyed it much but I found I liked this superior version. By the time we started the story telling I had drunk enough of it to feel relaxed and festive.

'I was glad that it did not fall to me to start since I needed my idea to shine the brighter by contrast with other familiar versions of stone-age life. I was not disappointed: the first stories all revolved round men waving firebrands and communing with spirits in a world cobbled together from museum displays on 'early man', American Indian religion as portrayed by Hollywood, and memories of camping with the Boy Scouts.

'At the fourth draw the winner – or loser, depending how you look at it – was Maya. I was naturally paying a lot of attention to her words.

'"I've spoken to some of you," she began, "about the place I think of as hom; a small town or large village in South India. Although it aspires to being a town it has a rural feel to it, quiet with mainly single story, mud houses set along alleyways. It looks at its best in the early morning when soft light beams down through the smoke of morning fires and in front of each house there is a smooth layer of cow dung on which you will see an intricate, geometrical design in white – each one slightly different from the next. This is what you see if you walk round at six thirty or seven in the morning. If you want to watch the designs taking shape you need to be out even earlier, when everything is still a little indistinct in the dusty pink of predawn. Then you will see women and girls sweeping, cleaning, plastering and then completing their routine by kneeling down and tracing these lacy patterns with fine rice powder.

'"So far you have made your artists men, probably because you are thinking of the European art world. But when I think of art the image that comes to mind is of those women kneeling in the dawn. So, you will not be surprised that my story will centre round a woman..."

'As Maya developed her theme you can imagine how my confidence ebbed away with every word. She had beaten me to my idea and now I would only seem to be a feeble imitator. I hardly followed her story as I was anxiously trying to invent a new one which would have some other twist of originality. In my nervous state I finished up my cider and refilled my cup. My mind was quite paralysed and the cider seemed to help. Under its influence I began to identify some good new themes to work on. It would be all right after all, I thought, absently downing the next glassful.

'Need I go on? You have all probably guessed what is to come. The good themes began to tangle themselves up so I couldn't quite follow any one of them. Then suddenly the ground did an odd thing. It tilted itself up so I felt in danger of sliding off. As I was trying to get control of that hazard I realised something else disconcerting was happening to me, something which meant that, tilting ground or no tilting ground, I had to get away from the circle of firelight. I think I did manage to creep away without conspicuously bumping into trees or otherwise making a spectacle of myself, but I could not be sure. Certainly by the time I was actually sick I was in a dark part of the wood far enough down the hill to hope that no one knew what had happened to me. I was embarrassed that they would all think I'd bottled out of my turn but I was in no state to return. I wandered round in the dark until I felt better and then crept off to my tent bitterly regretting the one chance I might ever have to begin a chain of fantastical events which would end up with Maya and me as lovers.

'In the morning I didn't know whether to be relieved or humiliated that no one seemed to have missed me or my story. Maya, it turned out, was leaving before the next weekend to work on a Roman site and would not be coming back to our cave.'

Vernon came to a stop while we waited expectantly.

3

Interlude

When it was clear that no more was to follow, Leandro started to clap, saying, 'Look how you've redeemed yourself!' He indicated the circle of attentive faces. Some of the onlookers started to applaud too. Vernon looked surprised.

'I'm sorry I made a fuss,' he said. 'How could I be so stupid? This was more than half a century ago!'

I couldn't resist asking, 'Did you ever see her again?'

This was a mistake as my question made Leandro and his friends notice me for the first time and I was afraid I sounded childish. It wasn't quite the point, I knew, but I was curious.

'Did I ever see her again?' repeated Vernon. 'No, and yes. I heard she became a big wheel in India, an expert on the Indus Valley civilisation. I gathered that she'd married and had children. It may sound a bit ridiculous but I avoided meeting her. In fact I'll never know if the Palaeolithic was where my interests really lay or whether I steered clear of ancient civilisations because they were her area.

'Eventually, I was at one of those giant conferences that gather people from the whole discipline and I noticed she was giving a paper. Curiosity got the better of me and I went to hear her. A stately figure sailed into the room carrying a good deal of weight under a regal sari. At first I didn't recognise her, but when she started to talk I could see in her voice and mannerisms the ghost of my Maya. I made myself go up to her afterwards to remind her laughingly of our Mendip cave. She was delighted and told me how her time in England and the camp at the cave had meant a lot to her, but I could tell she had only the dimmest memory of the schoolboy who came at weekends.'

Vernon fell silent again and then added, 'I suppose telling stories is not such a bad idea.'

'And you've given us a great start,' said Radhika, the architect in the blue batik.

'He has.' Leandro agreed. 'Not only that but he's suggested our theme. We must take on Marion's challenge.'

'Oh yes. Let's settle on that,' Radhika urged.

'But we didn't even decide to tell stories,' complained Sven, the fair young man, Leandro's unobservant opponent in the bao game. 'No one except Vernon spoke, and he was against it.'

'He's not against it now, ' said Zehra, 'and we've all seen how it really did pass some time. I even forgot to listen out for our plane.'

'It's not the only way of passing time,' said one of the people I didn't yet know.

'We should take a vote on it,' Sven insisted.

'What on earth for?' demanded someone else. 'People can do what they like, can't they? No has to take part.'

At this Radhika broke in with a sharp, 'No!' before jumping up and saying with an air of authority, 'That's just a way of blocking the idea. It won't happen unless we all go for it. If it's a choice people will think they have to be really good, and no one will think that – except maybe you, Leandro, as telling stories is part of your work. If we all join in it'll be obvious that it's not a literary contest. So, I say we all do it. That will stop us thinking about the plane and then it will come.'

Something about the way this was said seemed to sway people because after that the argument shifted to details like whether to go along with the cave painting theme or not.

Frieda pointed out, 'The person, I suspect, who knows most about the topic has had his turn and his story didn't address the question. How can we tell sensible stories if we know nothing?'

'Stories don't have to be "sensible",' Leandro countered.

'But there's no point in a theme if we tell just anything,' Jalal said, ' and some of us don't even know what these paintings look like.'

'We can find a picture,' said Zehra.

'Wouldn't it be easier to tell true stories?' said Sven.

'That's what Vernon did, after all. He didn't even tell us the story he didn't tell about the women painters.'

Jalal, who had started fiddling with his phone rather than listening, muttered to Zehra, 'I'll try "cave painting"... if I can connect. The signal's very weak.'

The heavily-built white man who had arrived after me suddenly cut in saying, 'Women did not make those pictures.' He spoke in a foreign accent I could not quite place. 'Yes, women would put designs outside the house. Yes. That's decoration. It's for home, family – the life that is lived today. The cave pictures aren't like that. They're about …' Temporarily stuck for words, he gestured fiercely into the air before trying out, '… things beyond. It's about things beyond us. Like an icon. And who makes icons? Look anywhere in the world and you see, it's men who paint religion, war, death, creation …'

His bluster annoyed me but I was more annoyed with myself because the first women artists that jumped to mind, Tracy Emin and Vanessa Bell, weren't obviously the best counter examples. Then I remembered the ideal woman, whose work includes an unusually convincing version of Judith in the act of beheading Holofernes, but I couldn't remember her name.

While I dithered Radhika reacted instantly, throwing at him a lot of names most of which I hadn't heard of and clearly nor had he. She went on to complain:

'Even about the kolams – those designs outside houses – we don't put them there just to prettify the street. They are a kind of prayer, a visual prayer.'

'Yes, decoration can mean something,' Zehra agreed.

'I'm not even sure if decoration is ever *just* decoration,' Radhika mused, half to herself. 'Isn't the act of decorating in itself a form of worship?'

'Or people could chose to tell true stories or make up ones,' Sven cut in, to continue the earlier conversation doggedly ignoring the current one. 'Let everyone just chose…'

'I thought we'd decided on the paintings,' Zehra said.

'Perhaps a theme is easier,' Frieda conceded, abandoning her previous opposition. 'It makes it more of a game. Especially an impossible theme.'

'At least, if we're going to follow your Marion's challenge, then let's adopt her rule that it's not a competition,' said Sven.

Everyone was soon talking over everyone else and it looked as if nothing would come of the storytelling after all. I was glad, as the idea appalled me, assuming I would have to take my turn. Then, just as the group was beginning to break up, Jalal, who had wandered off outside, came back to say he had managed to connect for long enough to download a picture and he handed his phone round with a lively image of a red bison on it. The beast looked so bright and fresh on the screen that some people at first took it for a modern graphic.

Somehow, after this, agreement was reached. Sven gave up objecting and went to the bar for some straws, bent up the end of one and waved it in front of us before putting it back in the bundle. *Treacherous straws*, I thought, willing my fingers to pick a long one.

'Not me, please not me,' said Zehra, half joking,

but voicing my feelings exactly, as I told her in a quiet aside. She smiled and squeezed my hand.

Vernon, who had largely stayed out of the discussion, gave us a sympathetic glance and gestured for Sven to wait. 'Don't you think it's hard to expect someone to come out with a story straight away. Why don't we have a pause for lunch now and then start? But draw the straws now so the lucky winner knows.'

No one opposed that and Sven held out his straws. I wondered whether anyone would decline. Of the people who had not spoken, three had shown signs of being interested in the discussion: a tall, dark, craggy man whom I thought might be Somali; a young African who seemed to be connected with Vernon and another young man, almost still a boy, accompanied by an elderly woman dressed like a villager, whom I took, correctly as it would turn out, to be his mother. The most likely abstainers were two others who had also not spoken: a nondescript white man stuck into a game on his tablet which he'd paused only half-heartedly to hear Vernon's story; and a fat African in a suit who was sitting a little apart, tapping his brief case irritably now and again. If they decline, I told myself, I can do the same. To my slight surprise and distinct disappointment they both accepted straws and so I took one too.

My discomfort was postponed. It was Jalal, the engineer, who held up the bent straw looking politely embarrassed.

Leandro manipulated us all to gather into a circle while we had lunch, even bringing in those like the brief case tapper and the tablet player who had so far remained aloof. 'Lunch' was an exaggeration as the little bar had run out of everything except for coke, crisps and a few tired samosas. All the same Leandro managed to make the occasion mildly convivial, starting off by getting everyone to introduce themselves, a move which began to break down the divisions between old friends, the conference group and the rest of us.

I learned that the very young man with the mother was Tom Ulemu, a schoolteacher who was teaching in Mufalenge but was from the South. He looked so young he might have been still at school himself and I found it hard to imagine him standing up in front of a class, even of little children. He was the last born of a large family, which explained why his mother, whom we called Mama Ulemu, looked more of an age to be his grandmother. The young man with Vernon, Nyezi, was Tanzanian and was doing a PhD on prehistoric ecology attached to a large-scale study headed by Vernon. Although Nyezi was respectful of his boss there was something of a joking relationship in the way the two interacted. Frieda, the entomologist, proved to be not German but Austrian. Zehra mentioned nothing she had not told me earlier. About Dieter, I discovered that he had a long connection with East Africa and had known Vernon back when both were first working there. I also got the impression they had been friendlier then but that now Vernon in some way disapproved of Dieter. The fat man with the brief case was Magome, a local bureaucrat, exactly the job I would have guessed – that, or a bank employee. I'd had to deal with examples of both and I could imagine looking across a dusty desk with Magome, on the other side, bulging out of his chair and oozing with sweat and petty self importance as he repeated with smug satisfaction that it, whatever "it" was, couldn't be done.

Radhika, who just introduced herself as an architect, was challenged by Frieda for failing to mention that she was also a campaigner, a well known advocate for local materials and who had herself developed improved versions of traditional ones including a special kind of mud brick. Prompted by this, Radhika confessed to being a mud brick missionary and complained that, so far, her gospel had gone down better among a cultured fringe of the Bombay elite than among the people she aspired to influence.

The main surprise from the new introductions was that the remarkably black, gaunt, Soṃali was not Somali, nor even African, but was from Chicago and, more unexpectedly still, a Catholic priest who introduced himself as Mathew. Should we call him "Father Mathew", I wondered as the introductions moved on. The white man with the tablet, Reece, was a compatriot of Vernon's and mine, which I had guessed from his slight Midlands accent. He was here "on business," he said, without elaboration. The other businessman present, the man who had so far said nothing that I'd noticed except to relegate women's art to the merely decorative, turned out to be Russian and spoke fluent but heavily accented English. By contrast with Reece he willingly revealed the outline of a tangled CV that took him from a junior Soviet diplomat in Zambia, through other postings and, after the Soviet collapse, into a variety of speculative ventures based on his African connections, the latest of which had brought him here from South West Africa where he currently lived. His name was Kolzak, Zak for short.

Leandro the Golden, as I thought of him, also had a complicated back-story. His father had been a dissident Portuguese living in Angola who had married a woman from Cameroon and had chosen to take Angolan nationality after independence. The couple were killed in the last phase of Angola's long civil war when Leandro was away studying. His career in journalism began in Angola but he was now based in Kampala, attached to some international centre but also a peripatetic journalist writing for European as well as African media and known too, in Africa, Vernon told us, for his poetry and short stories. His position as our informal leader might be due to his personality but I guessed also had something to do with the way he linked different elements in the group. I was right in thinking that he and Vernon went back a long way together. In fact he knew Vernon originally as an old friend of his parents, which explained a certain family-like quality in their relationship. Through Vernon, he had met Nyezi. Dieter, he knew before the conference because of the connection with Vernon and because Dieter regularly visited East Africa as a consultant. The conference that had brought them together again was where Leandro first came across the others on the village trip, Radhika, Frieda, Sven, Jalal and Zehra. Leandro was the one person Zak had recognised, the link there being a connection through Leandro's father and old Communist networks from the time when Zak was a diplomat. The Ulemu mother and son were not previously known to Leandro but because he had enough of her language to talk with Mama Ulemu, who had no English and little Swahili, he was one of the few people here she could relate to. As for Mathew, he and Leandro had met once before at some event to do with debt. With Reece there seemed to be no connection, but odd remarks suggested they had already found one or two things in common.

While we were exchanging mini biographies Jalal kept staring at the bison and frowning. He soon started asking Vernon questions that made it clear he had never heard of Lascaux and although, as a civil engineer, he knew about rocks and rock strata, he had only the haziest notion of human prehistory. Vernon had to explain that the paintings were done not just long ago in the sense of before the British Empire or before the time of Mohammed, but so long ago that the earth was different and colder; that this was a time when there were no cities anywhere at all and also no fields, no vegetable plots and no herds of livestock, because no one anywhere had yet domesticated animals or planted crops.

Tom also hadn't heard of this before but seemed to find it less surprising than Jalal, perhaps because he had grown up, we heard, in an area where there are still a few hunter-gatherers who the villagers believe are remnants of the first people to occupy the land. Unfortunately, they also believe that they are sinister and not quite human. Vernon's task with Tom was to persuade him that there is only one kind of human alive now and that we are all descended from hunter-gatherers. Several of us who were familiar enough with the general idea of a progression from apes to humans and from hunting to farming were vague about the timescale and shocked to hear that people – that is people like us, Homo Sapiens – had spent something like twenty times as long hunting and gathering as they had farming and herding. I have to admit that I'd never really taken this in although I must have seen the figures somewhere. It does slightly destabilise assumptions about 'normal' life.

After a while Jalal strolled outside and could be seen pacing around with his phone. When he came back he showed us something else he had downloaded. An image of horses' heads, coloured black and looking rather like a modern charcoal sketch.

'There were some just of hands, red hands,' he said, 'but I lost the signal before I could download anything else.'

'Some of the earliest are hands, aren't they?' said Radhika who evidently knew a bit about the subject. 'They are amazing; they look so like the kind of thing children do now when playing.'

Mathew had taken Jalal's phone and was staring at the horses. 'Difficult to believe they weren't kept for riding,' he said. 'Looks like they were drawn from right close by; not like wild animals that you'd see from far away.'

'You'd see them close enough when you'd killed them,' Zak suggested.

'But these are very, very much alive,' insisted Radhika who had just been passed the phone.

'I don't recall any people in Palaeolithic art,' Frieda remarked. 'Nor plants. Only animals and only some of the animals they must have known.'

'What about the man under the bison that your Marion talked about?' asked Zehra who obviously had a good memory.

'It's famous because it's rare,' said Vernon. 'Human figures are very rare.'

'You mean in Europe?' challenged Radhika. 'But in India, aren't there scenes of people hunting or fighting?'

Radhika and Vernon then got side-tracked into some academic controversy until Leandro interrupted to remind us that we were hoping for a story, not a seminar. He turned to Jalal who began apologetically.

'This isn't easy. If you'd asked us to go back further it would have been better for me. I could have told you a story about deserts and seas coming and going – I can see them when I look at the layers of rock in a new cutting – but when we get to the first men, all I can think of is Adam and Eve and I suppose that now we don't quite count that as history.' At this point he glanced nervously at Mathew as if for confirmation from the only religious professional present. Mathew nodded vaguely and Jalal went on, 'Of course I'd heard of the Stone Age and cave men but, you know, I'd never pictured cave men as living in Europe. If I pictured them at all I saw them here, in Africa. Perhaps because people – I mean people like Vernon – say we all came out of Africa originally, although what I found odd, thinking about it, is why people left Africa at all and for places covered most of the year with snow. Yes, I know they didn't plan to end up in the snow, but what was wrong with Africa?' Jalal looked around for comment but saw everyone sitting expectantly, wondering if there was ever going to be a story.

'Okay. I can see I'd better begin,' he acknowledged.

4

Jalal's Story

Jalal jumped up and presented himself in front of us. 'Right,' he said. 'Here goes.'

'He doesn't have to stand, does he?' Sven cut in.

'Actually, I'm good. I like to move.'

He took a brisk turn round his patch of floor.

'Right,' he repeated. 'It's in three parts.'

He held up one finger and announced 'Part One', as he took a step forward and drew breath.

'It's late afternoon and hot, hot, hot. There's a river winding through grassland and a little band of humans is camped on its bank. The adults are dozing in the shade of some giant trees but down at the water's edge children are splashing in the shallows. A little boy picks up a handful of mud and throws it at his big sister who shrieks and reaches for a fistful to throw back. The mud battle goes on until the little boy gets a dollop in the face which makes him run off, sulking, to a place down river where there's a bit of cliff. He vents his anger by hurling a mud ball at the cliff making a "splat". He likes the sound and hurls another and another. Splat! Splat! Splat! Then sits on a rock with his chin in his hands glaring at the water.

'His sister splashes down to his rock to see what he's up to and starts to laugh.

'"Shut up!" says the boy, not moving. "Shut up!"

'"But look," she says, "look what you've done!"

'"What?" grumps the boy, not moving.

'"What?" She imitates him. "What?"

'The boy makes a wild animal noise at her. "Wraaaarrr!"

'"No. Look! Actually you've made a buffalo. Go on, look."

'The boy gets up and turns to the cliff where the girl is standing pointing at a splodge of mud.

'"Look! There's the head, that's his back and these," she points to where mud had trickled down in two leg-like lines, "are his front legs." She moves her finger along to another trickle. "And here's a back leg but where's the other one?"

'The boy thinks, walks over, puts his finger in the mud and pulls it down to make a line next to the back leg trickle. "There," he says.

'Other children drift over and look at the "buffalo." Soon they're all trying to make mud animals on the cliff face. The youngest ones quickly give up and swim away but the older ones keep on until the cliff is covered with mud patches roughly suggesting a buffalo or bear or elephant. They are still busy when the heat dies down and adults begin to stir.

'A woman with a baby on her back goes down to the water, fills a leather bag and walks past the children with the dripping bag on her head. The children call out to her, "Look Auntie, see what we've done. We've made a buffalo and an elephant. There! There! Come and see!"

'The woman takes a brief look at the cliff and says, wearily, "It's mud," and plods on.

A pair of young women pass by on their way to bathe, followed at a little distance by a young man with a fish spear pretending he just happens to be on his way to fish. The children run up to the young women and drag them towards the cliff.

'"Look Big Sisters, see what we've done. We've made a buffalo and an elephant. There! There! Come and see!"

'The young women giggle at the animal shaped bits of mud and tease the children. The man pauses behind them, looks thoughtfully at the shapes and then actually starts to improve them. Picking up a stick he tidies the outlines and scratches in some detail. "That's good, Older Brother," the children shout, and jump about. "More, Older Brother. Do some more." One of the young women picks up a chip of stone and starts scratching at a mud pat. The other one copies her but ignores the mud and starts to scratch at the rock. It marks quite easily and produces a better shape than the mud animals but takes longer and the children, getting bored, go back to chasing each other in the water. Only the little boy stays behind watching until a thought comes to him that makes him run off back to the place where his mother keeps her few possessions. There he finds some of the red powder used for body paint and he runs back down to the cliff where the three young people are busy, their plans for bathing and fishing postponed.

'Later, when the sun is low and everyone has left the riverside, an old, old man passes by and stops at the cliff now covered with reddish shapes which, as he stares, appear strangely to look like buffaloes and other animals. He does not like what he sees.'

Jalal spoke the last sentence to sound like a warning and paused for a moment before announcing, 'Part Two. A few weeks later.

'Since the afternoon by the river the animal shapes have become the cause of a big dispute. The old, old man who saw them as he walked past in the evening suspects magic and when he hears how the images got there starts to mutter about witchcraft. But many people are impressed and have been experimenting themselves with the new skill. Others have listened to the old, old man and are afraid. Now everyone has been called to a meeting to decide what should happen.

'First to speak is the old, old man. He moves only slowly to the point, talking first about many things which seem only slightly relevant until he gets to the creation myth that tells how the Spirit of the Earth made animals and humans out of clay and breathed life into them. Humans, he says, must not try to copy the work of the Spirit. It will bring disaster. People have no reason to play at creation unless they hope to gain power over others. No one has done this before and now the evil must stop.

‘The other side is put by another elder, the grandfather of the little boy who made the first mud buffalo. He also moves slowly and wordily towards his argument that making images of the animals is not copying the work of creation because no one is pretending to breath life into them. The things on the rock are not animals but only look like animals and he asks what a man sees when he stands by water and looks down. It looks as if there is another man looking up at him but there is no man.

‘The grandfather looks pleased with this point but it turns out it was actually a mistake. Because people think reflections are a bit weird. There are stories about people being misled by them and disappearing or being turned into a sort of evil replica. As he winds up his case people are shifting uncomfortably and muttering to each other. From then on the gathering begins to go badly for the picture makers. A few people speak for them but more and more come to agree with the old, old man and even some of the picture makers say they were wrong and it must stop. So the meeting ends with a decision that the pictures are dangerous. No one is to do anything like it ever again and anyone seen making the pictures must be brought to judgment.

‘Most people go away satisfied but a few of the picture makers are not. They start to hang out together and sometimes meet to draw on rocks in overgrown places where no one goes. The extreme reaction, the talk of danger, gives them the idea that there is something important about the pictures. Soon the making of the first one is remembered as a revelation, not a child’s game. They wind each other up to assume dark motives for the picture ban, but they are cautious because there are not enough of them to risk a fight. So, they look for secret places to draw and the search leads them to the best, most secret place of all, a set of caves. In the caves, the darkness and difficulty of working makes them feel that the old, old man was actually right that they are doing something special. But not witchcraft. Nothing like witchcraft. No, the drawings speak to the spirit world. They are like an offering, a gift, a gesture of respect. '

This sounded a bit final but Jalal put up his hands as if to say 'wait a minute' and continued.

'There's a bit more.'

He held up three fingers and went on:

'Part Three. Years later.

'The little band has split. After losing the argument the secret picture makers started to drift away bit by bit and now form a resentful faction. There is hostility between the two groups. Each blames the other for whatever goes wrong: a hunt that fails; a stillbirth; a wound that turns bad...

'The picture makers are still a small minority and have kept away from the others to avoid confrontation. But now there is a crisis. A hunting party from the picture-hating faction has returned with serious news. Everyone gathers round to hear, and the hunters tell how they saw a great storm on the horizon and hurried to shelter in a cave. At first they were glad to escape the storm but when they looked around what did they see? They saw a wall covered by the forbidden pictures!

'Those listening are fired up with rage. They had long suspected, long feared, that the picture makers had not respected the decision at the meeting. Now here was proof. Something must be done! Everyone who can fight grabs a weapon and a war party sets out to find the picture makers. The plan is to punish rather than kill because this is a time when people are not yet quite hardened to killing each other.

'The picture makers evade their attackers for a long time and when they are finally surrounded they put up such a show of resistance that the picture makers back off and offer to talk. So they talk but, as you can probably guess, the same old arguments are repeated and both sides are now surer than ever that they are right. It becomes clear that the two sides cannot live alongside each other. Well, luckily, they don't have to because there are plenty of places around where there are no humans yet. The picture makers agree to leave and to go far, far away, not stopping until they have gone so far that the others will never see or hear of them again.

'The picture makers gather their few possessions and depart, heading northwards towards a barren zone that marks the end of the known world. As they leave, a man believed to be something of a prophet makes this pronouncement: "You and your descendants will travel on for years, will travel for generation after generation finding no rest until you arrive in a cold land, a land of wind and shadows. There you will turn pale like dried bones in the sand and you will cover yourselves to hide this ghostly sight from each other. This is your destiny."

'When he hears this the leader of the picture makers is afraid but hides his fear with anger and shouts back, "Ghosts we may become but ghosts with strength, and we will return. Then you will eat dust and wish with all your heart you had never driven us away…"

'Okay. That's the end.'

There was a tentative clap or two and then Leandro applauded more firmly so that we all joined in. Radhika said, 'Thank you for starting us off.'

Jalal grinned and replied, 'Great to be done! Someone else's turn now!'

Sven turned to Vernon. 'Well, what do you say?'

'Yes, why not? Let's have the next story.'

'No, I meant about Jalal's. Is it a bad guess. A good guess?'

Vernon shrugged, 'Why are you asking me? I've told you we really know so little.'

'But more than us.'

'You may not know the things you would most like to know,' Frieda added carefully, 'but you must know a lot of other things, and you could say something about how a story fits with some of those other things.'

'It's a game, isn't it? I'm sure people don't want a lecture.'

'Of course,' Frieda conceded, 'and we'll all be silenced if we think our stories must fit with evidence we don't even know exists. But just for fun, Vernon, you could say one small thing after each story, just one small thing from your perspective. No?'

There was a buzz of agreement and Vernon gave in.

'One small thing only then. So, we don't know

if children played a part in cave art, but we do know that they were around in the caves at the time. Some of the handprints are of children's hands and in one cave there's a remarkable find which, for me, conjures a scene rather like Jalal's children fooling around by the water: it's a child's footprint in a patch of mud that evidently hardened and preserved the print for nearly twenty thousand years!'

In the quiet which followed, our attention was drawn to a parallel conversation that had been going on in low tones between Tom and his mother. Just as Vernon finished, the old woman raised her voice so that anyone who spoke her language would have known what she said. Leandro switched his attention to the couple, exchanged a few words with the mother and then turned to the son, dropping into English. It became clear that Mama Ulemu had been asking Tom what everyone was talking about and Tom had fobbed her off saying it wasn't interesting. Leandro dropped back into the, to me, incomprehensible language and was, I guessed, providing a more satisfactory summary of the situation which Mama Ulemu punctuated intermittently with nods and an appreciative or thoughtful 'mmm' before rounding on her son and giving him, I assumed, a good ticking off. The upshot of it all was that from now on Tom would try to translate the stories as they were told.

Satisfied, Leandro suggested we should move on and draw the next lot. Frieda put in a plea for a short break after the draw which was quickly agreed. Again I took my straw and again I was lucky. Zehra was the victim.

'Oh!' she exclaimed, holding up the bent straw. 'It's me. I'd hoped the plane would come and save me from my turn.'

Some of us laughed, and Father Mathew said, 'We are all hoping that.'

During the break Jalal went outside and strolled around in a carefree manner, tossing a little pebble in the air and then juggling with a pair of them. Zak and Dieter went out to smoke. Reece picked up his tablet but then put it down again, strolled over to me and made some remark of the 'how do you find it out here?' kind, to which I responded neutrally. From the way he asked the question I had a feeling I did not want to hear his views on 'out here' and so switched the topic to ask him if he had 'done' cavemen at school.

'If we did, none of it stuck,' he answered. 'But school and me didn't get along.'

'Oh!' I said, and reluctantly added, 'Why?'

'Either school was shit or I was shit. Whatever.'

I said something non-committal and asked how he'd got into doing business out in Africa.

'Joined the army,' he answered in a slightly aggressive tone, as if he assumed I would disapprove. 'It's what a lot of us kids did, the factories being closed and that. Didn't suit everyone but, for me, it turned me round. Found out I wasn't so dumb as I thought at school. Got some qualifications and that. But what about you? I bet you went to uni, didn't you? '

At that point Zehra edged up and said we were about to start and she needed to ask me a quick question. She wanted the names of one or two northern flowers, the sort that ice age people might have known. It made me realise I have no idea how ancient any of our flowers are but, pressed to name something, I thought that moorland landscapes have an archaic look and so suggested heather or thyme.

People were already drifting back. Someone placed a chair for Zehra and we all settled down ready to listen. Zehra apologised that her story was not the right kind of thing, but she'd have to tell it anyway.

5

Zehra's Story

'Far away and long ago in the time of the great cold there was a man called Storm Cloud who had two wives, Standing Heron, the older one and Thymeflower, the younger. Together with Storm Cloud's brothers and cousins and their wives and children they roamed the windy grasslands all summer and returned each winter to some caves in a sheltered gorge.

'Standing Heron had one son whom she called Rain's Gift because he was conceived in the rainy season after she had been married but childless for seven years. His birth, she said, was like the bright new grass that springs up when rain at last breaks a drought. Years passed again without bringing another baby and then two girls arrived in just two years but both died. Standing Heron doted on the son but she longed for a daughter too, a girl to hold close in the cold nights and who would help her with her daily tasks. The other women would often say that her co-wife, young Thymeflower, was like a daughter and that Thymeflower's children were like her own. They also said that when Rain's Gift was grown up and married his wife would be another daughter to her, a daughter who would stay with her always and not leave her for a husband as a girl of her own would do. All this was true, Standing Heron agreed, but inside herself she still grieved for her little girls buried in the cold, cold ground and she could not quite feel the same love for other children as she did for Rain's Gift. He returned her love, becoming more helpful as he grew, unlike so many boys who take to running wild just as they reach an age to be useful. Often he would fetch water or firewood without being asked and as soon as he started hunting for small animals he would always bring her a share of anything he caught.

'One year, towards the end of winter, Storm Cloud observed that Rain's Gift was reaching the age when boys become men and start to hunt for big animals with other men. He told Standing Heron and Thymeflower that they should make everything ready for his son to undergo the ceremony of reaching manhood which would be held, as always, at the time of the flying of the geese. So the two women hurried to work on the clothes Rain's Gift would wear as a man, fine clothes made from bison pelts and trimmed with patterns of white, black and coloured feathers. As they worked, the first warm sun of spring at last began to melt the snow and the men's talk turned to the reindeer herds that should soon arrive following the retreating snow.

Throughout the daylight hours the little camp was alive with tap-tapping as men worked on spearheads and women sharpened the knives they would use for cleaning hides. As the days became milder, children ran about more outside, their chatter competing with the tap-tapping of stone on stone.

'Then the geese came, great flocks flying northwards. Everyone stopped whatever they were doing and looked up to watch the welcome sight. A small party headed off down the snowy hillside to a lake where geese would settle for the night and become easy prey. Standing Heron watched with sadness as well as pleasure, knowing that the time had finally come that she must give up her little companion. The boy she had fed, teased and played with for so long must leave her side and turn into a man.

'The hunters returned with enough goose carcasses for the feast. The next morning the birds were plucked, a great fire made and the ceremony began, a simple one compared to those of later times. Rain's Gift, and the only other boy of his age, were each prepared by painting their faces and arms with ochre and were then taken away by the men to prove themselves in secret tests of which the last was to strip naked in the snow to clean their bodies completely before putting on adult clothing for the first time. When dressed they were brought back to the fire where the women and children, pretending not to recognise them, shouted abuse at them for failing to approach as strangers should. The boys, now men, tried to answer in kind but could not match the older women's coarse humour.

When this had gone on some time the men intervened and mocked the women for not knowing their own sons who were then reintroduced to them in a formal manner involving the recitation of their genealogy as if their mothers and aunts had forgotten who they were. After this was completed, everyone fell to dancing and feasting.

'Only a few days after this ceremony the first reindeer came…'

Zehra stopped suddenly because everyone's attention was drawn to the space outside the building where several lorries had just driven up and were now disgorging gun-carrying soldiers. The main contingent went towards the runway but a smaller party came clomping inside.

'Government ones at least,' Reece murmured to Leandro.

'What do you think it means?' asked Sven.

No one answered.

One of the soldiers was shouting at the baggage handlers who had reappeared from wherever they had gone, and another, evidently an officer, took a couple of his men and barged through into an area off limits to the public. The others positioned themselves around the edge of our space, bulging aggressively under their uniforms and clutching their guns in a ready-to-shoot posture.

Leandro went over to speak to the one he identified as being most senior but was unable to get much out of him. Their orders, it seemed, were not to say what was happening, not to say why they were there, in fact not to talk to the public at all. The man did, however, relent in so far as to tell Leandro that their presence had nothing to do with any of us, a double-edged comment since we might have hoped the military was there to secure the airport and make it possible to resume flights.

Nothing further happened, and after a period of tense waiting Leandro suggested that Zehra continue her story.

'The guns distract me,' she said, 'but I'll try.' She drew herself up and closed her eyes for a moment.

'The reindeer. Yes, that's where we'd got to.

'So, when the reindeer began to pass on the plateau above the gorge, Storm Cloud gathered the men and they set off at dawn up a steep path with the two new hunters, Rain's Gift and his age mate. Standing Heron followed them with her eyes as the path led them up and up, winding backwards and forwards until they reached the top and vanished from her view. The hours passed slowly but before the end of the day the party could be seen returning laden with their kill. The hunt was a success and there was fresh meat for everyone.

'So, spring began well and as the days lengthened and warmed, the herds of animals passing above the gorge got larger, darkening the thinning snow. Then came the time when the passing herds became less frequent, the sign for Storm Cloud and his family to prepare for their own migration to the summer hunting grounds. There they would meet other families, the sisters who had married into them and distant relatives. There would be feasts, dancing, storytelling. New marriages would be made, friendships strengthened, quarrels stirred up and quarrels settled. There would be long evenings full of the sound of drumming.

'Rain's Gift was already on the way to being an excellent hunter. He had grown to look like the man he was expected to be. His hair, which Standing Heron used to plait close to his head, now fell in the way of unmarried men, loose and curling on his shoulders. He no longer ate with Standing Heron but with the other unmarried men, but she would watch him sometimes in the light of his separate fire. Mostly he ignored her, absorbed in conversation, but every now and then he would catch her looking at him and make a mischievous face like the one he used to make when he escaped her in a game of tag. It was as if to say, "Look at me, I've really run away now..." Every time this happened her heart melted.

'Three days before the day chosen for departure one of the hunters who had been out looking for food came back to say that he had seen a small herd of auroch not far away.'

'Herd of what?' interrupted Zak.

Zehra looked rattled and quickly turned to ask Vernon, 'Isn't that what you said they were called, the giant wild cattle of the Ice Age?'

'Indeed it is,' Vernon reassured her. 'Actually, they long outlasted the Ice Age. It wasn't climate change but us that finally did for them – in the seventeenth century.'

'Oh. How sad! Well, anyway, they'd seen this herd of aurochs and it provoked a discussion among the men about whether to set out on a hunt. Some argued that it would be dangerous work and not necessary as there was enough small game around to feed them on the journey; others argued that it would be a good omen to kill such significant animals for a feast on the eve of travel. Soon the women got involved. Mostly they opposed because of the danger, but a few were in favour because they agreed about the omen. And so it went on, backwards and forwards with the older people citing different lessons from hunts they had known. Standing Heron said nothing. She was opposed herself but could tell her son wanted to seize this first chance to hunt something bigger and more exciting than a reindeer.

'Standing Heron walked away and went back to preparing the hides they would use for shelters on the open plateau. Eventually, everyone else drifted off. The hunters had won and the men prepared to leave at once, planning to spend the night out near their prey and to attack early, before the animals could move too far from where they had last been seen. Darkness fell on the half empty camp and Thymeflower and Standing Heron huddled close, holding between them Thymeflower's youngest child, a little girl still feeding at the breast.

'It was late the following day that one of the women looked up and saw, on the path high up in the gorge, some of their men carrying a burden. It was a burden that was plainly not part of an auroch or any other meat. She cried out making everyone look up. What they saw being carried could only be a man. Someone from the hunting party must be severely injured, although at least not dead. A death would have been announced by shrieks of mourning but the party was approaching in silence.

'The women counted the figures on the path and saw that three were missing. What had happened? Some of the older children ran to meet them while everyone else went to build up the fires, fetch water and trim lamps as it would be near dusk by the time the men got down. Before long some of the children came running back down. One, a nearly adult girl, flung herself in front of Standing Heron and asked forgiveness as the bringer of bad news. She did not look at Thymeflower so Standing Heron knew then that the victim was not her husband but her son. She touched the girl's head and pulled her up in silence. It would be shocking to everyone, and most of all to Rain's Gift, to cry when he was alive. So, she held her screams inside and walked out in the fading light to meet the men. Storm Cloud was in the lead and put his hands on her shoulders. She made to go to the improvised stretcher but Storm Cloud pulled her back and the bearers hurried on to the cave where they laid their burden in the sheltered area behind the fire.

'Standing Heron knew from the men's manner that they assumed death was only postponed. When she lifted the blood soaked covers she saw they were right.

'The events of that hunt afterwards became one of those stories told again and again, at length, but then what was told was brief and of that she took in only part. They had spent the night near the small herd. At first light they approached. There was one enormous bull and a few cows, calves and yearlings.

Some men lured the big bull away while the others rapidly attacked, wounded a cow and killed a yearling calf. The bull charged back in a terrible rage and the hunters turned their attention to confusing him, to prevent him concentrating his force for long on any one of them. Rain's Gift showed courage and skill in drawing the bull onto himself and then dodging the charge. In turns they played the bull like that, waiting for him to give up or to weary sufficiently for someone to aim a spear carefully, from close enough to kill. The bull did not tire but became more wary of the men's tricks, readying himself to turn when they leapt out of his way. Eventually, one man slipped as he jumped away. The bull spun round to gore the fallen man and Rain's Gift ran in to stop it in the only way now possible, by thrusting his spear into the creature's great neck. As it entered, the bull lurched and caught Rain's Gift with one of his horns and, driving the sharp tip deep, tossed him in the air. All the men now closed in and fortunately the bull was so troubled by the wound that he turned away to retreat, bellowing, towards his terrified herd. There was not much the men could do for Rain's Gift as the horn had ripped deep into his belly and torn his intestines. They wrapped him in furs and carried him back as fast as they could but, because they were not enough to transport the dead beasts as well, they left two men behind to butcher the carcasses and keep the meat safe from hyenas and crows. They would not abandon such hard won food.

'The whole family sat with Rain's Gift through the night. They were calm, as they should be, while life remained. Standing Heron behaved calmly as she knew she should but felt something else, something powerful and frightening, which flowed into her from her dying son. She could see he knew death was approaching and that he was not resigned although he acted correctly. When he had strength he said the things he should say, but behind his correct words she read surprise and outrage. Towards dawn he suffered a series of spasms and she saw the outrage intensify. He drew out his right hand that had been resting on the gaping wound and was thickly covered in blood. He raised it and with a determined gesture pressed it hard on the rock wall above him. He fell back and looked at the mark in a puzzled way for some time. Then their eyes met. The pain seemed to have receded and she thought he made that mischievous face, the "I've got away" face but in the dim light she could not be sure. He tried to speak but only managed to say, "the bull…" and then, quite suddenly, his life ran out.

'The family delayed their departure for the funeral and Standing Heron played her part as expected, but when it was over she told Storm Cloud that she would not leave for the summer hunting grounds. He was angry at first and kept away from her. Thymeflower whimpered quietly that she needed the older woman's support. Other people gave their opinions but Standing Heron went off into the woodland down the gorge so she did not have to listen. Storm Cloud found her there later, his anger a little cooled by this time, and they walked together a long way to a sheltered spot near where the stream at the bottom of the gorge became a waterfall. Storm Cloud was disturbed by her extreme reaction and more so to find her speaking not only the name of their son but also the names of the little girls, dead so young and so long ago. But she transmitted to him something of her feelings so that for a long time they wept together for their three dead children. When he got up to go Storm Cloud told her again that she must come with them the next day, but she said firmly that she would not and that Thymeflower would do everything for him that she could. He looked at her in a puzzled way and said, "She is not the same as you." Then they made love, long and fiercely beside the waterfall. The next day, early, the family left and Standing Heron was alone.

Not the same as you, not the same, not the same… The words went round in Standing Heron's mind as she sat looking at the hand stain on the wall. It was a good outline and sometimes she put her own hand over it and imagined touching her son's hand, which was like no one else's.

'The days lengthened and when she was not wandering in search of food she found herself looking at her own hand, also like no one else's. She was not sure why but she felt a need to imprint her own palm near his. So, she prepared some ochre, covered one hand with it and printed it on the wall near by. Later on she found herself thinking about the words Rain's Gift had spoken as he died: 'The bull…" Why? She was sure he did not just want to say that the bull killed him. He had no need to say that. Everyone by then knew what happened. It was more that he and the bull were bound together. She could not work out quite what this meant but in between wandering in search of food she found herself trying to trace the outline of an auroch bull. First of all, when she was down by the stream, she dabbled a faint image with water on the rocks. It had a bit of an auroch look about it, but was not right. She closed her eyes and tried to remember what an auroch looked like. Four legs, the hump, the great horns. She scratched something in the sand. As the summer wore on the doodles looked more auroch like and when she knew it was time she made up some ochre again and made her auroch outline on the rock near the two hand prints. After that she moved into another cave to eat and sleep because she felt it was wrong to do ordinary things there.

'One day when a cold wind brought with it the first flurries of snow, Storm Cloud and his family returned. Most of the adults were surprised that Standing Heron was still there and alive. No one had been known to spend so long alone. They had expected her to follow them to the summer hunting grounds and when she did not appear they assumed she was dead, although no one said so. They greeted her warmly but felt her chosen solitude was strange. When people saw what she had done on the cave wall they were not sure what it meant although they respected her decision to not eat or sleep in the place her son had died. No one else made a move to reoccupy that cave but they did not like the way Standing Heron spent a part of every day sitting in front of the pictures and apparently talking to her dead son. Some said she had gone mad because of the months spent alone. Others whispered with a shiver that she was trying to cross the line between the dead and the living and that perhaps it would be best to leave that place and find a different winter home. A few, including Storm Cloud, thought differently. One day Storm Cloud made up some ochre paint and put his own handprint on the wall by Standing Heron's. Then he called Thymeflower and their children to put their handprints too, a little way away from the others. After that attitudes began to change. The cave became a place where people would gather to tell and retell stories about important things that happened to them like the auroch hunt and the death of Rain's Gift. More people began to print their hands and after someone died, their children or husband or wife or, in the saddest cases, their parents, would touch the handprint and remember. After Storm Cloud died his children by Thymeflower painted another, larger and more lifelike auroch near his hand print, not because an auroch, or indeed any other animal, had caused his death but because, over the years, the red figure had come more and more to represent fate; fate that is the same for everyone and yet different for each person.

'Little by little these practices spread so that in time all the other people that wandered the cold plains made hand prints which, after a death, gave the relatives a place to grieve and ensured, long afterwards, their descendants would remember them and know that this person had once lived.

'The end,' said Zehra abruptly, with a shy smile.

Most of us clapped, which we seemed to have decided collectively would be the right thing to do for each story. The action brought me back to the present and I was glad to see that the soldiers had relaxed considerably since their arrival although the sound of our clapping made one or two briefly tense again. I noticed other people glancing anxiously at them as well as looking at each other to see of anyone was going to speak.

'Very touching!' said Dieter, in a way that might or might not have been ironic.

Mama Ulemu said something that most of us missed.

'You got a real sense of the snow and the cold,' said Sven. 'Have you been to Europe in the winter?'

'Not even in summer,' Zehra answered, 'but I hope to go sometime. When I was a child an uncle went to Sweden and brought me back one of those scenes in a glass ball that you shake to make a snowstorm. My snowstorm fell on a tiny house with a fir tree beside it. I kept shaking it and dreaming that one day I'd walk through snow like that.'

'I'm sure you will,' exclaimed Radhika. 'Although I wouldn't have known you'd never been north.'

Dieter objected. 'You had the hand print and the bison done at the same time but we're told the handprints came long before.'

Jalal jumped to the defence. 'It's a story isn't it?'

Leandro was only half paying attention because he had reacted to whatever it was that Mama Ulemu had said and the two were quietly talking. Now he broke off and announced: 'I have just heard something that is very interesting indeed. Mama Ulemu has been trying to tell us that she has actually seen the prehistoric people.' He allowed a dramatic pause during which we all looked obligingly surprised while Tom whispered something I took to be a restraining remark to his mother and she made a slightly indignant reply. Leandro went on.

'At least she has seen their spirits, that is the spirits of people who she says lived near her home long before the time of her own ancestors. So, not the spirits of the people in Zehra's story, who clearly lived in the far north, but perhaps the spirits of their contemporaries in Africa or of the people in Jalal's story who didn't leave. Who knows? But I suggest we listen to her. If no one minds we will make this her turn without drawing the straws.'

Tom was the only person who minded. He was embarrassed and muttered that his mother was illiterate, superstitious, would not be worth hearing.

'Let us decide that,' Leandro answered. 'As you are not interested, let me translate. I will do the best I can but you will need to help out from time to time.'

How literally he translated I don't know, but I was struck that she would speak for a long time with different tones of voice and gestures and expressions but all that would turn into just a few sentences of ordinary English. This is roughly her story as it emerged in translation.

6

Mama Ulemu's Story

'In our village usually the boys went out to graze the goats but my mother had no sons and so she sent me. Her next co-wife had three boys, all younger than me, but the oldest one went with me and we took his mother's goats as well. In the rainy season we took them up a small hill behind our village where there was plenty of grass and we'd meet other village children with their parents' goats. We'd just take them out in the morning and in the evening we'd come home. But in the dry season we all went further away. We took the goats up over the top of the first hill and on up into some rocky hills where there were little gullies with water holes and grass around them and trees growing quite thickly in places. It was far away and usually we would take food with us and stay a few days. It was a big area where the water holes were far apart and so we often wouldn't see anyone else. Towards the top of the hills were some caves but we never went up there because there were not many trees there for the goats to feed on and because the Old People were there.

'Our father and our mothers told us we did not have to worry about the Old People because they are not our ancestors and have no interest in us either to help us or to harm us. They are the spirits of people who lived in the deep, deep past, long before out ancestors arrived. But we children were afraid all the same. We heard that the Old People haunted the caves and if you went up near the caves you sometimes saw them passing. They wandered around, probably looking for descendants to bring them offerings, but there were none. No one knew what had become of their people, whether they had moved away to some distant land or had all died.

'The elder over there' – she indicated Vernon – 'has said that people went from Africa to the northern countries where white people come from now and so perhaps it was your ancestors that abandoned their forefathers' spirits there where we used to herd our goats. Perhaps, if you went there, they could talk to you and you could bring them peace. Or perhaps they would possess you. How can we know? Perhaps their people all died, the children and the parents, leaving no one to honour the dead. We have heard of such things. Even now we have heard that such things happen. In that case the Old People will be there forever.

'We never went up to the caves even though it was sometimes cold at night and we could have sheltered in them. We were afraid. Even lower down where we stayed I was afraid. It was very quiet and the pale, empty landscape was lonely. Now and then you might startle a small antelope but there were not many wild animals. I suppose they had been hunted. Lions had disappeared in our grandparents' time. There were hyenas and possibly a few leopards, although no one had seen one or known one to steal a goat for some years. We were careful of snakes but you didn't often see or hear one, especially in the dry season. So, we were more afraid of the Old People than anything else. Very occasionally we caught a glimpse of them – one or two tall figures would appear far away behind a rock and then vanish again. But the sight made me shiver and my little half brother, if he saw one, he'd run to me and cling on to me.

'One day near the end of the dry season I saw far away a strange cloud and, after I looked at it carefully, I knew that it was a dust storm approaching. Sometimes the first rains bring such a storm, although usually it comes more slowly, clouds build and then the storm breaks. This was so sudden that it was strange, and I thought it may be an unusual, terrible storm and we should shelter and drive the goats to shelter. But the gully where we were camped was shallow. There was nowhere to go except the caves of the Old People. *We can't go there*, I thought, but then I thought our parents have told us we don't need to fear the Old People. So, I said to my little brother, "Hurry! Help me drive the goats up to the cave where we will shelter." He started crying because he was afraid of the caves but I said, of the two terrors, the storm will be worse. So, we rounded up the goats and drove them over the stony ground where already a hot, dry wind was whipping dust in our face. "Hurry, hurry," I said, and I picked up a stick and beat the lingering goats to drive them on as the dark cloud was near. The sun went in and a hot wind blew stinging dust into our eyes but we were nearly there. I took my little brother's hand and dragged him onwards, stopping now and again to run after one of the goats, and at last we reached the dark arch of the cave. Inside, a rock face sloped down to a sandy space and I chased the goats down into that space and pulled my little brother down the rocky slope to a ledge where we could sit. It was cold and still inside but, despite the cold, something told me the place was inhabited. Beyond where the goats were it was dark enough to hide anyone or anything. The goats milled uneasily and suddenly made a dash for the entrance as if startled by something in the darkness. I chased them back and they huddled together at the bottom of the slope. My little brother whimpered and clung to me. As the full force of the storm arrived outside, the light dimmed and even less of the cave was visible. I thought I saw a movement in the dark beyond the goats but when I looked there was nothing. I turned back to watch the dust whirling at the entrance and a little later I noticed behind me a tall figure, leaning against the wall and also looking outwards. Terrified, I turned to look at him but he was no longer there. Then I noticed there were two people behind me, sitting by the entrance. I froze and did not shift my eyes. The nearer one turned and looked past us towards where I had seen the standing figure. Then she – I think it was a woman – slowly turned back and I saw she was braiding the hair of the figure in front of her. She should have seen us sitting in between her and the tall man but she made no sign at all that she saw us. Slowly I turned my head to get a better view but, like the other figure, as soon as I looked straight at her she was gone. I didn't say anything to my little brother.

'Outside there was lightning and then thunder. Soon it began to rain very hard and the rain settled the dust so that it became a little lighter, but only a little as night was coming on. My little brother wanted to go home but I knew there would be thick mud everywhere and in the dark and the rain we would certainly lose some of the goats. So, we stayed all night in the cave holding tight to one another, too frightened to sleep much, but shortly before dawn I slept properly and woke again to see the first pink light filling the outer part of the cave. The rain had passed and the colour of the light indicated it was a fine morning. Then I noticed there were two men standing by the entrance leaning on long spears. I was no longer afraid and wanted to know who they were. So I addressed them in a tone I hoped they would understand was respectful. But they made no reaction at all. A third joined them and, silently, they left the cave.

'One of the goats was missing when we drove them out and I hope that the Old People had taken it as an offering. I was glad that my parents had been right that these spirits could not harm me, and now I felt sorry for them that they have no one to care for them.

I felt a great sadness to think that whole lineages can be destroyed so that even the memory of them dies.

'These may be the foolish words of an old woman but your talk about an Old People who left paintings in caves made me think of this time.'

After translating the last lines Leandro said something to her, which I assume was reassuring as she smiled a crinkly smile.

'Tell us more about what these people looked like,' asked Sven.

'They were tall,' she said, 'tall and thin.'

'Light skinned or dark? And what did they wear?'

'They were naked and they were pale, but not pale like you people,' she indicated Sven and Vernon who were near her, 'but pale in a different way, maybe because they were spirits. You people may have got pale because of living in a cold place. So, not pale like you but not dark as I am. They were naked, except I think they had some jewellery about them, but I could only see them from the corner of my eye. When I looked straight at them they were not visible.'

Vernon nodded and said, 'Sometimes I feel like that during a dig. When we have found things that shed a little new light on the people who lived and died there, I start to see – almost see – the people, especially if I linger on site alone when the day's work is over and the place is still. I'm consciously puzzling over some small detail and then, suddenly, I get the feeling that the people are there with me, present in all their richness and complexity and that I only have to pay attention to know what they are really like. Then, of course, the moment I pay attention they are no longer there. I am alone thinking about a few flints and bones.'

No one added anything, partly because new activity among the soldiers indicated something might happen. After the initial bluster of their arrival they had relaxed into a bored torpor, but in the last few minutes they had straightened up and grasped their weapons again.

7

The Decision

The soldiers' activity was soon explained by the sound of an aircraft engine, at first distant but drawing closer. Then a little plane flashed down the runway, vanished and reappeared taxiing up to the terminal. What a cheering sight! Everyone gathered their luggage and some hopefully approached the check-in counter. Outside, a trio of officers stood to attention as a large, uniformed figure, evidently a senior officer, descended the steps from the small plane. There were salutes and greetings. Some soldiers ran up and started unloading crates from the plane, while the officer and his entourage swept into the waiting room where more saluting took place. One of the officers from the greeting party shooed us away from the doorway where we were poised to head to the plane. There was a brief consultation between officers and then most of them went out of the other door to where the lorries were parked. Leandro and Magome, the bureaucrat, followed them. Meanwhile, a couple of airport staff reappeared with some luggage that they took out to the plane, ignoring us completely. The next moment two men in civilian clothes, accompanied by soldiers, strode through the waiting room and out towards the plane. They boarded, the engines started again and the plane taxied away and was soon heard taking off. We stared at each other astounded.

Leandro and Magome were still outside near the lorries but in a few minutes Magome returned on his own, sweating and fanning himself. It was the time in the late afternoon when the heat pools up around buildings and the sun is not yet low enough to promise relief. He sat down heavily, overflowing the small chair.

'Plane is coming,' he panted without conviction. 'They are saying plane is coming soon.' He offered no more information.

An officer stamped into the room and yelled an order at the soldiers who had started to slouch again. Instantly, they straightened up, clicked their heels and marched out behind the officer. There was a revving of engines and the lorries and military vehicles drove off, leaving nothing behind but dust.

Leandro slowly crossed the empty parking place and came back inside, apparently untroubled by the heat. We turned to him.

'It's hard to tell,' he began, 'whether they have no idea themselves what is going on or if they just don't want us to know. The commander refused to say anything about the coup but kept saying we should stay here and a plane will come. He kept saying, "It'll come today" although it seems to me unlikely as it's already late and the runway's not lit. Certainly, the plane that's just left couldn't get to the capital and back before dark. I pointed that out but he snapped that it wouldn't be that plane coming back for us because that one is a military one, his manner implying that the plane was, like him, very busy and very important, much too busy and important to do anything for civilians.'

Leandro told this as if we should be amused but our situation seemed to me to be getting less amusing every moment, a feeling accentuated by the rest of the story.

'So, I tried asking the commander if we should retreat to Mufalenge for the night but this made him snap again. He said we shouldn't even think of it. There are roadblocks and the town's under curfew. I suggested he could have us escorted through the road blocks and I think he gave this a flicker of thought before dismissing it, blustering, increasingly crossly, "Plane will come. Plane will come!" That was it. He then turned his attention to the troops, bawled a few orders and got into his vehicle.'

His account was met with silence except for Vernon who said, 'Oh!' and Dieter who asked, 'You think it's true about the road block?'

Leandro answered obliquely. 'Something is definitely not right. If there are no hostile forces near, why is Mufalenge blockaded? And if there are, why did the army move off when you'd think the airstrip would be a key place to defend?'

'It stinks,' agreed Reece.

Leandro glanced at his phone as he went on: 'I think we should quickly make calls – if anyone has a signal. Try to get hold of someone who has a grip on what is really going on – or at least someone in Mufalenge who will know about the curfew. I suggest everyone goes out to check for a signal and, if anyone has one, we pool contacts.'

We all complied except Frieda, who said she doesn't carry a mobile, and Mama Ulemu, who extracted a basic handset from her clothes and gave it to Tom.

Jalal, predictably, had the best signal and quickly got through to a cousin in the capital but the cousin didn't know much. The coup had failed according to the TV, but the capital was still tense with the army patrolling empty streets. Jalal then passed his phone to Leandro as he couldn't think of anyone else to call. Reece evidently had a signal but went off out of earshot to make his calls. By holding my phone up high I managed to get a ringing tone for my NGO's Mufalenge office, but not an answer. Although unhelpful, this was not necessarily worrying since it was getting late, around the time the office would normally close. The signal faded before I could dial any other numbers.

Back inside, we shared fragments of intelligence. No one had managed to establish anything much more about the coup or whether there was fighting in or near Mufulenge but one thing which seemed certain was that staying the night in a comfortable hotel in town was not an option. The roadblocks were real and, although a curfew was not in force at the moment, there were vehicles going round with loud hailers announcing it would start at sundown. No taxi was prepared to come out, for any price, and even the personal acquaintances that one or two people got through to confirmed that it was impossible get in or out of town. So, that meant we'd all be sleeping on the waiting room's concrete floor and, meanwhile, there was the problem of dinner. The little bar was not only closed but had been stripped of anything much to eat. The airport staff had vanished after the soldiers left.

Leandro, remarkably, had already thought about food and had found out earlier from the airport staff that there was a village with a small shop not far away and he volunteered to walk there if one or two others would join him. He set out with Nyezi and Zehra just as the sun touched the horizon, and they returned in the dark with raw materials for a meal. The plan was to invade the kitchenette used by the absent bar staff and now padlocked. Mathew (or Father Mathew) volunteered to sort out access and proved surprisingly adept, carefully picking the lock rather than using force. Reece joked that in a former life he must have been a burglar, a comment which drew more of a laugh than it might have done if we hadn't been treating Father Mathew with that respectful embarrassment that people often show in front of a priest.

The supplies included a scrawny live chicken which Mama Ulemu took charge of and quietly killed, gutted, plucked, chopped up and turned into sauce with the help of tomato puree and a few chillies, while Tom boiled maize flour to make a thick porridge. While this was going on Leandro and Reece seemed to be in deep discussion. Then the lights flickered and went out leaving us in a darkness not quite complete but complete enough to be disorienting. Fortunately, apart from phone torches, we had between us two proper torches, and the shoppers, being well aware that power cuts go with crises, had bought another torch, matches and candles. When the meal was eventually served, by candlelight, Leandro remarked that all we were missing was some beer, whereupon Magome surprised us by producing a large bottle of local spirits and put it in the centre for all to share. The evening at once felt more companionable and as we raised a toast to the shoppers, the cooks and Magome, I found myself almost forgetting that everyone in this odd assembly weas to me a complete stranger.

Over our improvised supper Leandro and Nyezi told us what happened in the village. Their arrival had been uncomfortable as the villagers, clearly nervous, reacted to unknown visitors by approaching with pangas. Before any heads were chopped off Leandro managed to explain our situation, but the atmosphere remained cool. The shop was shut, no one knew if it might open or had any suggestions about supplies. Only slowly, as they chatted and exchanged information about the army's passage through the area, the villagers began to relax. Tea was offered and, after more chatting, the owner of the shop turned up, opened it and, despite complaining that his stocks were low, agreed to sell some rice, maize flour, the candles and a few odds and ends at rather inflated prices. The chicken was offered by someone else at an even more unreasonable price.

Gradually, it emerged that the reason no one was keen to sell food was that rumours were circulating about the approach of insurgents – or bandits – and the villagers were thinking of taking to the hills with whatever food they could carry. From listening to the radio and phoning relatives in better connected places they had reached the conclusion that the rumours were probably true.

Leandro went on to say that those reports, combined with the odd behaviour of the army, suggested to him that there was a real possibility that insurgents would arrive to take over the airstrip with unpredictable consequences. It was not clear who these insurgents were, but rebel forces that had been operating for months in a few areas had a reputation for indiscipline and violence. Given that the road into Mufalenge was closed, our situation seemed at best precarious.

Leandro paused to let us take this in before starting to explain about a possible solution. The eastern border of the country, he said, was much nearer than the capital – a mere fifty miles by the most direct route on forest paths. We could walk there, where we would at least be safe, and from there make whatever onward travel arrangements we needed.

'Walk?' Dieter exclaimed. 'You did say, "walk"?'

'People do walk, you know, to get places,' Radhika said. 'A lot of people in the world do a lot of walking, just like they've always done. There are villages in India – maybe in Africa too – that aren't even on a road. But let's hear what else Leandro has to say.'

From the rest of his account we gathered that the

walk might take three days, the terrain we'd be crossing was hilly but not mountainous, there was a good track used by local people and it should be safe as we'd be travelling in the opposite direction from where the rebel forces were assumed to be. So, Leandro summed up, the walk would not be easy but perhaps better than staying with diminishing supplies beside the undefended airstrip.

We looked at each other in silence before breaking into anxious discussion. Could we all walk so far? What did the older people think? Vernon and Dieter were probably the oldest and both assured us they were regular walkers and could manage. Mama Ulemu, Frieda and Zak, the late arriving Russian, were clearly not much younger. Tom spoke for his mother, asserting she would have no trouble as she regularly walked twenty miles to her sister's village. Zak was completely confident. Frieda said she walked a great deal in town but was not sure about forest paths. Judging from appearances, the least fit person in the party was Magome with his considerable bulk, and while he claimed at length that he had no problem with walking, absolutely no problem at all, he could not recommend the plan for entirely different reasons: we would have to abandon our luggage; there would be no GPS signal and even if there was, our phones would run out of charge; there would be nowhere to eat, no roadside cafès, no shops; and if we made it to the border most of us didn't have entry visas and would be turned back. These were reasonable objections which began to sway opinion against walking until Leandro began to demolish them: he had a good idea of the route which people in the village had described in detail; Reece had a standard compass not dependant on power; we would pass by a few villages where we might get food; the shopping party had, in any case, bought supplies for three days; and, as for the border, it is hardly patrolled where we would cross and the authorities would be helpful. Our eastern neighbour, he pointed out, was a well-ordered country and one in which he and Vernon had influential friends. While he conceded that we would probably lose our luggage, we'd be likely to lose it anyway if the insurgents arrived and in that scenario not only our luggage but also little things of value like phones and laptops that we could carry with us.

When most of us were persuaded that the walk was manageable, the big question remaining was whether we were really endangered where we were. About that it was harder to reach a conclusion since the discussion was based on little more than one person's guess against another's. The women early on favoured walking, perhaps because we felt more threatened by the ill-reputed invaders. The men were divided. Magome stuck to his objections and Dieter agreed with him. Mathew, who settled the Father conundrum by claiming to be happy with plain Mathew, was neutral. Tom did not volunteer a view but, because his mother clearly wanted to walk, he muttered, when asked, that walking was best. Reece hardly took part because he kept coming and going trying to make calls. Jalal and Zak were both personally keen to get walking but couldn't be sure it was sensible. Nyezi and Vernon were biased because they had friends across the border and knew that, once arrived there, it would be easy to get a direct flight home. Sven refused to come down for or against, but kept saying we shouldn't just guess but should go over every bit of evidence to weigh up how likely it was that the insurgents would come. After persisting for a long time he eventually got attention by demanding rather forcefully, 'Do we even know if there was an attempted coup?'

We all turned to him.

'What makes you say that,' asked Mathew.

'You think it was invented?' suggested Radhika, 'to cover up something else?'

'I'm just asking,' he replied. 'I'm thinking, a few months ago there were riots about the price of food. The cost of food is still a problem. So, could it have been another riot and they called it a coup?'

'To justify bringing in the army?'

'Perhaps. It is the kind of thing a government might do. Some of you know more about the situation here than I do and I'd like to hear what you think.'

'Well, Leandro,' said Vernon. 'You're the journalist. What can you add?'

Leandro shrugged. 'Sven has a point. During the riots the government played down the food situation and blamed the UDR for stirring it up. '

'UDR?' queried Frieda.

'The main opposition party,' Mathew explained. 'Union for Democratic Reform, headed by Sowele, former prime minister and once President Banze's big buddy but now, since he broke away, enemy number one.'

'I regret my ignorance,' Frieda apologised, 'I knew very little about this country before I was invited here and then I did do some reading, but it was more directed towards its termites than its politicians.'

'Apt comparison,' Dieter quipped.

'So, can someone tell me about these parties, what difference is there?'

'Not a lot,' Dieter sniffed, 'apart from who gets the kickbacks.'

'If that's all.' Mathew speculated, 'wouldn't Sowele have done better to stay in bed with Banze?'

Zak jumped in. 'Perhaps not possible. There can only be one man at the top. A former ally is a deadly rival.'

'It was when the old president finally retired,' Dieter went on. 'That was the issue: which of them would get the top job. Banze got it and Sowele wasn't pleased.'

'It wasn't quite like that,' Leandro intervened. 'True, their politics don't look very different now but back then they were. It was more than just a personal power struggle.'

'Forgive me for butting in,' said Reece, 'but can someone tell me where this is going? Does it have anything to do with deciding whether to sit on our arses here or go tramping through the bush?'

'It might,' Frieda rejoined. 'Leandro was trying to answer about the coup. Let him finish and we'll see.'

Leandro continued. 'The key questions for us are: was there an organised coup? If there was, was it linked with the insurgency in the northwest? If the answer to both is "yes", we could be in for a lot of fighting, a civil war even, and as the northwest hot spots are not far away, staying here is high risk. On the other hand, if what happened was a food riot in the capital and some unconnected bits of border violence in the northwest, then probably all we have here is unnecessary panic.'

'Okay,' Reece agreed. 'But do we need to know all that about the Banze Sowele split?'

'Maybe not,' Leandro admitted. 'Perhaps I was going back a bit far but…' he hesitated, 'the past casts a long shadow.'

'Yes,' Frieda agreed with feeling. 'And if we are in that shadow, would it not help to know more?'

So, encouraged by Frieda, Leandro went back over a tortuous history, only bits of which I already knew.

At the country's first election the National Liberation League (NLL) won an overwhelming victory based on its role in the independence campaign. For the next half century it won election after election and set up the party leader as, effectively, president for life, making nonsense of the multi-party constitution. When the glow of independence wore off, dissent began to simmer, but because the NLL seemed unbeatable it took the form of factions within the party; factions based on personality, regional loyalties and also, according to Leandro, around policy. The independence project of centralised, quasi-socialist development was disliked by sections of the governing elite and also came under pressure from outside, from the usual suspects like corporate business and the International Monetary Fund. This was when Banze and Sowele, once young comrades in the independence movement, emerged as possible future leaders representing different factions. Banze was for retaining a managed economy; Sowele for liberalisation. When the president finally decided to retire and Banze and Sowele were identified as likely successors the IMF made no secret that it wanted Sowele, but the President favoured Banze and fixed the party machine to give him the job.

In an effort to keep the party united and to placate the IMF, Banze made Sowele prime minister and adopted a compromise of token liberalisation while avoiding major cuts to services. Within a few years, however, relations between the two deteriorated. Banze gradually side-lined Sowele who then left the NLL, set up the UDR with his influential allies, tapped into some rather shady sources of finance, and absorbed one or two small parties to form a significant opposition. He marketed himself as the champion of democracy and modernisation, and picked up support from various disaffected groups, particularly trading on grievances in the north and northwest, one reason why the history might provide clues for us.

The UDR grew rapidly until it nearly won an election and that was when Banze did his about turn to embrace liberalisation and rebrand himself as a pragmatic moderniser. After that there was little to chose between the parties in terms of policy and Banze shifted his attention away from development goals to tightening his grip on power. With privatisation under way, foreign creditors lost interest in regime change and the UDR lost some of its most generous backers.

Dieter objected to Leandro's gloss on events and we had to cut short an impending argument by asking about the discontent in the northwest. Here again the past cast its shadow as tensions there go back at least to the colonial period. At that time the remote northwest was home to a group of pastoralists who became notorious for their fierce resistance to colonial rule. When they were finally defeated many fled into the neighbouring territory to escape reprisals. After independence, when some returned expecting to resettle areas by then occupied by farmers, land disputes inflamed old hostilities and sparked a wave of atrocities which was quickly stamped on and hushed up. Things seemed to settle down for a generation or so, but in the last few years an insurgency resurfaced and was presumably behind the incidents around Batawe including the blown-up bus.

That was roughly the background that everyone who knew anything about it agreed on but, unfortunately, it didn't answer the key question of what was behind the current upsurge of violence and whether Sowele was involved as the Government alleged. Leandro thought that a more likely explanation was the recent discovery of coltan, resulting in illegal mining and a lucrative smuggling racket under the protection of armed gangs. We agreed that coltan might be the key but that it didn't necessarily rule out Sowele's involvement.

'So, let's put all this together,' Reece suggested. 'We know that Sowele had a reason to mount a coup, since his prospects of defeating Banze through the ballot box have faded while he may have enough of a following to bring off a coup. But we still know diddlysquat about what really happened in the capital. Similarly, we know that some mess of historic grievance and resource cash is probably behind recent fighting in the northwest but we still know diddlysquat about the extent of it. We assume the military convoy that rolled though here had something to do with the coup, or the northwest, or both, but it's not more than an assumption. Come to think of it, we only assumed it was even under government orders. It might have been supporting the coup – if there was a coup.

'So, I'm sorry, Sven. We have looked at it from all angles as you asked, dug about in the murky past but we don't seem to have got much further. It was a guess and it's still a guess. But it's a guess we have to make.'

He came to a stop and waited.

Radhika spoke first. 'For me it's not a question. If the insurgents come they are likely to do just anything to us, and we have no evidence that they won't come. Well, I just can't risk what might happen. It's too horrific. I'll walk.'

There were murmurs of assent. Even Dieter now said we should leave but be ready to turn back if we found out before long that the plane wass coming.

Sven turned to Magome, the other main objector, and asked what he made of the discussion. Until then it had not occurred to me that we had failed to consult the only three people present who were actually citizens of the country we'd been discussing at such length. Tom, it is true, probably lacked the confidence, and his mother the language, to contribute much; but Magome had lived through that recent history. Now he cleared his throat and addressed us slowly.

'Well, I have to say,' and he indicated Leandro, 'he knows quite a lot, a lot of things about our country. I won't say that he's right in everything, but he knows some things. Yes. He did quite a good job. And this Englishman here,' he now indicated Reece, 'is practical. He says that we need to know what is happening just here, and that is a very big difficulty. We don't know what is happening here. Will the plane come? Will the bandits attack?' He rambled on a little and then concluded, 'I think the points have been made. It will be better to leave. We have food. It is not so far. Yes, friends, we will walk!'

With his conversion the decision was made and we agreed to leave the next morning shortly before dawn.

After that there was a quiet moment when some of us, I at least, were looking around to chose a patch of concrete to lie down on. In this pause, however, Zehra remarked that there seemed just time for another story. No one opposed this. The candles were still burning cheerfully and the concrete floor was not strong competition. Magome produced another bottle of spirits, saying he couldn't it carry it fifty miles. So, we drew lots again and this time Reece won – or lost, depending how you look at it.

I thought Reece might duck out or get away with a one liner joke, but he made no complaint and seemed to have a story more or less ready.

8

Reece's Story

'You aren't all going to like this one,' he warned, addressing this statement mainly, I thought, at Radhika and me. 'In fact, it may not be the best story for this moment, but I made it up when we thought we'd all just be sitting round here and as I'm on now there's no time to change. So, here goes.

'You'd think it would be a man's world, living with wild animals, hunting and that stuff. Well, it was most places, most times. But once, somehow, the women ganged up and took over. They didn't rule the men – that might have been tricky – they got rid of them, most of them.

'People weren't painting in caves then and they didn't live in them either. They lived in warm, thatched houses in villages with big fences round them to keep out wild animals – and later on, the men. They weren't painting in caves but they did paint patterns on their houses – round the doorways and that – and they painted their bodies.

'People talk about women as the gentle sex. Bollocks! Oh, excuse me. Must mind my language. Anyway, those women weren't gentle. Once they'd got rid of the men they wanted to keep things that way but couldn't do without men completely – for obvious reasons. So what did they do? They killed most of the male babies at birth, letting just a few grow up and unlike the girl babies, the boys who were spared didn't grow up with their mothers. The women didn't trust each other not to end up wanting to protect their own sons. So, they swapped boys with another village. When a boy was weaned he was sent away and quite likely never saw his mother again. When they reached puberty they were taken away one at a time, taken far from the village and left to fend for themselves, alone. Many died and the women said that those who survived were the strongest and cleverest and so the best to breed from. Every so often the women would go out and look for one of the boys now grown into a man and take him back to the village where he'd be put in a special house and kept like a prisoner but pampered so that he thought he'd hit paradise. The women would take turns to get laid by him until they got pregnant. Eventually, the man would be killed – gently – first drugged and then suffocated. So there was no struggle and no mess, nothing that might be noticed by any boys in the village at the time because, of course, the women didn't want the boys to know what was in store for them.

‘The one snag was what to do with boys between being weaned and being old enough to have a chance of surviving in the wilderness alone. The women didn’t want the boys to grow up with the girls because they might like each other too much and the girls wouldn’t want them to be taken away later on. They didn’t want the boys to take part in village life, to learn their customs and everything because they would start to belong and resist being kicked out; even some of the women might not want them to be kicked out. The girls and boys and those women might leave the village and start living as in the old days, and if that happened there would soon be enough men to come and attack the women living without men and put an end to their rule. At first they locked the boys together in special houses, but that way the boys got very friendly with each other and talked about their situation. In one village they staged a revolt, burnt down their house and ran away together into the wild where for some years they were a danger. News of the revolt got around and then the elders – the old women – decided that each boy should be kept in a small shed on his own. But this did not work out because the boys were so miserable they got sick and too many died. So, the elders had to think of something else.

‘What they decided was that each boy would stay in a house with a woman and her daughters but would be treated differently from the daughters. While the mother and daughters all slept together on a good pile of furs the boys would sleep alone on the other side of the house. They wouldn’t be allowed to play with the girls and would be given all the nastiest household tasks to do on their own. To make sure they did not became part of a family they were moved about between houses. The mothers told their daughters terrible stories about boys and men so that they would keep away from them, and they also told the boys that the other boys were very dangerous and they had better not go near them. They told them that boy children are not proper humans until they have gone through a solitary trial which they would start when they were old enough, and that after the trial they would come back into the village and live a wonderful life. To reinforce this tale the boys were allowed to peek into the special Man-House to see whatever man was there being pampered and caressed. The children swallowed these stories because they didn't have much of a chance to see they weren't true. There were never more than a few boys in a village at any time. They were all of different ages so they weren't natural playmates and, because they were treated roughly, they behaved roughly, which seemed to prove the point that they were dangerous. The longer this way of life went on, the more people thought this is just the way things are – society all female; men, very few of them, lone beasts wandering around, a hazard best avoided, except for the one or two "tamed" for a purpose.

'Well, those boys who survived, they did live in caves and generally hid from each other believing, as they had been told, that other men were dangerous. It was a lonely life and when they weren't hunting there was nothing much to do. They hadn't been allowed to join in games and anyway you can't play games on your own, not the sort of games the girls played – you know, chase and acting things. But one thing they had sometimes helped with was decorating the doorways or, at least, mixing the colour for it. So, some of them hit on the idea of decorating the caves they lived in and they found it passed the time. One thing led to another. They spent a lot of time watching wild animals as their lives depended on knowing how to stalk them for food and how to avoid being attacked by the dangerous ones. As they had no human company, they came to feel a sort of companionship with the animals, even the ones they feared, and began to do crude drawings of them. Sometimes one man would come upon a cave in which there were pictures that someone else had done and that seemed like a kind of message. They would add an animal and maybe see that later someone else added another.

'One day one of these men approached a cave and saw another man was there drawing. He hid outside, fearful, but soon saw the man was looking at his own drawing, sort of copying and improving on it. The more he looked the more it felt as if he and the stranger were connected. At last he decided to take the risk of making contact and very cautiously said, "That deer you are looking at, I put it there."

'The stranger started and grabbed his spear but the first man rested his own weapon against the wall and asked, "Did you do those?" pointing at a pair of reindeer. The stranger edged away but also put his spear down and answered, "Yes."

‘To cut a long story short, they stopped expecting the other to attack and agreed to work together now and then on the paintings. Slowly they got less wary and started to hunt together, eat together and, in time, told stories about their childhoods. So, it dawned on them that everything they had been told was lies. They were puzzled, then sad, then very, very angry and when they calmed down they began to plan.

‘The next spring, the time when older boys were dumped in the forest, they watched out and followed any women taking a boy out, and when he was abandoned they captured him, persuaded him they would do no harm and took him to their cave. That way they saved several boys from the dangers of living in the wilderness alone. They became a little band living together and in time, as their numbers grew, some men split off to form another little band, but they all met up now and again.

‘When they talked about the life in the villages something that kept coming up was the subject of the so called “redeemed” men, living in luxury in the Man-House. They began to ask each other what happened to them later and decided that they should allow one of them to be taken and “redeemed” so that he could report back.

‘After a bit, a party of women came into the area on the look out for a new candidate for the Man-House and the men laid low, except for one of their number they’d agreed would make himself available. I’ll just call him Big because the women didn’t bother to name boys and I guess the men hadn’t got round to inventing names yet but just gave each other tags like Big, Small,

Black Hair, Scar etc. So, Big was sunning himself on a rock, deliberately making himself visible and the women saw he was a fine, strong, good-looking man and approached him.

'It happened that the women were from the very village that Big mainly grew up in and he recognised some of them although they did not recognise the boy now grown into a man. Back in the village he found it very strange; instead of being kept apart, fed on leftovers and bawled at, he was now seated on a pile of furs, brought the best food and praised. After a day or two one of the young women stayed with him and began to softly touch him and whisper sweet things. He felt a fire in his thing, something he'd sometimes felt before without quite knowing what it was, but now it began to truly blaze. As the girl touched his thing it leapt up as if it had a life of its own. Although he had not ever seen humans making love he'd seen the wild animals at it and now took in what she was asking. As he penetrated her she squeaked in pain but did not try to stop him, and in any case he could not stop. Then suddenly it was over. He fell back panting, not thinking about the girl until he saw she was bleeding and crying a little. He stroked her arm and she made an effort to stop crying. Then she got up and left.

'Other girls came to him. Some shyer than others, but soon he was well able to take the lead. He worked out that it was difficult for girls the first time but once that was over they had some pleasure too. After a first time he'd not see that particular girl for a while but then she would return and stay with him for a few days and usually other girls would come and go, playfully competing to have sex with him. They would sometimes go out to a nearby river and wash and sit in the sun. He tried to get them to tell him about their lives but they giggled and said nothing. He was not very bothered as he was having a good time.

'One day a girl came whom he felt he knew. After a little he realised that she was a daughter of a women whose house he had lived in and he remembered that she had been kind to him sometimes, getting bawled out herself for talking with him or giving him a little present. He could tell she was now quite nervous and he was very careful with her, working up very slowly to the moment he would enter her. Only when it was over he asked her if she remembered him. Her eyes widened in surprise. He told her how he remembered her little presents and they laughed about how she'd been punished for them. Then she said she had to go.

'As usual, time passed before she came back but when she did, she behaved quite strangely. She stroked him and lay with him with apparent pleasure but when he was close to climax, instead of egging him on, she pulled away and made him come outside her. He was angry and didn't believe her when she said there was a reason for it and it was because she cared for him. He tried to send her away but she persuaded him that she would be in trouble if word got out that she wasn't pleasing him. So he just turned his back on her and they slept.

'The next day she was affectionate but distant. When he started making love to her she made him pause, snuggled very close and whispered in his ear that it was true there was a reason he should not come inside her but that they should make it appear as if he did because people – 'women, you mean,' he said – might be watching through the rough fencing of the wall. For the same reason, she said, brushing his face with her long hair, she was whispering because she was not supposed to tell him such things.

'"But you've told me fuck all," he said bluntly.

'"Ssh!,' she whispered, kissing him lightly. "I'm only to tell you things like how much I like you and how beautiful you are – nothing about what happens beyond this house." Then aloud she said, "Yes, your eyes are so lovely, let me kiss them again." She kissed them and then whispered quickly, "But this isn't just what I have to say, as I do really like you."

'In these short, whispered snatches of conversation she told him that she would be with him for nine days but they would not be alone often and when other girls were there she would not whisper anything but endearments. She promised that if he kept up the pretence of penetration and was careful not to refer to anything she'd told him in front of others, then on the seventh day she would tell him the reason for her prohibition.

'Big was intrigued and longed all the more to make love to her. – I suppose I'd better give her a name,' Reece said interrupting himself. 'Let's call her "Bold"... no, that sounds like "Bald". "Brave?" Maybe not... makes you think of Braveheart. Oh well, it doesn't matter. "Flame." I'll call her "Flame".

‘Big longed for Flame more than the other girls. In fact his services to the others got a bit perfunctory and when Flame hung back to let the other girls enjoy him he was irritated. When any of the other girls was in the room Flame tried to avoid his attention until it was dark and they could hope his withdrawal would not be noticed. Or sometimes, if they all went together to the river, they would slip behind a bush and return laughing.

‘So the days passed, and when the seventh day came Flame woke Big early when the other girl with them was still sleeping. In case her sleep was light, Flame complained aloud it had been hot in the night and suggested they went right away to the river. He followed her out through the village passageways where women were doing their morning chores, sweeping out their houses and setting fires. She joked with one of them that they’d had a busy night and couldn’t wait for a bath.

‘She took him to a pool above the one where the women usually bathed and looked around carefully to see that they were alone. Then she told him that he was in danger, that the women would kill him when he had got enough of the girls pregnant and already several girls’ periods had stopped. That was why she would not let him come inside her, because the more girls were not pregnant the more chance they would delay killing him. Also, she would no longer see him if she became pregnant. Big was shocked, even though he and the other men had suspected something. What a fool he had been indulging himself and forgetting everything else! He got up preparing to run right then but Flame grabbed him, warning that there were women on watch around the village who would be suspicious if they saw him running and alone. She said they should go slowly together up the river as if engaged in love games and if they met anyone she would say they were going to pick wild strawberries that grew up high on a grassy hilltop. On the far side there was dense forest and they could go a little way in and, if no one followed them, they could go on and get away. She had even hidden some food and two spears at the edge of the forest because they would need to hunt and perhaps defend themselves.

'"I must go with you," she said, "because they will know I helped you and…" she hesitated, "because I want to be with you – always."

'Big sat down again on the rock and thought. It was a bit of a puzzle. In the last few minutes he'd learnt first, that women had been murdering men as a matter of routine and were planning to murder him and then, that this particular woman, Flame, wanted to trade her comfortable life in the village with her mother and sisters to be with him forever in the wild, alone – as she thought – not knowing that men now lived in bands. But, before he could think this through, she was saying that any moment other girls might join them and then they would have to give up leaving that day, and who knew when the elders might decide that Big's life should end?

'He got up and indicated she should go ahead as she knew the path. She reminded him this must look to any observer like a lovers' stroll. So, they linked arms and went up the valley unhurriedly, picking flowers now and again and kissing. This was fortunate because just when the valley became steeper they were hailed by a woman perched up on a rock observing the surroundings. But Flame laughed and chatted with her, saying that they were just going up to the waterfall a little further on, and asked her to tell the other girls if she saw them to come and join them and bring some food so they could party up there for a bit. The woman seemed quite unsuspicious and casually wished them good fucking. They checked before they turned the next corner that she was still seated on her rock. They hurried on beyond the waterfall and then turned off, up towards the grassy hilltop and the strawberry beds. It was still early and no one was picking there. They looked around carefully and then withdrew into the forest, stopping to be sure that no one was following them. Then they collected the weapons and food and set off at a jog along a narrow forest path. By evening they were sure they were safe.

'It was a two day trek back to the caves where Big's band lived and as they walked they talked for the first time, freely. He told her about the other men and she told him how, as a child, she had suffered to see the boys so cruelly treated but learnt to hide her feelings as she got older, although she then started to worry about the future when she might have a boy baby and have to give it up.

'Back at the cave the stories that they both told filled the men with anger and horror. They resolved to bring the rule of women to an end and set about gathering the other male bands and making a war plan.'

Here Reece changed his manner into a finishing up mode.

'Well that is more or less it. As you can guess, the men were victorious. They killed the older women, the elders who presided over the infanticide and the – manicide? – the killing of the men. What do you call it?'

'Homicide,' said Frieda tartly. 'Yes, the same for any murder – because man is assumed to encompass woman. As in *The Ascent of Man*, for instance.'

'Well, anyway,' Reece resumed, clearly not interested in the linguistics, 'they killed the old women and took the young ones prisoner to share among themselves. They found quite a few of the young women were secretly glad to see the end of women's rule as some had suffered when boy babies were taken away, and others wanted more from a man than they got from occasional visits to the Man-House. The men imposed discipline on the women, willing or unwilling, and resolved that never again would women be in charge. Ever since, for thousands of years – until the last hundred or so – they have been successful.'

Here Reece looked pointedly at the women and at Sven, whom he had evidently spotted as a likely gender traitor.

'Going back to our story, the men moved into the villages with the young women and first of all they shared the women casually, but this led to fights. So, Big, who was generally looked up to as leader and had already made it clear that Flame was only for him, suggested they bind each woman to a particular man who would be the only one allowed to fuck her and would be responsible for controlling her and her children. There was a bit of arguing, especially when it came to deciding who got which women as no one wanted the snappish or frigid ones, but because there were plenty of women to go round – remember a lot of boy babies had been killed – it wasn't a big deal as everyone got at least one good one.

'Okay, if you are worrying that the paintings don't appear much, I'm just getting to that.

'Things took time to settle down and some of the men were worried about living with women, afraid they would take to murdering again. Others were more confident they had the upper hand but all agreed that they shouldn't forget that women could be dangerous, that men must stick together. Big suggested that the men should meet together every so often, away from the women, and renew the bonds they'd had when living in the wild. The obvious place for these meetings were the caves where they had lived before and where the paintings would remind them of the time when animals were their only company. More than that, the paintings had worked like a sign from one lone man to another, carrying a message that beat the fear of each other and broke the spell of the lies they had grown up with. So, it seemed important that they should go on painting, and decided that women should not be allowed to enter the caves or witness the paintings.

'In time, the events which led to the men's secret gatherings in the painted caves were forgotten but the traditions persisted and passed on the knowledge that women are dangerous and men must band together.'

This was said with the tone of finality and we clapped as had now become the convention, but rather limply, and the silence which followed felt negative.

Frieda was the first to speak. Adjusting her glasses and adopting a quizzical tone she said, 'Of course now, with IVF, women could manage it so much more smoothly. At least,' she added, with exaggerated thoughtfulness, 'I suppose there would need to be one big slaughter in the beginning but after that everything could all be arranged quite humanely.'

'Wouldn't the sperm banks need restocking from time to time?' asked Vernon, picking up Frieda's manner.

Some of us smiled, others looked a bit blank but Radhika was indignant.

'I don't even think it's funny,' she complained. 'That tired old patriarchal plot! How often have we heard it? A woman besotted with a male hero betrays her home for him, her family or her country. Think Medea; think Ariadne. It doesn't make much difference that here she's betraying her sex. The point is that a woman is so besotted with a man than nothing else figures.' Radhika sounded angry in a way I wasn't sure was reasonable, as hadn't we agreed to play a game? But I was impressed that she seemed more at home with people like Ariadne and Medea than I am, although you'd think they are more my heritage than hers. I tried unsuccessfully to think of Indian mythological women to fit the betrayal theme. Even Holika, the witch who tried to kill her virtuous nephew, was doing it for her evil brother, not for some desirable outsider and, as far as I remember, no sexual passion was involved.

While I was flicking through my mind for the exploits of famous wicked women I slightly lost the thread and picked it up again only as Zak was appealing to Vernon for his comment.

'Is it possible?' he asked. 'Was there ever a society run by women? I know a woman can rule sometimes. There have been powerful queens like Catherine the Great. There was your Margaret Thatcher. But they depended on men. They did not give power to other women. The Amazons were not real were they?' The idea seemed to bother Zak.

We all turned to Vernon but before he could answer Sven pointed out there had been no comment on Zehra's story nor on Mama Ulemu's.

Vernon countered that there was not much he could say about either. 'Mama Ulemu spoke from her experience, something I'm no more qualified than anyone else to comment on. Zehra's story revolved round what was going on in her characters' heads, which is also beyond my sphere of supposed expertise. As for the action part of her narrative – the hunting and migration – that seemed more or less consistent with the evidence.'

'Thank you,' said Zehra, obviously pleased. 'I was thinking of somewhere like the Serengeti but cold. Now what about Reece's?'

‘He’ll knock it,’ predicted Reece, but Vernon began mildly.

‘Actually, Reece covered himself by being vague about the timescale. If he’d had the women’s rule lasting ten thousand years then you’d expect to find a corresponding distribution of remains, far more women than men, burial grounds containing only women and maybe, somewhere nearby, remains of male infants. But the only indication of time he gave was that the women’s rule lasted long enough for it to seem the norm, and that isn’t very long. If you think of England, now most people ...erm...’ He paused looking for an example. ‘Most people, for instance, take motorways for granted even though anyone over 60 remembers the country without them. And that’s in a society where we not only have a mass of records but are long-lived compared to Palaeolithic people.’

‘Or compared to Africans now,’ put in Nyezi. ‘And you can see the affect of shorter lives; British people talk about their empire as if it was yesterday, but for most Tanzanians it’s almost faded into the time of the ancestors.’

Zehra didn’t agree, but instead of arguing, Nyezi protested that he hadn’t meant to divert people’s attention and wouldn’t Vernon finish what he had been saying?

Vernon picked up the thread reluctantly. ‘My point was only that if the events Reece related had taken place but the women’s rule had lasted just a few generations, the chances of finding evidence for it would be, to say the least, slight. So, there is no evidence for a female dictatorship – but that doesn't mean it didn't happen. The only part of the story that obviously conflicts with evidence is shutting the women out of the caves, since, as I've said, there are women's and children's handprints in them. But, of course, that doesn't mean women were always there. They could have been permitted in special circumstance or they could have defied the ban now and then.'

Soon after that the conversation faltered and we all settled down as best we could to sleep. I had not ventured to say anything but I was left with a feeling of unease. Whatever was it that put such a horrible story into Reece's head?

9

The Road

It was dark and there was a slight chill when we set off on an earth path that skirted the runway and then led through straggly bush. Now and then Leandro checked a piece of paper on which he'd written down a series of landmarks to look out for: cross paths, large trees or places where the bush grew more or less densely. We knew that we should come to a road quite soon which we had to follow for about three miles, and Leandro was anxious that we should get this behind us as soon as possible since it was the part of our journey where we were most exposed to possible troop movements.

Our path joined the road quite suddenly, apparently where Leandro had expected it would. We stopped for a five-minute rest and then increased our pace, keeping our ears tuned for any approaching vehicles. The moon, which had cast its mysterious monochrome light over the bush when we started, had now set and there was a faint hint of light in the east, which spread all too rapidly as we hurried on. The road had a strip of potholed tarmac in the middle and wide, dusty stretches of laterite each side on which we walked in order to be near the bushes in case we needed to hide from passing traffic. The road ran boringly straight across the flat scrubland but as the light increased I began to reinterpret what had seemed like a layer of darker sky as a line of hills. Long before we reached them the road took a distinct turn to the right and Leandro stopped, peering into the scrub in front of us. This bend was apparently where we were supposed to find a path but it took some time of walking back and forth until Nyezi pointed out a faint track ahead and we left the road with a sense of relief even though not a single vehicle had passed.

We went on through the same flat landscape for another mile or so until we reached the foot of the hills, which rose suddenly from the plain like land emerging from water. The slope facing us was only moderately steep and was corrugated by miniature valleys formed by streams, now mostly dry. Our track could be seen more clearly here, a narrow, stony line winding up the side of one of the more pronounced valleys where very soon the grass and scrub gave way to a light woodland of wiry trees. We plodded up slowly, in single file, until the gradient slackened off and Leandro called a halt on a rocky bluff that provided a great view across the land we had left below. We would rest here for ten minutes, he said. Some of the party were visibly in need of a break. Magome, sweating profusely, had fallen behind along with Dieter who was flushed and panting. It was not very hot yet and at this elevation there was a pleasant breeze. Once we'd sat down no one spoke for a long time and I became aware of an unfamiliar quiet: the complete absence of air conditioning, fans, or even the most distant echo of traffic, radios, people pounding grain, children playing. Neither birds nor insects filled the gap, perhaps because it was the wrong time of day, so that the only sounds were the faint sigh of wind through leaves and the occasional rustle as someone fidgeted.

When we moved off again our footsteps at first sounded deafening by contrast although none of our shoes made much noise and some made none at all. The route continued slightly uphill until we reached a gently undulating plateau where the trees grew straighter, taller and closer together, forming a fairly continuous green and gold canopy. On the ground, however, there was little undergrowth so we could see quite far around us and there was no need to keep rigidly to the path although, of course, we needed to be careful not to drift away from it. Now and again, at the top of an undulation, there would be a crown of boulders and the trees would thin so that there was more of a view. As we passed one of these places I clambered to the top of a moss-covered rock to look out over the forest stretching out in all directions. As I stood there I suddenly noticed I was enjoying myself. It was good to be released from the futile wait, to have left behind the airfield with its dingy building, the barren expanses of beaten earth and tarmac, the endless sitting. My body was responding to the exercise and my senses to the constantly changing scene. I have always liked walking and exploring unknown places, so for me our journey was like a holiday trip, a little adventure. I felt a twinge of guilt that I was having fun while others were weary, hot or anxious, but I couldn't help the way my spirits lifted as the morning went on. There was something familiar, not only about the rhythm of walking but also about the landscape and I realised it reminded me of Epping Forest where my parents had often taken me walking, as a child. The wood had an eerie resemblance to the more open areas of oak or beech in the early autumn when the foliage is also green and gold and enough leaves have already fallen to make a carpet on the ground. To be as bright and dry as here it would have to be a very fine day in a warm, late September. But the visit that came most to mind was instead on a day of mist, which by late afternoon turned to drizzle, making my brother sulk. I remembered tramping along on the sodden leaves, on a path that seemed endless when, suddenly, we emerged into a clearing with a little wooden tearoom where bright lights shone. Soon we were all sitting with our hands round steaming mugs and I had the jammiest jam doughnut I'd ever eaten. Unintentionally, past and present merged so that I caught myself looking forward to that little café where we'd all have tea and buns, only to wake out of my daydream and recall that there were no English tea rooms hiding in this forest and that before nightfall we would be unlikely to pass any kind of café, tea stall, or even a house. I experienced a pang of loneliness and nostalgia but it passed by the time we stopped for lunch, a rest and the next story. For we decided, after hardly any argument, that the stories should continue.

We sat down on the slopes of a semi-circular hollow and ate biscuits, which the shopping party had bought, supplemented by snacks anyone still had with them. It was not a satisfying meal but better than nothing. Then we lay back in the deep shade and listened to Mathew who had drawn the short straw this time.

10

Mathew's Story

'I guess I'm going to let you folks down,' he began, 'but I've been thinking about it this way, and that way, and I can't do it. I can't think myself back into those times you've been talking about. Can't do it. I'm a city boy. I only really knew Chicago and New York until I came here. Well, except for church activity trips to the wild – or what we call the wild, which isn't like here but more of a park with marked trails and rangers around somewhere. This is the first time ever I've been somewhere that feels like real wilderness, where no one's going to drive up in a four-by-four to collect you if you break an ankle.

'It was great to hear those stories earlier. I was staggered, Zehra, the way you talked about snow even though you've never touched any. I could feel the cold! And you got me believing in your character, Heron? No, Standing Heron wasn't it? But I can't do that. So,

I've been rooting round in my brain for something I can talk about that might offer a bit of a clue. Better than a complete cop out and you did say it was okay to tell anything we felt we could.

'So, I grew up in Chicago in a big project on South Side. It wasn't too bad when I was little. I was the first child and my mom and dad tried to make a go of it. And they did for a few years but after the third child my dad disappeared and my mom struggled to pay the rent and feed us. Like lots of the kids on the project, I dropped out of school as soon as I could and joined the neighbourhood gang. It wasn't a big gang but, like most, it was affiliated with bigger ones. I was a new boy with some of the other kids I'd been in school with. We didn't do much – a bit of petty theft but mainly drug peddling for the older guys, and they let us hang out with them which made us feel we were men. The part of it I liked best was doing graffiti. I had a great buddy called Dave and we always did it together and we got to be quite good at it. The graffiti, you know, like most big city graffiti, marks territory for one gang or gang alliance and there are little symbols in it, but rudimentary – not that sophisticated.

'I guess you are thinking I'm going to say that the cave paintings were just like modern graffiti – marking territory – but I'm not. If those paintings had anything to do with marking territory I'm sure it wasn't like the Chicago graffiti, linked with violent turf wars. In the time of the paintings there was plenty of space wasn't there? Even if people then were divided up into tribes with territories, and even if they fought over territory from time to time, they wouldn't surely have needed to be fighting or threatening all the time? The kind of turf wars you get in big cities, I reckon, only happen in big cities, and then not even in all big cities. You get them where people are crammed up against each other, where there are different communities – like in Chicago: Blacks, Whites, Hispanics – where the communities are separate but near enough to bump into each other, and where there isn't enough opportunity or money to go round. So, in Chicago, where there aren't a lot of great jobs to be had – or not for the sort of people who end up in gangs – the most likely way to make money is from crime, especially the drug trade, and so the gangs fight over access to that. Violence may blow up more at particular moments, like when a gang leader's killed or a population gets moved from one area to another, but the tension's there all the time. The graffiti are everywhere, and so are the dealers and the thugs. There's always a trickle of beatings, threats and some killings that pollute everyday life for everyone. If you're a young man, most of the time you're either hyped up to be aggressive or you're scared. So, I'm not thinking it's our graffiti in themselves or the gang culture that goes with them which might throw light on the cave paintings, but something else I'm coming to.

'As I said, Dave and I got to be quite good with the spray can. Most of the graffiti round Chicago are pretty crude. I don't know how many of you have been there but if you haven't I'm telling you, don't think murals or great street art. Most of it is wonky writing and a few symbols or sketches roughly drawn. What Dave and

I did wasn't art either but it was an improvement on most of the scrawls and we began to get a bit of a name for it. Because we cared about what we did we got extra angry when one of the rival gangs scrawled all over our work. So, then we hit on the idea of tagging up high on buildings in hard to reach places so they wouldn't get written over. I've seen that in some places it's pretty routine to put graffiti in challenging places that make people ask, "How on earth did they get up there?" but not so much in Chicago. Most of the scrawls are down at street level just where anyone could do them. So, when Dave and I started doing them up high we got a bit more notice even than we had before.

'Then we got kind of hooked on the climbing part of it and lost interest in doing them just anywhere. Instead, we looked for more and more difficult to reach places and the difficult to reach part became the point of it. It's this I think might be a clue as to why your cave artists put their paintings not just in caves but, I gather, right back in caves where there is no light. Perhaps the point was that it was difficult to get in and to work there. Anything hard to do has special value.

'That's it folks. That's my thoughts.'

At first no one remembered to clap, perhaps because his talk was short or not quite a story or because everything was different sitting out under the trees. It was Vernon who remembered first and when proper appreciation had been shown he commented.

'Actually, although Mathew dismissed it, one of the ideas experts have come up with is that the paintings may have had something to do with marking territory.'

'He didn't completely dismiss it,' said Frieda, 'he just said it wouldn't have been anything like marking gang territory in a modern city.'

'What's the good of territorial markers stuck in a cave?' asked Reece, the first time he'd joined in the post-story discussion. He had seemed a bit more switched on to Mathew's account than to the previous ones.

'That depends,' replied Vernon, adopting his quiet professorial voice. 'First of all we don't know that the paintings were only in caves. They could have been all over the cliff faces as well because there they wouldn't have survived 20,000 years of sun and rain and frost. But again, the point might have been having them in the caves. They could be the more powerful for being unseen. You'd need to know how the people doing them think of territory, or how they think, full stop'

'I don't get it,' Reece complained. 'A sign works best where no one can see it?'

'There are circumstances in which it could do.'

'Like?'

'For example, suppose those images are sacred and have something to do with the way God or some such power has made connections between areas of land and groups of people. As long as all those people know the images are there and share the same beliefs about them, the presence of the images could control where people wander or where they hunt, even though the images themselves are hardly ever seen, maybe even more so, as there's a mystique about the unseen.'

'The Ark, of course, was hidden, ' Frieda pointed out. 'The Ark of the Covenant was covered by a veil and even the priests were not allowed to see it. The Beth-Shemites couldn't resist having a peep and God struck them dead.'

Reece was still sceptical. 'You mean people were so scared of a picture in a cave they wouldn't go after a nice fat deer if it ran onto someone else's land?'

'I doubt if they thought of the land as being owned quite like 'my land', 'someone else's land'. And scared? Scared, or respectful?'

Reece looked unconvinced and moved away from the circle to smoke.

'What about Mathew's idea about them being in difficult to reach places? Do you think there's anything in that?' asked Sven.

'No reason why not,' Vernon answered neutrally, 'but switching for a moment, something I'd really like to know,' and he turned to Mathew, 'is how you got from spray painting walls in Chicago to being a priest here?'

I'd been thinking exactly the same thing, but Mathew was evasive. 'I'm not sure that's got much to do with painted caves,' he said. 'I've had my stab at that. Better get on to the next person. Or is it time to move on?'

There was a mutter of protest and after a bit of arm-twisting he gave in.

'Okay. Like I told you, Dave and I got more and more ambitious about where we put our tags. We had the idea that the best place of all would be on bridges over a freeway – real skilled stuff to get up there and every passing car sees what you've done. So we managed one, and our stock in the gang went up again. We did another. We thought we were champions and so good at it we stopped being afraid. Well, on the next bridge something happened. It was so quick I'll never understand quite what it was, but I lost my balance. Dave grabbed me and pulled me in just enough for me to clutch at something but that effort unbalanced Dave and he fell. My grip only held me long enough to see him go. You know, in movies people fall off sky scrapers and dangle for ages hanging on to little ledges by their finger tips until, miraculously, they get saved; but in reality, unless you're a gymnast or top class mountaineer, you need something like a real handle to hang onto and even then your arms won't hold your weight for long. So, I fell just after Dave but he went right down onto the busy road while I had the luck to land on a big truck and not bounce off. Dave was killed instantly. I was so badly hurt they thought for a time in the hospital I'd not walk again. Lying there I had all this time to think about Dave. We were really close. Where I lived we were always hearing of kids getting shot and you might think we'd be used to people dying young, but that doesn't mean no one cares when it happens. I was gutted, completely gutted. Add to which, I felt it was my fault Dave died and wished it had been me not him. That guilt was worse than the fear I'd be crippled for life, but that was also pretty bad. So, I lay there wishing I was dead and hoping I'd get just enough better to get to the subway and jump under a train.

'During this time my mom came to see me, but not often, and when she came she was just moaning about how terrible it all was, which wasn't the most helpful thing anyone could do. A big guy from the gang came once and promised they'd see me okay if I was crippled, but no one else much came. Except there was this Catholic priest, Father Aiden, who was a sort of chaplain at the hospital and, although I'd never had anything to do with Catholic religion – my mom had raised me a Baptist but by then I wasn't anything – he'd spend time with me, bring me comic books and nice things to eat. He didn't talk about God much and that was a good thing because if I'd thought he was after my soul – not that I knew I had one then – I'd have wanted to run a mile or done the next best thing you can do when stuck in bed, clammed up. He was a good man, that priest. I wasn't his business and there were plenty of Catholics there with plenty of problems to keep him busy. He wasn't black either and that struck me. He was going out of his way to be nice to me although I was nothing to do with him.

'When it turned out that the doctors could fix me after all, he started talking with me about what I was going to do when I got out and told me about a community that was run partly by Catholics but by other people as well, which tried to turn round bad kids like me – he didn't, of course, say 'bad kids' – providing somewhere safe to live, getting them enrolled in evening classes, that kind of thing. I went there when the hospital kicked me out. I got better, started getting some education and things went on from there. I began to want to know about God and started to ask people, mainly Father Aiden, as I knew he wouldn't take advantage. I could trust him to back off if I backed off and not to railroad me about what I ought to do. I liked the Catholic God better than the Baptist one, as He seemed better on giving people second chances, or even third ones. That was important for me because it wasn't all as easy as I'm telling it. I didn't get faith all at once and, even when I did, I didn't necessarily act on it. Anyway, I converted into the Church and not long after that I came to know that I wanted to get deeper into it, maybe give my life to it. I had to do a lot more studying before I went to the seminary, but I'm lucky in that I learn easily and they are short of priests these days so you get encouragement if you can show even faint signs of a vocation.

'Okay, so one thing left is how I got here, Central Africa, so I could end up with blistered feet sitting round with you lot in this wood. That's easy. The diocese I'm attached to has a special link with the Church here. I guess there was once a mission, the old kind of mission station for converting the "heathen". But now we have an exchange scheme. So I'm here for a year and a priest from here is serving in my parish. And what's good about it is we each think we've got the best deal.'

This wound up Mathew's account; and if some of us had questions we kept them to ourselves as it was time to start walking again.

The afternoon was uneventful. The wooded plateau continued relatively unchanged. The main excitements were that a few times we saw antelope dung, once the people in front saw a pair of antelopes and twice we came to small dry streambeds where Leandro, Tom and Mama Ulemu looked unsuccessfully for water holes. This was a worry as we were running short by then but not quite a disaster because there was another source of liquid. We discovered this when Leandro suddenly halted, conferred with Mama Ulemu and then walked over to where a large, thick-stemmed vine was wrapped around some trees. He felt the vine and asked if anyone had a hatchet or a decent knife. Reece produced a formidable knife and Leandro hacked at the vine, which proved to be full of a watery sap, better for drinking than grubby waterhole water, only rather tricky to guide into our water bottles. While we were fiddling with the vine Mama Ulemu found some leaves which apparently have some use as Leandro had us all picking them.

Towards evening we found a good flat place to sleep and Reece set about making a fire. Radhika volunteered to cook and I to help her, although, as she remarked, 'cooking' was a bit fanciful, given our resources. We had taken a large pan from the airfield kitchen and we now used it to cook rice. The purpose of the leaves, it turned out, was that they could be eaten like spinach. Radhika grumbled that the shopping party hadn't thought to get any onions, garlic or spices although they had bought a few tins of tomato puree. As we worked she burst into an improvised, comic song on the lines of 'Oh for an onion' in which I quickly joined, causing some mild amusement. At least someone had thought to take salt from the kitchen, without which the meal would have been irredeemably bland. We were all hungry enough to enjoy our rice and greens, eaten off large leaves, and afterwards Nyezi revealed that the shoppers had bought some fudge-like Indian sweets which stood in very satisfactorily for a pudding.

It was still early when we finished and, as leaf plates make for no washing up, we were quite ready for the next story. This time the task fell to Nyezi.

11

Nyezi's Story

'I should pass,' Nyezi protested, 'because I know too much. Yes, it's true; I should have raised this before we began. I was going to but then I missed the moment. The point is, how can I make up a story when I know most of the things I think of couldn't have happened? Vernon had the problem too, of course, but Vernon didn't make up a story, did he? What he said was interesting – interesting to me because I knew part of it – about the school and the Mendip dig – he'd talked about that before, but he never mentioned romance or getting drunk!' Nyezi glanced pointedly at Vernon before continuing. 'Vernon could have told the story he'd been planning to tell to impress the Indian beauty. It must have been good if he thought it would seduce her. But he didn't tell it, did he? Probably now he knows the story couldn't be true and that's why he didn't tell it. So, it's clear that, to be fair, I should pass on my turn too.'

'What a total bloody cop out,' said Reece. 'I'd say that knowing something about it – unlike the rest of us – you've got a head start.'

'Absolutely,' Radhika agreed, 'it must be easier the more you know. How can it not be?'

Nyezi frowned a little theatrically and wagged his finger at us before answering, 'Cupules, take cupules – they're one of my big problems …'

'Yes?' said Radhika expectantly.

'Cupules,' Nyezi continued, 'are manmade little hollows in rocks that could be the earliest traces of art. Some predate cave paintings by thousands of years. Yes, thousands. So, you see, if I'm asked about the origins of art, it's cupules that first jump into my head.'

'Well, tell a story about your – what did you call them – cyoopyools?' Reece urged. 'Who gives a shit if it passes the time?'

'Yes, but these cupules are more of a puzzle than the paintings. Not everyone agrees they are art, but no one's been able to suggest a likely practical function. If they were all bored into horizontal surfaces they might be grinding areas, where people ground seeds or nuts, or they might have been used as containers. But they aren't all horizontal. Most are in vertical rock faces and some on overhead ones. They're not arranged in patterns – or not what we would call a pattern – which means they don't look like art. But they must have been important to the people who made them because, whether functional or symbolic, it would have taken hours and hours of grinding to remove so much stone.' He stopped briefly to check that we were all suitably bewildered. 'The worst thing about them,' he continued, 'is that there are accounts of hunter-gatherers in the twentieth century making cupules.'

'Why worst?' interrupted Mathew. 'Sounds like a gift: cupule makers who can tell you what they're for.'

'Wait,' said Nyezi. 'The oldest cupules were made maybe a hundred thousand years before the twentieth century ones. So, the purpose might be completely different. But one thing the modern accounts do tell us is that explanations can be unexpected.'

'Like what?'

'For instance, that the purpose is to make a bird lay eggs.'

Mathew mulled this over before responding, 'Okay. It's true that wouldn't be my first guess! How does it work?'

'In Australia there are – or were – people who pound rocks in a ritual to make the cockatoo lay more eggs. They're interested in the eggs because they eat them. The rock is said to be the body of the mythical cockatoo woman, and the dust of the rock rising in the air fertilises female cockatoos. So, the cupule in that case is a by-product of producing stone dust. Then again, there were some Native Americans who pounded rocks to produce rain. Those explanations aren't the kind of thing you'd think of, are they? Especially the cockatoo one? And if you did think of them there'd be no way of knowing you were on the right track unless you could ask someone. Even then you might misunderstand. Anthropologists working with living people get things wrong. So, what hope have you when there's no one to ask?'

'Good try!' laughed Vernon, 'but you can't have it both ways. First you plead too much knowledge; now it's that you don't know anything.' He turned to the rest of us. 'It doesn't stand up, does it?'

'No,' said Sven. 'There's no getting out of it.'

'Nyezi, you must have thought of something you could make a story from,' Radhika gently urged.

Nyezi sighed, 'I knew Vernon would take a hard line. But I thought some of you would see my point.' He shrugged. 'Well, if I have to, I have to. And perhaps, after all, knowing too much doesn't matter. As someone said earlier on, knowing about something isn't at all like living it. That reminded me of when I came to London for my PhD (thanks to Vernon who helped me find scholarships to make it possible). I knew what to expect. I knew all about climate zones and habitats. That was my subject. But that didn't stop me finding the beginning of winter a shock. I couldn't help fearing that the trees, when they dropped their last leaves, were really dead. Yes, I know trees drop their leaves here too, but it's different. They aren't all bare at the same time, while those trees in London, black skeletons against a grey sky, were quite…' he groped for the right word, 'threatening.

'Then, as the weeks went on, when night kept eating further and further into the day, I could understand how easy it would be to think the end of the world was coming; and how you might feel, when the light starts to return in January, that you'd had a lucky escape, that God had relented. Yes, you observe it happening year after year, but unless you know why it happens, you can't take it for granted, can you? A pattern can change:

deer come to drink at a water hole every night, until one night they don't. A man hits a target ten times and then misses.

'The Tube was another London thing I thought I knew all about but seeing it was something else...'

'You're procrastinating!' said Vernon.

'He is,' said Frieda, 'but now I want to know about the Tube.'

'Those long, long corridors with people moving through them, all at the same speed like a church procession! Always more and more people as if they are being manufactured somewhere, in an underground people-factory that turns them out fully-grown. You don't often see babies or children in the procession. Then, the first few times I saw the train come in it seemed almost indecent. You are looking into a round, dark hole fringed in grey bricks like fur. You see a pinpoint of light, then two beams. Then a monstrous red thing rushes out, thrusting into the space of the station. Of course, after a few days it was just a train but now and again that first impression would come back.'

'You're still procrastinating,' said Vernon.

'Don't be unfair,' Radhika reproved him. 'Let him get there in his own way.'

'Thank you,' Nyezi said to her. 'But he's right. I should get on with it. I did think of a story in case you all insisted. Here it is.'

He adjusted from chatting to narrating mode and began.

'Many thousands of years ago, in one of the bands of people who hunted across the uplands and the valleys of Southern Europe there was a man called Tokheidi, known for his dreams. Everyone in the band was interested in dreams and people would often recount a dream that seemed significant or entertaining, but Tokheidi was the champion dream teller. Almost every night he had a dream worth telling and, unlike most people who would get so far and stumble, he could tell dream events as if they had happened in the daytime world. They were so clear that some people wondered if he cheated and made them up, or parts of them. This mattered because stories were just made up by men – or women – and had no purpose except to pass time, but dreams came from the spirits who know the past and the future and can see what lies beyond the mountains or above the stars, and some of this knowledge is embedded in dreams, although concealed in a form that humans can rarely understand.

'Tokheidi was highly respected for his dreams until he told one that stretched the patience of his audience. In this dream he found himself in a strange land where people live in such numbers that they are like migrating reindeer, or swarming bees – so many they hide the ground they stand on.

'"Those people," Tokheidi said, "construct places to live in that look like pinnacles, cliffs and canyons, but made of ice. Not the ice of a glacier, white and rough, but ice like the smooth, dark ice on the surface of a lake. It was the oddest ice because to the touch it felt more like a smooth piece of flint – cool rather than cold." Tokheidi found it hard to describe what he had seen. "They live up and down these ice or flint cliffs," he said, "in spaces inside where everything is straight and nothing round. There are moving things that float up and down with people in them. On the ground outside there are boat-like things which carry people backwards and forwards faster than anyone can paddle a boat, even faster than a man can run."

'The listeners were already a little restless because the dream was so fantastic that it was hard to follow. Tokheidi himself seemed to be a little lost in it.

'"At first everything was confusing," he explained. "I couldn't see much except the glitter of the ice or flint and the great numbers of people moving around, backwards and forwards, in all directions and mostly ignoring each other. Because of the way a lot of them walked past me and past each other without a word or a gesture, I wondered if these were ghosts, if I'd come to the land of the dead. Some people say, after all, that the land of the dead is all ice and snow, and it could be very full of people because everybody ends up going there and, as far as we know, no one comes back or goes on anywhere else. So, the place would have in it far more people than those now living; more people than anyone has ever seen gathered together. I was afraid that I might be dead myself. I could not remember any reason why I might have died, but we do not know if the dead remember dying – or even living. But I was breathing and my skin felt warm to touch. So, I was encouraged that I, at least, was not dead.

'"As I wandered around I began to get used to the place and started to notice more about it. Now and then I would come to a grassy space where there were people sitting or standing – some alone but others talking to each other in a way quite like normal people. Some were even eating which could mean they were not dead.

'"I decided I had to try and talk to someone, but was not sure how. All this time no one had taken any notice of me but passed as if they could not see me. When I next came to one of the grassy spaces I looked around and I saw an old man sitting alone and decided to approach him.

'"As soon as I spoke, I saw that I was not invisible because he looked at me, not through me, and he did not seem particularly startled, from which I guessed I must have been changed in appearance to look something like the people of the place. My words, too, could reach him, which at the time did not surprise me although people from very far away usually speak differently and this place, if it exists outside of dreams, must be very, very far away, or some mention of it would have reached us. After all, we have heard of the Great Water which is like a lake but so vast no one can see the far side. The Great Water is far away but we have heard of it, we have met people who have seen it and we know that, if we walked westwards for some days, we could see it ourselves.

'"So, the old man and I could talk to each other although some of the things I said to him seemed to make no sense, and certainly some of the things he said to me made none at all while others made sense but were hard to accept. After offering respectful greetings, I told him that I came from far away and needed someone to explain things to me. He answered kindly that he had time and suggested I might like to sit down. In the grassy area there were some well-made and neatly finished wooden things that people were sitting on. He was the only person on his and so I sat beside him. He asked me where I came from and I told him our lineage, but he kept asking about a place so I told him we winter in the area of the Three Gorges, which did not satisfy him but he stopped asking.

'"The old man and I talked for a long time and he told me many things, some too strange to understand, some not important and some which you are about to hear. The main thing I learned will amaze you as it did me. In his place, when people acquire more wealth than others, they do not give it away; nor do other people expect them to. Honour and influence is won just for having the wealth, not for giving it. Yes, I can see you think this is impossible but it is what he told me. Not only do the people-with-so-much-wealth keep it to themselves but they use the influence they have to get more, taking valued things away from the people-without-wealth. So, the people-with-so-much-wealth acquire more and more and the strangest thing of all is that the more they take the more they are honoured and respected and the more everyone else does what they say. I told him that was hard to believe and asked why the others don't just go away leaving the badly behaved people-with-so-much-wealth all alone. The old man in his turn asked me where would they go? Of course, I said they would go to wherever they thought looked right or where someone who was a good dreamer was told in a dream to go. The old man laughed and asked again where I came from, a question which, just as before, led nowhere because that place of my dream, if it exists, must be too far away for anyone to have heard of the Three Gorges. But the old man said that my place must be a happy one and that I was lucky to live there. He then remarked, sadly, that I should beware because his people might one day arrive at the Three Gorges and change everything. I said that we would fight, them and if there were too many to fight we would go somewhere else. I added quickly that, of course, I'd be happy to welcome him as I could see he was not like the people he had been telling me about.

"'All this time I half wondered if he was making fun of me. It is easy to make fun of a stranger and I was very much a stranger there. But I decided he was not making fun because he explained, with a sadness that seemed real, that he was old and things had not been quite the same when he was young because some people at that time thought, like we do, that a person should be respected for giving away rather than keeping wealth. But they failed to change the way other people thought and now there might be no chance ever to change as the people-with-so-much-wealth were eating up the world. Eating up was not exactly what he said but it seemed he meant something like that. As caterpillars can strip a plant bare, these people leave a trail of destruction. Not only do they eat all the food and drink the rivers dry but their fires are so big and so many that their smoke hides the sun. Whatever he meant exactly, his words made me afraid. And that was when I woke."

'The listeners had become more and more restless as Tokheidi talked. Some had walked off but most stayed to the end so they could ridicule this nonsense. They were extra keen to dismiss it because Tokheidi had such a reputation for having significant dreams. Someone suggested that Tokheidi was right when he thought the old man was teasing him. Someone else suggested Tokheidi was teasing them, but a third objected that no one could think up anything so fantastic as these upside down people who admire taking, not giving. He said it must be that the spirits had decided to have a laugh. Perhaps they were fed up with Tokheidi's demand for dreams or had decided to test him to see if he could recognize a joke if they sent one. The phrase "upside-down people" appealed to the listeners and some of them started to fool around, standing on their heads and laughing at the notion.

'After this Tokheidi's reputation went downhill. No one could forget his upside-down people and sometimes when he passed by, someone would do a headstand and everyone around would chortle. Tokheidi was so depressed both by the mockery and by the memory of his dream that he could not laugh with them at all. He withdrew into himself and spent a lot of time alone, sometimes disappearing for days at a time.

'As time passed, however, one at a time, some of the men who were present at the dream telling and some who had only heard about it came to seek him out and ask questions about the dream and what it could mean. Secretly, many of the listeners had been troubled by it and, however much they mocked, they could not get out of their heads the idea that perhaps such upside down people really existed somewhere and in large numbers. At first Tokheidi shared his thoughts cautiously with each person in turn but, on the tenth occasion that someone turned up furtively, as if coming on him by chance, Tokheidi told him about the other nine and refused to say anything else unless he went and collected the others so they could all talk about it together. After they had met a few times and talked around the question and looked at it this way and that way, they agreed that the dream was a warning about the coming of strangers who eat up the world, who pitch themselves against the spirits and in doing so would cause a catastrophe so great that there might be no survivors. It was a dreadful thought, but they also agreed that the catastrophe was unlikely to happen soon since there was no sign outside the dream of any such strangers. However, they agreed they should not forget about it because there must be a reason for the dream.

'Those meetings soon attracted more people and, among those who went to them, Tokheidi had not only regained but increased his prestige. He was expected to suggest some course of action and after a while he had a dream, which he told. It was a very short dream in which he was standing at the edge of their village near one of the guardian signs, an impressive bull. The people of that area painted animal images round the places they settled to bring protection and blessings. Each animal was associated with different powers and the more impressive the painting the better they worked. So, the skill of painting was greatly admired. Now, in the dream, a huge fire came raging towards the village and destroyed everything. When the smoke cleared there was no sign that there had ever been a village there except for the guardian bull which, miraculously, was untouched. Tokheidi experienced a great sense of relief that the bull was still there but as he looked at it the rock turned black as you would expect after a fire and the bull vanished.

'When he told the dream he suggested the fire was the prophesised catastrophe and the survival of the painting perhaps meant they could survive it. But then why did the bull crumble into soot? Perhaps it was a warning. Perhaps it means the people might or might not survive. Or it could be a simple reminder that paintings do not last. Fire, floods, rock falls destroy them and every winter takes a toll so that, as long as a village site is used, the images are usually repainted every spring. When a site is abandoned for good the images eventually vanish.

'Tokheidi and his followers talked about how all things pass and if their band came to perish in the prophesised catastrophe then there would be no descendants to honour them and no sign by which even other people might remember them. It would be as if they had never lived. There was a long silence and then someone pointed out that the pictures done during temporary camps in rock shelters last much better than those on more exposed rocks at the edge of villages. Some rock shelters contain images painted by people so long dead that no one knows exactly who painted them. They are often faded but still readable. Others in the group nodded their agreement and someone added that the more sheltered the rock surface the better the paintings last. Gradually, as the group thought this over and talked about it, the idea came up that images painted right inside caves would last even better, perhaps for many, many generations. If they were done deep enough down they could even survive fire. Tokheidi then understood the meaning of the dream of the bull. It meant that people should deliberately paint where the paintings would last longest so that when the catastrophe struck, if any of their descendants escaped death, the paintings would still be there as a guide to help them reconnect with the spirits and remind them to honour their ancestors. And if all their descendants perished? That was a grim prospect, but still the paintings would exist to bear witness to their lives if any thinking beings should remain alive somewhere or be created in the future to re-people a devastated world.

'After this, Tokheidi and his followers began to paint a cave in the nearest of the gorges. At first other people laughed at them and made jokes about how it must be the upside-down people who gave them the idea of painting in the dark. Most people, however, began to take it more seriously when they entered the cave and saw a great bull, like the one in the dream, hovering on the rock wall in the light of a rush lamp. Eventually, everyone in the band came round to the idea and started to believe that these hidden signs could even ward off the feared catastrophe.

'As the little band travelled around and mixed with other bands, the practice spread, and wherever it was taken up it was passed down the generations and the more it became embedded in a way of life the more its origins became hazy. The story of why the paintings must be done had variants, but all agreed that it was to protect against a threat; most included something about an ancestor and a dream; and most agreed that the threat was the coming of terrible upside-down people who might destroy the world. That would be the end of everything and this is the end of my story.'

As Nyezi finished I became aware that our fire had burnt down to faintly glowing embers. Jalal got up to put on more wood sending a shower of sparks into the darkness. 'Blow on it,' said Nyezi, 'or it won't catch. It's too near to going out.' Jalal knelt and blew carefully under the new bit of branch until there was a burst of flame.

Radhika was first to comment. 'A good story even if it's not quite playing the game.'

'Not playing the game? Why isn't it?' complained Nyezi.

'It's not trying to be plausible. How could someone from a world without even fixed villages dream a city?'

'You can dream of places you've never seen.'

'Yes, but made from bits of places you have seen, just stuck together differently.'

'Not always.' Zak cut in. 'Revelations can come in dreams.'

'I'm sorry' said Frieda, 'but I can't take seriously stories that depend on the meaning of a dream.'

Zehra disagreed. 'Dreams can have a meaning but the reading of the dream in the story didn't feel right. I know people who can read dreams and the meaning usually isn't what it appears to be but often the opposite,'

'Like a funeral predicts a wedding,' agreed Radhika, 'or an infant suckling predicts imprisonment.'

Reece grumbled to no one in particular, 'I don't get the ice cliffs. If this guy can visit the future why can't he talk like he's there? Why is he stuck with "ice cliffs"?'

Frieda cut across the fragmenting discussion to say, 'If we are going to have another story perhaps we should ask Vernon for his comment and move on.'

We turned to Vernon who said rather quickly, 'What can I say? Dreams don't leave a trace. But personally, I like the notion that we have become upside-down people.'

No one added anything and so lots were drawn again and Dieter won. He hardly reacted, and as soon as we were ready he began.

12

Dieter's Story

'There is no need to wonder when these events took place because the same, or almost the same, scene would have been repeated for thousands of years – no, even tens of thousands. Of course, there must have been a time of change when the rituals evolved and another when people were ceasing to observe them. But my story starts one day of one year during the long period that passed when the rituals had been elaborated and were fully observed.

'It was early summer and the snows had melted. In the Valley of the Great Cave, people were preparing the Ceremony of Succession. They had been arriving from everywhere, often after travelling for weeks, and their shelters, arranged by tribe and clan, were strung out all along the riverside down stream from the Meeting Place.

'In the Meeting Place people were busy with different tasks. Some men were fixing the timbers of a rough platform while others were preparing animal carcasses for roasting. Women were building the cooking fires or grinding and mixing red ochre for body painting. Gradually, as the tasks were completed, people drifted over to a place on the riverbank where men and women were gathered separately, waiting. Everyone knew that the important work was taking place inside the cave in the cliffs above them.

'Towards the end of the afternoon an eerie sound echoed across the valley from the cave, the wailing of a horn. Immediately, those who had not yet joined the gathering came hurrying over as the clan chiefs stepped out from the crowd and walked into the river where they washed ceremoniously and, on leaving the water, put red-ochre markings on their faces and bodies. Next the other men washed in age order, the elders first, and afterwards went to their clan chiefs who marked them in the way they had marked themselves. As the sun reddened, each chief led his clansmen up to the cave mouth where they sat down in a rough circle except for a few men from each clan who were carrying drums and went to sit together at the cave mouth. Lastly, the women, girls and young children bathed, marked each other, and settled at a discrete distance.'

Dieter paused to interject, 'Don't assume from this that I am some unreformed misogynist. Societies just are gendered and throughout known history it's men that held most power. Accounts of states run by women, like the Amazons or Reece's murderers, always turn out to be essentially myths or fantasies. I think the game is to offer a past that at least is plausible and that is what I am doing.'

'It's your story,' said Radhika, 'and you have the floor.' No one else commented and Dieter picked up the thread.

'The horn sounded again to announce the first act of the Drama of Succession. The drummers began a persistent beat, which built an atmosphere of tension, until a figure in a huge antlered headdress burst out of the cave and danced into and around the circle. It was a shadowy presence only dimly visible in the dark, a spirit momentarily inhabiting a man. Suddenly, the dancer, stopped and addressed one of the chiefs in a voice that was terrifying and not quite human, demanding to know why these humans dared to approach a place sacred to – and here he gave a string of titles and epithets which I reduce to "Creator and Mover". The chief delivered a formulaic answer and the medium rounded on another chief with another challenge.

'So, through the long night, a routine of question and answer forced the chiefs to repeat the origin story of the Succession, a convoluted narrative which I will deliver in an extremely abbreviated version because I think you do not want to spend the whole night listening.

'After the Creator and Mover made the Earth and the Sun he told them to mate and their union produced the different creatures of land, water and air; but none emerged quite fully formed. Each pair of creatures was presented to the Creator and Mover to be finished and told how to live – the reindeer in herds, the lions in prides, the ants in heaps all working together, the crows in pairs and the rooks in flocks. But when the first pair of humans emerged they were so excited to see the world and curious to find out what it contained that they ran off before the Creator and Mover could complete them That is why to this day humans have hair only in a few places rather than a coat all over. But worse still, because they had not been told how to live, in the beginning they wandered around doing whatever they felt like and they often felt like doing things which made other humans angry, so you would never find more than one or two together. No one had respect for anyone else and if two humans had an argument, most frequently, one would kill the other. The Sun thought these unfinished creatures a good joke and laughed at their antics and so did most of the other animals, but the Earth wept for them, her last children, and asked the Creator and Mover to catch them and finish them off. But now that they were scattered around the world this was not so easy, so the Creator and Mover said the humans would have to make do with their incomplete bodies and would have to work out for themselves how to live. Earth was sad and asked the animals what to do; none could think of anything, but promised that if they had a chance they would guide humans in a good direction.

'One day two men met at a water hole and argued about who would drink first. Because both were big strong men neither was sure he could win a fight and, while they hesitated, Earth opened up and swallowed the water. While they stood amazed, a crow sitting on a tree above the water laughed at them and said Earth swallowed the water so it would not be polluted with a man's blood. The men thought about this and agreed that if the water came back they would draw lots for who would drink first, and Earth let the water flow again.

'The men drew lots and drank in turn but did not quite take in Earth's message. They went their separate way each wondering how to be sure he would win a fight in future.

'Not long afterwards one of them met a bear and thought, *Bear is a very strong animal. I will ask Bear to lend me some of his strength.* So, he asked and Bear agreed, on the condition that the man and his children would never eat Bear or Bear's children. The man accepted and said, "Now make me strong."

'Then Bear said, "How will you keep your promise if you don't know who your children are?"

'So, the man thought for a bit and said that he would make sure any woman he mated with mated only with him and he would teach their children never to eat a bear. "Now make me strong."

'"I have done enough," said Bear, "Because, if you do what you have just promised, you will become strong. Goodbye." Bear began to lumber away but stopped to call over his shoulder, "Don't forget. If any of your descendants eats Bear, your line will end.'

'The man went away and did as Bear said and that was why men and women started to marry and how the Bear Clan was founded. To help his descendants understand and remember their debt to Bear the man drew a bear on a rock, which became the first of the bear pictures that his descendants always made wherever they went.

'The other man in the argument over the water hole met a bison and thought, *Bison is a very powerful animal. If I were like Bison I could always crush any man who challenges me.* So, he asked Bison to help him and Bison agreed on condition that… and you can guess the next bit.

'So, the Bear and the Bison Clans were born and when lone men saw how much better those clansmen lived they asked other animals to help them, and that is how all the other clans came into being and man began to live in families and clans with clan chiefs to settle disputes and make decisions. After a time it was noticed that certain men had a special ability to communicate with the clan guardian spirit, and so these mediums also specialised in creating the images of the guardian spirit.

'Humans began to multiply because they no longer kept killing each other, but as their members increased the clans began to collide and fought bloody battles over trivial disputes. These times were in some ways worse than those before because the battles might wipe out almost a whole clan.

'At first, each clan imagined one day it would win completely and the slaughter would be over but, eventually, they all came to accept that none could prevail. Then the spirit mediums began to report that the Earth was angry about all the blood spilled on her; so angry that all the chiefs would have to combine to propitiate her. Now all the clans recognised some of the same sacred places, and the most sacred were certain caves, orifices of the Earth, from where her powers came and where it was strictly forbidden to shed blood. So, the chiefs agreed to meet in one of the caves and make offerings together to placate the Earth. In preparation for this event the painter-mediums painted the clan images on the cave walls.

'When the offerings were being made it happened that mediums from the Bear Clan and the Bison Clan became possessed, simultaneously, by a spirit more powerful than any of the clan guardians, a spirit emanating from the Creator and Maker himself. In their trance they demanded that all the clan chiefs should recognise one of their number, who was shortly to be revealed to them, as having the power to arbitrate between the clans and settle all disputes for a period of three years. At the end of the three years they were to return and a new Arbiter would be revealed. The mediums then revealed who was to be the first Arbiter by taking burning torches and holding them to light his clan image.

'The chiefs had to accept this message and at once honoured the chosen Arbiter, and the mediums then laid down a set of rules for how men and women were to live. There were many but I'll mention only one, that a man must take his wife not from his own clan but always from another, a rule that meant the clans could not survive without each other.

'From this time onwards the chaotic fighting ceased. The Arbiter ensured they lived in peace and prosperity and every three years his authority was renewed through the Rite of Succession. Humans had at last acquired the knowledge they missed at birth and although they remained unfinished physically, they learnt to make up for this by painting on their bare bodies or covering them up with various materials to ward off heat and cold as well as to improve their appearance. The other animals no longer laughed at them but began to look up to them.

'This is the essence of the story that unfolded outside the Great Cave, reaching its conclusion only as dawn was breaking. By then the ritual of succession that had meanwhile been taking place inside the cave was almost complete and the people were called in to participate in the final act. They advanced slowly through narrow passages and painted chambers until they reached an immense chamber with bays and alcoves and domes, which the torchlight failed to reach, and a floor heaving with rocky mounds and treacherous pits where darkness also lurked. Here the mediums moved around illuminating one painted beast after another, narrating the virtues of each clan and the achievements of past Arbiters while suspense mounted, until they came to the painting for the newly-chosen Arbiter under which they lit a fixed torch and raised their torches to show the painting, a mammoth, gleaming in reds and blacks and rippling with power. The chief of the Mammoth Clan moved forward to receive the headdress and outer clothing of the previous Arbiter.

'There were still a few ceremonies to complete and, of course, a great deal of cooking to be done before the feast was ready but at last the festivities began and, with much eating and dancing, lasted until exhaustion set in. Over the next few days the clans mingled to revive friendships, arrange marriages and exchange news and gifts before they began to leave, fanning out to their different hunting grounds. Just a few families remained behind with the Arbiter to look after the sacred area where people would come if they needed disputes settled or advice on other matters. There was a sadness in the parting, but everyone knew there would be another gathering and that the cycle of gathering and parting would go on and on like the cycle of the seasons.'

When Dieter finished we applauded briefly and some of us fed the fire while we waited for comment.

Sven began. 'It's a bit Hollywood, isn't it? Torchlight, chieftains, possession?' He did not mean it as a compliment.

Reece remarked, 'For a movie it could do with more blood and fewer spirits.'

'No,' Zak disagreed, 'the spirits are right.'

Frieda adopted her impish look and said, 'I'm glad to see that Dieter's people had read their Hobbes!'

Vernon and Leandro chuckled. I was mystified for a moment as at first I'd pictured cooker tops, and by the time I realised she was referring to the philosopher of a 'nasty, brutish and short' state of nature, Dieter was in full spate defending his version of a social contract.

'If the culture of the painted caves lasted for more than ten thousand years it must have been stable, really stable. When else has there been a time when art changed so little? The longest lasting art tradition

I can think of in historical times is in Egypt under the pharaohs. That should be a hint. What do we know about Egypt? It had religion, hierarchy, authority all linked. You don't get stability without those three in some form.'

Sven, visibly ruffled, retorted, 'What sort of stability did the kingdoms of our very Christian Europe bring? One bloody war after another: coups, invasions, massacres. Only an equal society could be truly stable.'

'On what evidence?'

'The most stable countries now are the more equal ones, like Sweden, Finland, Japan… '

'I thought Japan was rather authoritarian,' Radhika objected.

'England's very unequal but quite stable. ' I dared myself to contribute.

'The funny thing is,' said Vernon, 'forty years ago Dieter sounded a bit like Sven.'

Dieter ignored us all and continued, 'You can see it in the paintings. So yes, the paintings look naturalistic and spontaneous but actually they aren't. They're not like pictures drawn from life because they're all profiles. That's not how you see an animal, the profile with the legs nicely arranged so they are all visible. That's what you think you see, or ought to see: body, head, horns, four legs, tail – not the animal but your idea of it. Then, they're all similar. That says to me that the artists learnt from looking at other pictures, not from looking at the animals. Yes, they look spontaneous because lines curve freely, there are smears of colour, and the affect reminds us of a hasty watercolour lightly brushed in the open air. But a hill can remind you of camel but that doesn't make it a a camel. No one lightly brushed those paintings. People worked carefully, following rules handed down generation by generation. That suggests order, tradition, authority – and that allowed the culture to go on and on.'

There was a pause in which the crickets sounded loud. Sven looked sceptical but apparently decided not to add anything.

'Maybe we should think of sleep,' said Leandro.

'What about Vernon's comment?' I asked, surprising myself by speaking again.

'About the paintings,' Vernon responded quickly. 'I agree, certainly, that they aren't as naturalistic as they seem, that they convey an idea of the animal rather than an eye's view of it. Yet the creatures are thrumming with life, often in motion and, even when still, they look poised to move. So, it seems to me that whoever did the paintings wanted a lifelike look but their model of how to do that probably evolved one painting to another. What would be great to know is exactly why they wanted that lifelike look.'

'And a connection with authority?' prompted Radhika.

'I've agreed they seem to be following an artistic tradition. I think that's pretty clear and you could say that tradition's a kind of authority, but you could have that without a system to enforce it. People don't necessarily need boss figures to make them follow traditions.'

'He's not right, then, is he, about the long duration and authority?' Sven persisted.

'Ah,' Vernon sighed, 'that's another difficult one. Let's not get into it now.'

It was sleep time. Leandro suggested we keep the fire burning and set a watch just in case of animal or human disturbance. Leandro, Nyezi and Reece volunteered for two and a half hours each.

Once everyone had stopped talking and settled down the crickets again seemed almost to roar, while the forest was full of alarming squeaks and crackles. It was also getting cold. I took a long time to fall asleep and lay, alternately admiring Leandro in the glow of the fire and staring up at the few stars which showed through the trees. It probably seemed longer than it was because I never noticed the watch change and was surprised to wake from a deep sleep to find that the sky was starting to lose its blackness and people were already stirring.

13

Water

Breakfast was a disappointment. We had saved rice from the night before, carefully protected in the pan with its heavy lid firmly on and the pan suspended from a tree branch, but ants had found their way in. We ate what we could, picking through the grains and rejecting fingerfulls too thick with insects. As for drink, the shoppers had thought of tea and sugar but we had only three cups between us. Some of us shared the sweet black tea, passing the cups from hand to hand. Others declined.

We walked on through a forest that remained so similar, hour after hour, that I had the impression we were going in circles, an impression I could not shed even though I saw Reece checking his compass now and then. After about four hours, the scene at last changed. The ground began to rise and became rocky while the tree cover thinned, exposing us to the full heat of the sun. Not everyone was finding the going easy. Footwear was a problem as no one had been expecting to walk instead of fly. Mathew had mentioned blisters laughingly the night before but now he, Magome and Zehra all had to stop to plaster bits of their feet. Vernon, Nyezi, and Reece were well shod in light boots, the first two, presumably, as they needed to be comfortable on excavation sites. Mama Ulema was only wearing flip-flops but did not complain, while Frieda, in light trainers, and Radhika, in ordinary sandals, were managing without apparent discomfort. I was fortunate in that I was wearing a good pair of trekking shoes that I'd put in my luggage because they were one of my more valuable possessions.

We did not have to climb far before we reached a ridge from where we began to drop downhill and, although the ground remained rocky, the forest thickened up enough to provide continuous dappled shade. Soon, through the trees, we started to glimpse open space and then, suddenly, we came out on the edge of a small valley where a wide stream wound, glinting through lush plots of millet, maize and bananas. There was no sign of houses or people although there must have been a village somewhere nearby. After pausing briefly to look around and enjoy the perspective of green, cultivated land, we followed the track, more marked here, between the fields and through a fringe of tall reeds, to reach the riverbank at a natural ford. The water was sparkling clear and, after our long dry journey, seemed almost too beautiful to be real. A little upstream we could see, on a high bit of bank, a spreading mango tree which Radhika proposed as our lunch spot. There was a bit of a path along the bank and we pushed our way, rustling through reeds, to where the tree cast its dark shade on a carpet of fallen leaves. Under the bank was a deep pool, which moved some of us to think of bathing.

The men tactfully went on in search of a separate spot and, as soon as the reeds closed behind them, I stripped off and waded into the water. It felt surprisingly cool. I launched myself and started to swim around delightedly, encouraging the others. Frieda laughed and followed me in, her body looking thin and fragile in its nakedness but not marked by age unless you looked closely. Zehra at first went in modestly wearing a cloth wrapped around her, but after a while she let it slip and tossed it onto the bank. Mama Ulemu stood in the water to wash, chatting to us cheerfully although none of us, except perhaps Zehra, could understand anything she said. Radhika hesitated to do more than paddle because she said she could not swim, but I showed her that I could just stand even in the deepest part. Soon she too was naked, splashing and laughing while Frieda, Zehra and I swam happily in circles. After a while Radhika decided to wash clothes, saying the sun was so fierce they would dry by the time we moved on. She went to get from her bag a little bar of laundry soap, and offered the use of it to us all as she shoved her blue outfit under water. At that moment Mama Ulemu said something sharply to us and then called out across the water. We looked up and saw a dark figure of a man among the reeds on the far side. Zehra grabbed her cloth from the bank, Radhika hastily covered herself in wet cotton while Frieda and I sank down in the water, hoping we were only visible from the chin up. There was a halting exchange between the man, Mama Ulemu and Zehra, after which he walked slowly away upstream.

'I think she told him to go and talk to the men,' Zehra explained, 'although I'm not sure how well they understood each other. I got only the odd word.'

Unnerved by the suddenness with which the man appeared, we all got partially dressed while we finished our washing and spread it out over the reeds to dry. We were still arranging it when we heard Mathew from somewhere near the tree call out, 'Hi, Ladies. Are you decent? Can I join you?'

The men, he told us, had walked some way past shallows until they came on another, even deeper, pool and were bathing there when they met the man who had startled us. They too did not see him arrive but first noticed him, as we had, silently watching. Greetings were exchanged guardedly and a stilted conversation began. They had limited common language and, not surprisingly, the man was suspicious of this oddly assorted bunch of strangers turning up unannounced on his village land. Gradually, however, Leandro, Vernon, Magome and Nyezi, between them, managed to win the man's confidence and convince him that we were neither marauding bandits nor agents of some distant power with designs on their land.

'But the reason I came back now is to tell you we will be a while longer because we are fishing. The village man had been fishing when he spotted you people and now he's going to help us to catch some fish. Can you let us have a cloth to stand in for a net? And could you make a fire and cook a little rice in readiness? We've decided to make a long break here. Only don't use up too much rice as the man is also going to give us some sweet corn. He asked us to his village but we excused ourselves as it is somewhere over there,' and he waved vaguely across the valley down stream. 'Too far off our route. And also we gathered that food is short around here and so feeding us all, as they would probably feel bound to do, would be a strain on resources.'

Zehra gave Mathew her half dry cloth and we went off to collect wood, of which there was a fair amount scattered along the bank, presumably left by the last rainy season floods.

We were sceptical about the chances of the men catching anything, but we got a fire going, cooked the rice and settled down to wait. Mama Ulemu soon wandered off somewhere. Zehra and I sat companionably dozing while Radhika and Frieda returned to a conversation they had left unfinished at the building conference. One of the biggest difficulties Radhika encounters when promoting her mud bricks is the assumption that buildings made from them are extra vulnerable to infestations, especially of termites, or white ants as I used to call them before corrected by Frieda. Apparently they are not ants at all but a relative of cockroaches. I couldn't help remarking that cockroaches are one creature I would not miss if some one found a safe way to exterminate them. It was a silly thing to say in front of an entomologist and Frieda gave me the sort of look you give a bungling child. She left Radhika to demolish the notion of 'safe' extermination while she restricted herself to mentioning that one of many reasons to be grateful for cockroaches is that they recycle decaying vegetation into nitrogen, which feeds plant life. I absorbed the information in remorseful silence and the conversation switched back to termites, which are Frieda's specialism and are of great interest to Radhika for their real ability to undermine buildings as well as for their reputation for doing so. The two women shared strong opinions about the hazards and limitations of mass destruction and Frieda had started to explain new approaches to control when my attention was distracted by a bird darting along the river. I wondered if it could be a kingfisher as it looked a little like one except that it was not turquoise but a shade of deep ultramarine blue. Zehra saw me staring at it and remarked 'Kingfisher,' just as it dived. When my attention returned to the termite conversation it had shifted to considering the insects as creators rather than destroyers. Frieda talked of the internal beauty of a termite mound, constructed to enable the nest beneath it to breath, while Radhika praised the creatures for providing inspiration to her profession and talked excitedly of a building in Harare that she longed to visit, famously based on the termites' technique for cooling their nests.

'Except they got it wrong, ' said Frieda.

'Wrong?' echoed Radhika, surprised.

'Yes, the building was based on an assumption about the mounds which turned out to be false. But don't worry.' Radhika was looking disappointed. 'The building is still experimental and uses a low energy cooling system that owes something to termites even if it was based on a mistake. What does it matter if it isn't like a termite mound? And what we now know about the termite mounds is even more interesting than the old story…'

She was interrupted by the men returning. They had not been very successful and by their own efforts had caught only three fishes not much bigger than sardines, but they had persuaded the helpful fisherman to sell them a more trout-sized one that he had caught. Even so, there was not going to be much of a fish dinner for sixteen but we started roasting them anyway, and just then Mama Ulemu returned and held out another fish more than three times the size of the fisherman's. Everyone laughed. Her catch put everyone else's to shame.

Although short on quantity, the fish was delicious and how delightful it was to be eating under the mango tree, watching the glinting water below. When I went down to wash the smell of fish off my hands, I lingered to admire the view along the river, a silver band curving away between shivering reeds towards a hazy line of hills. The kingfisher was nowhere to be seen but high above in the clear blue sky some great bird of prey was wheeling. I wished we could stay there but already the washing and cooking had taken up too much time. Leandro decreed that we should move on, skipping an after lunch rest and more stories.

For the first hour or so we walked on along the valley, passing through cultivated fields and patches of lush scrubland until we reached a major bend in the river where the path carried straight on and began to climb the valley side. I said a sad goodbye to the water, wishing there was time for another quick swim. It was a long climb, steep in places, and by the time we reached the top, or at least a place where the hill levelled off, the sun was not far from setting. Several people were showing signs of exhaustion and we stopped to make camp there, even though we gathered that we were now well behind schedule.

As lunch had been more substantial than expected we just had maize porridge for supper with black, sweet tea. We drew the straws and it fell to Tom.

Tom was obviously ill at ease but adopted what I thought might be his school teacher manner and began quickly.

14

Tom's Story

'Once people used to eat only vegetables and small animals, but one day two brothers were out hunting and they didn't catch anything so they were hungry. Then they saw some buffalo grazing and the elder brother said, "Listen Little Brother, I'm very hungry and we haven't found anything to eat but if we killed one of those buffalo we would have plenty to eat and to take home with us."

'"But we never kill buffalo." said the little brother. "They are too big and it would be very difficult."

'The elder brother said, "It is true that we have never killed a buffalo before, but now we are going to kill one. It is true that it will be difficult but I have a plan to trick the buffalo."

'They went very quietly through the grass up to the buffalo, which took no notice of them because humans then were not known to kill anything larger than a rabbit. When they were close the buffalo raised his head and asked them if they wanted something from him.

'The elder brother said, "Buffalo, I am very sorry but we have heard some bad news about you and have come to warn you."

'The Buffalo thought it was very kind of them and at once asked what they had heard.

'"Crow told us that your life will end very soon and we feel sad that you will disappear from the world and be forgotten."

'Buffalo was very worried by this because crow is a bird who can tell the future.

'Then Elder Brother said, "We can't prevent the future that crow has told us about but, if you like, we can make a version of you that will last forever and mean that you will be remembered by all your kin and all the animals, so that you will not vanish and be forgotten."

Buffalo said that was a good idea and asked him to do it.

"Ah, but then you have to give us something in exchange."

Buffalo asked what he meant and elder brother said, "We are very hungry and we will do this for you if you allow us to kill you now, just a few hours before your death is foretold, and then we can eat you and that will help us to make the picture which will last forever."

Buffalo thought for a while but, as he believed that his death was coming very soon anyway, he agreed but said, "My spirit will watch, and if you do not carry out your promise I will curse you and all your descendants."

'The buffalo lowered his head and allowed the brothers to put their spears into his neck.

'They ate very happily from the carcass and took meat home.

'Younger brother said, "You had better carry out your promise or we will be cursed."

"Buffalo is dead now. He will never know whether we keep our promise or not."

'Younger brother was just about to point out that the buffalo's spirit would be watching when elder brother was seized with such a terrible pain he thought he might be dying. He was terrified and at once got to work on the portrait and, as he went on, the pain got less until finally, when he had done a really good job, he felt quite well again. That night the buffalo's spirit came and admired the painting and went away satisfied and his family came to admire the likeness.

'Then the rains came and then the snow – you have said, I think, that the paintings are in a place where there is snow?' Tom said this looking anxiously at Vernon. 'Then the rain and the snow washed away the portrait.

'When the buffalo's family saw that the picture had gone they called his spirit to come back and the spirit of the buffalo was very angry and said to the brothers, "You lied to me. I will now curse you and your children."

'"No, no," said Elder Brother, "Wait and see. We made a mistake, but I promise we will make a better picture of you that will really last for ever."

'He did not know how he was going to do that but younger brother had been thinking. First of all he thought they might make a shelter for the painting but he knew the shelters they could make would hardly last more than one or two rainy seasons. Then he remembered how, when the rains were very bad, the people would leave their shelters and go into one of the caves up on the hillside. A picture would last very well there, he thought, and suggested that Elder Brother paint the portrait in one of the caves. Elder Brother did this and the buffalo spirit was satisfied. He came back every year to check, and the portrait was there as bright and clear as when first painted.

'Everyone who heard about this took it to heart and so, when next the people needed to kill one of the big animals – and they learned how to do it without exactly asking permission – they painted a picture of it in the cave to make sure they wouldn't be cursed. So, it became the custom that people killed and ate the big animals but the animals that were killed lived on in spirit in the cave.'

Tom finished and Zak exclaimed, 'You see, spirits are important! I said so.'

For once Vernon spoke without being prompted. 'Well, Tom, you've touched there on one of the theories archaeologists have played with, that the purpose might be to placate animal spirits.'

Tom looked pleased until Vernon went on. 'But there's a small snag with the idea that it's to do with killing for food, because in many cases the animals depicted aren't ones that the people were eating – that is as far as we know from food remains.'

Tom's expression changed. 'I got it wrong then. I'm

sorry,' he said, with the air of a schoolboy being ticked off, or a very junior master found wanting by the head teacher.

'Don't worry,' laughed Zehra. 'It's not a test. We can't be expected to know that sort of thing.'

'Of course not,' Vernon agreed. 'As I said, the general idea behind it, seems rather plausible.'

Reece objected that if people painted every animal they killed for twenty thousand years they would have needed a lot of cave space.

No one seemed keen to respond and we drew the straws again. This time my luck ran out.

15

Nita's Story

I hadn't yet come up yet with anything worth telling and hesitated between pleading to pass and muddling along somehow. No one else so far had reneged. Nyezi had tried, but when Vernon pushed him he gave in quickly enough. Everyone had taken their turn, even Jalal and Reece, who didn't strike me as having much of a literary background; and Mama Ulemu, who probably had not been to school at all. I twisted the straw round my finger and decided I must muddle through for long enough to be seen to have done my bit.

'I've had the same trouble as Mathew,' I began, aiming to postpone the moment as long as possible.

'Like Mathew I can't think myself into such a different world. Seeing how he managed instead by drawing on his own life, I've searched mine for a clue but the trouble is, unlike Mathew's, my life's been quite unexciting, almost as far as you could get from being a hunter-gatherer living with mammoths and cave lions.'

'I wouldn't say mine really offered a clue.' Mathew interjected.

'It made a story at least.'

'Every life is a story.'

'Maybe, but not one you'd want to hear. I mean, the town I come from – one of those 1940s new towns near London – is a byword for a boring place, a place where people go to live in a semi-detached house with a partner, two children, a car and a dog, where a trip to the supermarket is entertainment.'

I suddenly changed course, disconcerted that I was reproducing this old cliché. 'Mind you, that's snobbery – to say a place is interesting only if rich and famous people live there or if it's a hotspot of deprivation and violence.'

I stopped again as I had meant to make a few jokey remarks not start a rant. My sense of being challenged had conjured memories of feeling challenged by self confident Londoners who talked as if London – especially North London – was the only place to live.

I went on more quietly. 'I mean it's not a bad place to live, especially for a child – big gardens, quiet streets, bits of wilderness in among the houses, decent local school... but not a likely setting for drama. The same with my family – the kind of family I bet most children would choose if they could, but not story material: loving parents, happy with each other as far as one can tell, neither married before, both in decent jobs – Dad's a GP and Mum teaches chemistry – one brother, a bit of a pain at times but not bad as brothers go...

'So, all I'm saying is that my own experience doesn't offer much in the way of leads, but I can see you're waiting and I'll just have to go with something that's a bit random.'

Unpromising though it was, my life had yielded up a few thoughts. One was attached to a moment on a fine February morning when I was about ten years old. A friend and I had a den, under a gorse bush on a bit of heathland near some allotments. My parents had one there and my friend and I would often go with them, help dig a bit and then escape to our den. This particular morning my friend hadn't come, so I went to the den alone and sat outside in the sun. Patches of frost remained here and there but the earth had started to warm, the air was still and the sky, an even intense blue, spread out far, far behind the yellow gorse flowers. The moment affected me deeply; it was a sensual experience so perfect that I wanted to stop time so it would last forever. Later, at home, I tried to recapture and freeze that feeling by painting the gorse and sky. I made several attempts all of which fell so far short of the memory that they only increased a sense of loss. I failed, but the attempt offered a possible clue in the idea that art can rescue us from time. Unfortunately, I couldn't quite relate this to the cave paintings.

Another memory seemed more promising as it featured a wild animal. It was from a few years later when I was returning home after clubbing in London and had caught the first morning train. It was just beginning to get light and there was a slight mist. The walk from the station takes you through a patch of woodland along a rather twisty path and, as I rounded one of the bends, I came face to face with a huge fox. I expected it to turn and run but instead it stood its ground with one paw raised and gave me a fixed glare. I glared back, first just surprised and then frightened. I told myself that such a small animal would never dare attack a fully grown human, but I was uncomfortably aware that even little dogs can savage a person if they choose. After what seemed an age the fox turned away and stalked off unhurriedly into the brambles.

That fox image was very clear and I noticed something that made it quite different from the cave paintings. The most memorable part is the fox's face – turned towards me with two eyes locking with mine. But the animals in the cave paintings aren't looking at you – or the ones I could remember aren't. Like Dieter pointed out, both head and body are in profile. That distanced them from my fox but set off a train of thought that gave me my attempt at a story, which I forced myself to begin.

'After a very bad day's hunting a man was walking home thinking over the day's failures; how he had tracked several promising deer but every time he got close enough to cast his spear the animal looked up, saw him and bounded away. While he was preoccupied by this problem he came across a lion sunning itself. The moment he saw it he dodged behind a tree but too late. The lion had spotted him and got up, stretched, and started to approach. Terrified, the man climbed the tree but the lion leapt up after him. The man climbed higher and higher until at last he reached a point where the lion decided not to follow but lay down along a fat branch and waited. The man spent a long time clinging on uncomfortably until some deer came past and the lion abandoned his watch to chase after them.

'The man reached home very late and sad that he was bringing no meat for his family. All they had to eat were a few woody roots his wife had dug up and some slightly bitter berries the children had picked.

'He told his wife about the failure of his hunt and of his near escape with the lion, and she told him that the children had been chased by an elephant when they were picking the berries and had also had a very narrow escape.

'"Something is not right," said his wife, after thinking for a while. "There are too many days when you do not make a kill and too many times when we are threatened by some fierce animal. We must do something about this."

'"I have been going out for longer and longer," said the man, "and making my spears better, with sharper heads and smoother shafts which let them fly better. What else can I do?"

'His wife thought for a while and then said, "Why don't you consult the wise old woman who lives on the far side of the long hills?' People say that she can talk to the animals and knows so many things about them; she may know what to do."

'The man did not really believe that an old woman could help him, and he did not much want to travel all the way to the other side of the long hills, but because he was ashamed that for many days he had brought back so little meat, he decided he would do as his wife suggested.

'The next day he travelled across the plain and over the long hills and searched here and there until he found the old wise woman who lived alone with her pet hyena.

'He approached her, told her about all their troubles, and offered her a small deer he had managed to kill on the way. The old woman listened carefully and said she would help him but he should go away and come back later as she needed time to think about it.

'When he came back he found her sitting together with her hyena in front of a stone on which she had scratched the shape of a lion. She motioned him to sit down, which he did, although slightly disconcerted at the way the hyena looked at him and twitched its tail.

'"You must divert the eyes of your prey and the eyes of those who would prey on you," the wise woman said "I will teach you how to do this, but first you must make a promise."

'The man was afraid he was going to have to promise always to bring her a share of whatever he managed to kill, but she asked something much less troublesome.

'"You must promise that you will never, ever use what I am going to teach you against another human being."

'He promised that very readily because he did not think of fellow humans either as food or danger. At that time it was rare for human beings to attack each other, and cannibalism was unheard of.

'"If you ever break this promise you and your descendants will lose the power for ever." The old woman looked at him very hard before she went on. "Secondly, you must keep this a secret from all animals because if they know about it they will not be affected by it."

'The man didn't see that as a problem as he was not in the habit of talking with animals. So, he got ready to learn the old woman's wisdom.

'"You must make a likeness like this," she began, indicating the scratched outline of the lion. "Make a better likeness if you can, but make it of whichever animal it is you want to have power over. You must make it so the animal is looking away, looking where it will not see you. You must never show the animal looking at you, because that will give it power over you. That is the first thing you must do. Then you must breath life into the likeness. Blow on it seven times and recite the verses that I will teach you; blow on it seven times again and while you do this you must concentrate on what you want to happen; if you want the lion to pass by, or if you want the gazelle to keep grazing."

'The man stayed with the wise woman until he had learnt how to draw various animals and had memorised the verses. Then he went home and taught his wife everything the old woman had taught him so they could work together to put it into practice.

'For several months all went well. The man was successful in his hunts and neither he, nor his wife, nor their children suffered dangerous encounters with any animal. But then there came a time when slowly, slowly the old problems returned.

'Eventually, the man returned to the wise woman beyond the long hills to ask what could be going wrong.

'The first thing she asked him was, "Have you tried to use the spell on a human being?" He assured her that he hadn't. "Have you tried to make a likeness of a human?" He assured her that he hadn't. "Well, in that case you must have revealed the secret." He assured her that he hadn't but this time she didn't accept his answer. She called her hyena, whispered some instruction in its ear and the hyena sped off into the long grass. To the man she said, "You must wait." And she went away to attend to some other business.

After a long time the hyena came bounding back and the wise woman had some consultation with it, after which she rounded on the man.

'"You have been careless and let the animals know the secret. I thought this must be the case. You have let them see you making the likenesses and you have left the results just anywhere, where they can see them. All the animals now know what you are doing and can resist it. You have been very foolish but you are fortunate that animals have short memories, except for the elephant, and it happens that no elephants have passed your way recently. So, in time you will regain the power, as long as you never again let any animal see what you do."

'When man returned to his wife they spent a long time wondering how they could make sure no animal ever saw them making a likeness again.

'"You will have to keep watch while I draw and make sure no animal comes near enough to see," the man suggested.

'"I don't think that will work. I can't stop the birds from flitting by or a squirrel from scampering overhead. Even a rat could probably slip past and see."

'"I could hide under a big bearskin."

'"Perhaps. But you will look very odd hiding under a bearskin and the animals might be suspicious; and if they are suspicious they will surely find a way to peep." She looked thoughtful and then went on. "But that gives me an idea. You know the caves where we go to shelter in the winter sometimes? Some of them go back deep into the earth far beyond where we stay…"'

I broke off the story here.

'You can all guess what happens next. The plan of drawing in the cave works very well. They get better and better at making the pictures and pass the skills down to their children, who in turn pass them on to all their descendants, with the strict rules that they never show animals looking at them and never, never, draw a human being.'

I sat back nervously, relieved to have got through without completely losing my thread. After the customary applause, Radhika spoke encouragingly. 'That makes a lot of sense – representation as power, a bit like the male gaze.'

'Certainly,' Frieda agreed, 'the story was fine, but I was more interested in the prologue about you, Nita. You were suggesting we would find your background boring because you lived somewhere safe and pleasant with parents who are alive, love each other and are loved by you. So how is that boring? Surely the more unusual a state of affairs is, the more interesting it should be? And in the world as it is, a background like yours is, I'm afraid, not very usual. So, why would it not be interesting?'

'Because there's no story in that.' Reece stated, as if it was obvious. 'Nothing much happens.'

'No,' Frieda responded sharply. 'That's not true. Things don't "go well" by themselves. They have to be made to go well and that involves, thought, imagination and work.'

'And it takes so little to make them go wrong,' Radhika agreed. 'It takes years to build trust between communities but one small act of violence to destroy it all.' She thought for a moment and went on. 'You can see it in less emotive things too. Like a metro. Think what it takes to have enough trains for passengers, running on time and safely. That's complicated and interesting. To make a train crash you just need one person, any person, with no ideas and no skill, to chuck a concrete bar on the rails.'

'But it's the riot and crash that makes the headlines,' said Dieter, 'and you'll never change that.'

Frieda made an exasperated gesture and Sven was boiling up to speak when Radhika turned to me to say, 'But Nita, I suspect you've left out one very conventionally interesting part of your story. Presumably your parents are not entirely typical of couples in your town?'

I bristled. I tend to react badly when strangers try to pry into my origins. But I quickly softened, as her manner reminded me that Indians are generally obsessed with origins and it amused me think this ultra-sophisticated professional was behaving like any old Calcutta granny. I laughed and said, 'I'm afraid it's not Romeo and Juliet. After he qualified, Dad went to Calcutta to do an elective and met my mum who was just finishing a BSc. Although Mum's family isn't from the jet-setting Anglophone elite, they're quite progressive, keen Gandhians, steeped in Tagore and all that. They were worried, of course, but not opposed in principle. Mind you, they had several daughters to marry and, of course, with Dad, there was no question of dowry.'

Radhika smiled at this.

'On the other side, my English grandparents are Christian Socialists, ideologically committed to anti-racism and if there was a time when their feelings didn't quite match the ideology, there was nothing to show for it by the time I knew them. We all get on.'

Radhika looked as if she had more questions but, thinking we had heard enough about me, I asked if we were going to have another story that night. Most people were in favour, but Zak prompted Vernon to comment before we moved on. To my relief he just said something about secrecy being connected with control.

I felt more relaxed now that my turn was over and settled back comfortably while the draw took place. It revealed Leandro as our next story-teller.

16

Leandro's Story

'If you listen carefully to the wind you can sometimes hear strange and unexpected things. For the wind picks up words in passing and whirls them around for ever until sometimes they recombine, and those who are attuned to hear may pick up an echo of what was said. This is how I can pass on to you something of this story that was told some twenty thousand years ago. It seems that the man who told it was at first speaking to a welcoming host.

Leandro paused for affect and then began.

'My name is Born in the Year of the Summer Snow. The Pointy-Chin people complain about the length of my name and if I were one of them I would probably be called Borny or Snowy because that is the way of the Pointy-Chins. They are always in a hurry and think that speaking a name properly is a waste of time. They are wrong, because a name is important and every name has its meaning and its reason. My name recalls to people the season of my birth, events that took place around that time, and people now dead who were living then. These events and people are part of me and so it is good to recall them whenever I am spoken to or mentioned. Something everyone remembers about that year is the strange weather that occurred in the season of the longest days when it is usually warm and sunny. That year, I have been told, began like others with snow and ice, clear days and storms until, as usual, the snows softened letting new grass and flowers thrust up into the light. But when the white of the snow was finally gone, and the plains were covered with flowers, and humming with bees, the skies unexpectedly darkened. For some days clouds like grey rocks pressed down and then it began to snow and went on snowing until the whole world was white again like in the dark season, except that the flakes lay lightly on top of the grass and flowers. No one remembered such a thing happening before. The Pointy-Chins – there was a small band of them that passed just afterwards – the Pointy-Chins, of course, said that it meant something; not that the weather had turned cold, as anyone could see, but something else, something that only a special person could know. The Pointy-Chins find these hidden meanings in anything and everything. A crow lies dead on a man's path and it means, not that the bird's life ran out in that place but that someone wants to kill the man; a stone breaks off the cliff and it means, not that the thaw is freeing rocks previously frozen but that a dead ancestor is angry. A man can't sneeze or fart without it being a sign.

'Why am I saying this about the Pointy-Chins? You will understand when you have heard me out. You asked me to tell you why I and my family left our home, now far away; why we passed on beyond the homes of the neighbours we met and with whom our children marry; why we now come among you, who are hardly known to us, although you are true people like us. We are grateful for your hospitality. It will never be forgotten that you have welcomed us although we have no children in common. I told you that we will leave you soon and that when we leave you we will not go back to our home but will go on to places unknown to us where the people, if there are any, will be even more distant from us than you are.

'Our home is in a valley that runs up into the Big Hills and anyone wanting to cross the Big Hills would find that following our valley is the easiest way to go. We walk up the valley at the season of meetings, as there are neighbours just beyond the Big Hills where some of our daughters are married. Otherwise we do not go so far. But the Pointy-Chins pass through one way and then the other, many of them, every year. Occasionally we meet and exchange some greetings, and occasionally they ask us about the weather or the game. They do not speak properly, of course, but they have a few of our words and we have a few of theirs and one way and another we can get them to understand, "There is snow on the hills," or "There are no mammoths nearby." Everyone thinks they are strange looking people – almost people, but not quite people. You must have seen them occasionally: tall and thin with foreheads like a cliff instead of gracefully sloping back as ours do, and with those jutting chins from which comes the name we use for them. Since I was a boy I have been more curious than most people, and I sometimes go a little way with them and try to ask things, and that's why I began to think that they are stranger inside than they are outside. The first odd incident happened when a group was camped near our home for some time and I used to see one of their boys quite often. One day I caught a ground squirrel. I was going to share it but the boy grabbed it from me and ran back to the camp. I ran after him and saw him give it to his mother. She said something and I could tell that she was asking him where he got it and instead of pointing to me, who was not far behind him, he indicated that he had hunted it himself with great difficulty. I was really surprised. Why would he say something that was not? What did it matter who had caught the squirrel?

'Not long after that I asked the boy why he wore a duck's foot on a leather string round his neck. I'd seen several other Pointy-Chins wearing them. Perhaps they found them decorative, although to me they were quite ugly. At first I didn't understand what his answer was as it was so unlikely. Eventually, I worked out that he was saying it protected him so that if he met an angry lion, the lion would not touch him; if he trod on a snake, the snake would not bite him. He got very cross because I didn't understand for so long and when I did I laughed. Why would a lion worry about a duck's foot when lions will eat a duck whole? How would a snake even see he was wearing the thing? The boy was so cross he not only shouted, but also threw a stone at me.

'When I was grown up, if there was any need to talk with the Pointy-Chins, I was often called on, because the time I'd spent around their camps as a boy meant I was quite good at it. The more I saw of them the more I was worried by them, and tried to explain to anyone who would listen why we should all be worried by them. People took no notice, saying that the Pointy-Chins may be odd but that is a problem only for themselves; that they have been passing through our land for generations and nothing terrible has happened; they move on and take their oddness with them. I was sure that people who speak like that were looking away from many signs – true signs, not Pointy-Chin signs – that there was reason to be afraid. I argued that our grandparents say that in their own grandparents' time there were hardly any Pointy-Chins, that people knew about them but rarely saw any and had no need to understand their speech. Now we see them every year and even in my lifetime their numbers have increased. When we work the same hunting grounds there have been troubles. They move on, it is true, but they come back. They move because they are restless, not because they are on their way somewhere else where they will stay.

'Now let me talk about the depictions.'

Here Leandro broke off to speak as himself for a moment.

'"Depictions" is a poor compromise because the meaning of his expression, as I understood it, has no simple equivalent. The best long hand I could think of would be something like, "exercise-of-skill-to-experience-more-deeply-and-honour-what-we-see". I hope you prefer my botched short cut.'

Some of us nodded and Leandro waited a moment or two and then sat back and resumed where he had left off.

'Firstly, let me say how happy we were to see your depictions. We were overjoyed, after so many days struggling through arid scrub, when we saw on the cliff face that brilliant frieze of trees and stags. We knew then that other true people had been there and perhaps were living nearby. Then we saw beneath us your green valley with its river and tall trees, taller than we have at home, trees like the ones depicted on the cliff above, and then, as you know, on our way down we met and greeted some of you. As we approached again we took delight in the depictions on and around your shelters. I see you like to repeat – trees, stags, and trees again. We have not seen that before. We try to depict things as we see them although we never quite succeed, I admit. But we will talk of all that later as it may take some time. Before the pleasure of that talk I must continue with my story because you may need to know what I have to tell.

'It was the easy time of year. The snows were gone but the reindeer still passed by and everyone had time to talk and play. As we do, and I'm sure you also do, many people were decorating our shelters and were renewing the depictions on the rocks and trees that the winter snows had wiped away. A troop of Pointy-Chins was near and they watched us and muttered to each other. They seemed to be troubled by our work, staring at it not with pleasure but more as a person examines the snow on a hillside when an avalanche is likely, or studies the dark clouds of an approaching storm. One of them came and sat with us and asked what the meaning was of this work. We answered that it has no meaning other than to celebrate sights our eyes have enjoyed. The Pointy-Chin, I could see, because I know a bit about their expressions, thought we were saying what is not. No one except me could see that, so the others went on laughing and talking about this leaf or that bison leg, why it is done the way it is. Some of us offered to let the Pointy-Chin try to do as we do, but he still thought we were saying what is not and went away silent.

'Some time afterwards I noticed that man and some other Pointy-Chins going in and out of a cave above our valley home, not one of the caves low down where we retreat sometimes in winter but one of those higher up, which we hardly go to unless occasionally to shelter if a storm happens to break when we are near. As the weather was fine they clearly weren't using the cave for shelter and I wondered what had drawn them to scramble all the way up there. But, as I have said before, the Pointy-Chins are strange people – if we can count them as people. One day I thought I would see what they found so useful about the cave and walked up, but cautiously, because I knew somehow that they would not like to see me there. So, I walked up, keeping out of sight, and slipped into the cave without a single Pointy-

Chin noticing. There were no Pointy-Chins in the first space but I could see a light ahead, smell fire and hear echoey voices somewhere further down into the earth. We do not like the deep inside of caves, but I decided I should find out what these people were doing and so crept quietly to a place where the rocks opened out and they had made a small fire. Quickly, I ducked behind a boulder where I was in deep shadow and could hope to see without being seen. The fire was not the only source of light because, as well, some of the Pointy-Chins had torches in their hands – rather well made torches, I noticed, better than ours, providing a more constant, yellow flame. The scene revealed by this light was quite extraordinary. By a smooth surface of rock two Pointy-Chins were holding up torches while a third was marking the rock with charcoal and one or two more stood by, watching. All of them were men, which did not surprise me because among Pointy-Chins men and women usually hunt separately, sit separately, and seem generally wary of each other.

'I watched for a long time although my position was uncomfortable. There was a cold drip of water on my back, the smoke tickled my throat and I was afraid all the time that if I coughed or made a noise I might be discovered. The man with the charcoal was trying to draw a bison but he was not skilled and it was a botched job; all the same he smeared some ochre onto it to make it look a bit more real. I couldn't understand much of what they said to each other but I picked up a few repeated phrases like, "Legs too thin", "It will not work", "It is not yet like the work of the Squat-Things".

“Squat-Things” is a phrase they use for us, although not to us as it is rude. The meaning is not quite squat things but it comes partly from the different way we look; the “Thing” suggests something we do not have a word for. It suggests we are neither people, even a kind of people, nor quite an animal, but some other kind of creature which has something to do with the dead crow on the path. I can see you do not follow and I know it is difficult. Let me say it another way. Just as the dead crow makes them afraid even though it is not a threat, so they are a little afraid of us – not afraid that we might attack them, which could be something to be afraid of, but just afraid – afraid because of who we are. When they speak to us, if they have to call us anything, they call us something like “strangers,” which is quite respectful.

‘The scene in the cave did not at once make sense to me. Why would they go to the trouble of working in the dark when they could work anywhere? Why are they struggling to copy our work far away from it when they could sit with us and copy? Over time, from watching them watching us work and from more secret visits to the cave, I came to understand that it is like the dead crow and the duck’s foot. They think our pictures mean something other than the picture and they think they have some effect, like to make something happen or to stop something happening. They particularly think the animal images have this meaning. Why especially the animals I have not quite been able to work out, but perhaps because we pay so much attention to them and because animals can be dangerous but also are our food. For whatever reason, they were copying only the animals. I see you think this is comic. So did my family when I told them what I had discovered. It is comic but also serious. When they managed to make better copies in their cave, then I noticed they began to behave differently in our presence; less respectful, and as if the slight fear they had of us was gone.

'As I said before, at this time it was very noticeable that their numbers were increasing. They have children every year which must be unfortunate for them as their children do not grow up any faster than ours so that they are burdened when they travel and always have to find a lot of food. The result is, however, that a troop grows quickly. Because of their numbers they hunt hard and when they were in our area we found game was sometimes scarce. They began to interfere with our lives. We found them sometimes taking animals from our traps. Their practice of saying what is not made things difficult. One time they told us they had seen deer heading down the valley when we found out later the deer had gone up the valley. If they told us where they were planning to hunt we found that, instead, they were hunting where we went to avoid them and that even then they were watching us to see where we would pick up a trail.

'I advised several times that we should move away and go in search of a place where the Pointy-Chins were still few but people were happy in the place we all knew and raised all sorts of objections to moving. We discussed the problems with our neighbours who mostly had similar experiences, but none wanted to move. When I talked about the secret paintings in the caves they only laughed.

'Then there came a time when some of us walked over to speak to our neighbours in the next valley and found they were not there. Indeed, the place they used to live was occupied by Pointy-Chins who told us they had just gone away. Afterwards, I said that I did not believe that those neighbours, with whom we marry our daughters and with whom we had often discussed moving, would just go away like that without visiting us. Wasn't it more likely that the Pointy-Chins killed them? They could have done, as there were many more of them in the area. When I suggested this, most people said it was not possible, that people hardly ever kill other people. Only occasionally, if someone becomes very angry, there may be fight in which someone is wounded so badly that death follows. Or we know that occasionally a person becomes mad, behaves not like themselves and indeed not like any true person, but then their relatives gather round and prevent anything terrible happening. I said, yes, it is unknown among us that people would attack a whole family but we have seen that the Pointy-Chins are strange, they say things which are not, and not only to us but to each other. I could see people were finding it hard to think such a thing could happen but, at last, there were some voices for leaving.

'Before enough people were convinced, the disaster struck. I had continued to watch unseen the progress of the Pointy-Chins in the cave although it worried me to see them doing what we do, but so strangely, toiling in the darkness instead of sitting in the sun. Only two or three particular men seemed to be engaged in the copying, which again made the scene strange since in the season of image making more or less everyone takes part even if some are busier and more skilled than others. Here, just the two or three men stuck to the work while others held the torches or made comments, but they didn't change places, and, as I said before, no women were even in the cave at first although later on I saw some from a distance going in, carrying food. After a time I probably became less careful and one day was seen leaving the cave. The man who had seen me let out a terrible cry and then, suddenly, several of them, shrieking in the most horrible way, were running after me. I deliberately did not run to our shelters because I guessed that these shrieking men might be a danger to my family, so I ran up the valley side where I soon outran them and disappeared into some long grass and scrub. I then turned back and hurried down by a different route towards our shelters to warn everyone.

'Stay listening, but I must stop a moment because I can hardly speak of what I saw. The pain still burns inside me. My tears will never stop. The shelters were smashed and some of our family lay twisted and bloodied on the ground. I could not then see exactly who was lying there although I could see some small children and thought I recognised my mother. I did not wait, as I saw the rest of our family, some carrying children, running down the valley followed by crazed Pointy-Chins. I rushed downwards and when I drew close I seized small rocks and hurled them at the Pointy-

Chins causing one to fall, another to stumble and the others to stop, undecided whether to pursue me, pursue the others or help their injured brothers. The pause was long enough for my family to get away and eventually I was able to catch up with them. There was both pain and joy. My wife was there, unharmed, and our two older children but our youngest was among the dead and so were both my mother and my father and my uncle. My young unmarried cousin, the beauty of our family and the joy of my uncle, was dead, like her father. Her mother was alive and my brother and my other cousins, but my brother's middle child was dead and one of the cousins had lost a child.

'That was where my story ended on the night I told it to the people by the Quiet River, who received us with great kindness if some puzzlement. I hope they will think over what I told them and pass it on to other true people so that they may be forewarned about the Pointy-Chins. In my heart, though, I fear that there is nothing we can do. I might be wrong about the fate of those neighbours who disappeared and it may be the Pointy-Chins attacked us only because, in their strange way of thinking, I had attacked them by watching their secret work. But even if they do not intend to attack us they multiply so fast and hunt so recklessly – they even kill pregnant deer and those with young – it could happen that one day there will not be enough deer for them and for us. Perhaps neither they nor we will survive, and who will then celebrate the leaping stag, the bending grass and the soaring eagle? Who knows? The world is very large and there may be many people in it like us or like the Pointy-Chins or different again. If so, I hope they may be like us.

'Whatever will come for the rest of us true people, I and those I have loved are near our end. I now speak only to the wind. My grief must talk even if to the empty air.

'After we left the village by the Quiet River we travelled on again searching for a place we could settle, but did not find anywhere with good water that was not already the home of some true people. Then we started to see Pointy-Chins again. They could not know anything about the rage of the other Pointy-Chins against us, and mostly they ignored us, but we avoided them as much as possible. As we travelled, the land became drier so water was often hard to find and the soil dusty. When we moved on past the area where we saw the Pointy-Chins we came to a hilly, barren place where we saw no people and no Pointy-Chins but also found hardly any water and little game. My old aunt died there of fatigue and grief. Eventually, we came to a wide river along which there were many trees like the ones by the Quiet River. There was some small game about and fish in the river but we found no village nearby and saw no depictions anywhere. So, we thought we might make this place our new home and decided definitely to stay for the winter. But with the winter came a large number of Pointy-Chins and some camped not far away. We were glad the snow had covered the paintings we had done in the autumn and which would have signalled our presence. We did not want to risk settling again on a route used by Pointy-

Chins and so, when the snow melted, we went on, up onto a hard dry plateau where white rocks forced their way through the earth as the ribs burst through the flesh on the corpse of a rotting mammoth.

'We struggled with hunger and thirst until everyone was weak. Clambering down a rocky place my brother fell and broke his leg. We had to stop there, where we had no water, and so my cousins went with our water skins back to the last place where we had found a spring. They never returned. I went back and found the water but no sign of the cousins. I heard a hyena cry and thought perhaps the beast had surprised them, attacking, because in this barren place there was not much for the hyena to hunt. By the time I returned everyone had been without water for so long that my youngest nephew had died of thirst. Despite our best attempts at care, our brother fell into a fever and after a few days he also died. We covered his body with stones and went on, finding only lizards to eat. If this rocky waste goes on much further we may all die here. We have just reached a ridge, which I hoped might be the end of it, but beyond there is only a precipitous slope dropping down a little way to more of the barren plateau.'

Leandro slowed the narration now and gave it a tone of sombre finality.

'A wind got up, whipping dust into our faces. I have found a little shelter by a pile of white rocks where the few of us left are resting precariously while I sit on the ridge and howl a lament for my family, and not only for my family but for all true people.'

This was evidently the end and applause was followed by a gloomy silence broken eventually by Frieda, who said, 'It is probably fortunate that only one kind of human has survived. If you think of the horrors we perpetrate in the name of invented differences, think what we might do if there were real ones!'

This prolonged the silence until Vernon spoke, striking a very different note.

'I'm shocked, Leandro. You, a Golden Age-er! Really? I was a bit surprised by Sven, but at least in his Golden Age there's hope: if we once lived the right way up it's not our DNA that turned us upside-down. But what encouragement can we take from a Golden Age peopled by a long-extinct kind of human?'

Most of us had taken the story rather seriously and were startled by the way Vernon seemed to be teasing Leandro.

'On top of that,' he went on, 'I'm afraid designing your Neanderthals as a cross between Age of Reason rationalists and 19th century Impressionists sounds, well, just a touch far-fetched.'

Radhika was the first to come to the defence. 'Vernon, you're being too harsh. Leandro only implied they hadn't invented supernatural causes or magical fixes. That's possible, isn't it? You don't have to have been through centuries of philosophy and grand theory to reach the conclusion a duck's foot isn't likely to scare off a lion.'

'Well, I don't know,' said Magome, in that ponderous tone that suggests a person definitely believes they do know. 'You will find here that village people always believe those things.'

'I don't find that,' said Zehra quietly but curtly. 'Some do; some don't.'

Nyezi agreed, but added that it was anyway not quite the point. 'Magome's thinking of farming villagers but we're talking hunter-gatherers. You can't assume they'd think the same way. Sadly, there aren't enough hunter-gatherers left now for us to generalise about them. I've heard that some in Tanzania apparently don't believe much in the supernatural. They don't think the dead come back or that accidents are caused by witches…'

'But the Bushmen have shamans,' Zak interrupted, 'and shamans get possessed by spirits, don't they?'

Vernon chipped in, 'It's tempting to look for clues from today's hunter-gatherers but it may not get you very far. It's not just that they're all different but you can't assume any of them are anything like the prehistoric ones.

'Being a hunter-gatherer back then wasn't at all like being one now. Back then they could live on the best land, where getting food was so easy they'd have plenty of time for social life and the arts. We know they traded and probably travelled widely. How different from today's hunter-gatherers, marginalised by farmers, ousted from the fertile areas, confined to ever shrinking pockets of desert or dense forest…'

'Attacked by loggers and miners,' Sven muttered.

Nyezi challenged Vernon, 'But I've heard you talk as if they do provide clues!'

'Yes, yes,' Vernon agreed. 'I said it's tempting and I'm often tempted.'

Nyezi went on speculating: 'And we know so little

about Neanderthals we can't know they weren't like Leandro's "true people" can we?'

'We can disbelieve in them if they have incompatible characteristics,' Frieda objected. 'He presents his people as artists and lets his narrator talk of "clouds like rocks", "a landscape like a rotting carcass". From that we must assume they have imagination, and yet he also presents them as a people who do not lie, are mystified by lying. If you have imagination then surely you would understand a lie – you would not lack the concept.'

'Mmmmm?' said Radhika, suggesting she was unsure what she thought of Frieda's logic. No on else seemed sure and Radhika went on.

'At least Leandro's story tackles one puzzle – something Dieter also referred to – the way the paintings look naturalistic and modern, strangely different from the stick figures and geometrical designs of most folk art and yet, like folk art, they employ limited motifs, are largely one-dimensional and hardly develop over time. Leandro's idea, that the cave artists started off by copying from long lost art works that were genuinely drawn from life would explain the life-like look and the idea that they copied only the animals and then went on for centuries copying the copies, would explain the limited, repetitive quality and lack of development.'

Jalal, who had been looking sceptical, now ventured to speak. 'If those people had such a rational way of thinking, I mean being logical about the duck's foot thing, wouldn't they have worked out how to defend themselves? Why didn't they resist?'

'Not enough of them.' Radhika answered. 'Leandro

dealt that that. They were too good at birth control and were outbred.'

'Going back to the painting style,' said Nyezi, 'do you need such a complicated explanation? The folk art Radhika's probably thinking of, with geometrical patterns and little stylised figures, is made by people who farm – whether now or in prehistory. And a farmed landscape is full of enclosed spaces and repeated patterns: animal pens, houses, plots for this or that crop, furrows on a ploughed field… Maybe, if you live in that kind of space you come to enjoy repetitions and patterns. If you live on open land where grass merges into forest and plants and animals are just scattered about, you wouldn't so readily think in patterns.'

Dieter yawned and stretched pointedly before saying, 'All very ingenious, but Vernon was more on the ball with his comment about golden ages. He could have said they're just a kind of wishful thinking. Vernon won't be that decisive because he likes a quiet life. Always been a bit of a fence sitter. '

Vernon gave a slightly superior laugh and retaliated with, 'Better a quiet life than a harmful one.'

This was all said lightly but I felt an undertone of real dislike between the two men.

Leandro cut in amiably, 'I thought Vernon came down on me heavily enough. And for once he didn't wait to be asked. Anyway, I'll accept *nul points* for plausibility and we can go to bed.'

'Bed!' moaned Magome. 'You say "bed". Wouldn't my bones love one! They can't manage this stony ground!'

He started to heave himself up and appealed to Tom, 'Young man, can you lend me a hand?'

'Of course, sir,' the young man answered, and helped him up.

17

The Unexpected

No one slept well that night, probably because of the cold. We must be higher here than we had been before because after dark the temperature dropped noticeably lower than on the previous night. I was troubled less by the cold than by remembering Frieda's remark about cockroaches recycling dead leaves. The little rustling sounds which had previously seemed only mildly alarming now conjured images of giant cockroaches scuttling around beneath me and inevitably popping out to crawl across my face. I slept off and on but was fully aware of the watch changing twice and of other would-be sleepers fidgeting and hunting in bags for extra layers of clothes. People were up early and we got going before the sun was quite up.

We had walked on uneventfully for two hours when we saw smoke rising above the trees ahead. Yesterday's fisherman had told us we would pass a small village on our way and so it seemed likely that we were approaching it. Soon we came to a clearing and then Reece, in the lead, stopped dead and gestured to everyone to keep back under the trees. Something was wrong. On the far side of a field of cassava I could see traditional village houses, but some were damaged and a curl of smoke was rising from a blackened roof. There was no sound, no voices, no pounding of grain, no chickens clucking or radio playing. Reece, Leandro and Zak conferred quietly and then Leandro led us in silence a little way off the path where he indicated that we should sit down out of sight from the clearing or the path. Reece left the path in the other direction towards an area where the trees grew closer to the houses and we soon lost sight of him. After a long time we heard a chicken squawk. Then there was another long silence before Reece returned looking serious. The three men conferred again and then Reece told us what we had guessed, that the village had been attacked. There were two bodies but no sign of anyone alive, either the villagers or the attackers. As far as it was possible to tell, it was safe for us to enter the village where he wanted to look round a little more for clues as to what might have happened and where the attackers might have come from and gone to.

Whoever was responsible for the attack had not done much damage to the houses. They had apparently tried to set fire to one or two but it was a still day and, with no wind to fan the flames, the fire had fizzled out leaving patches of blackened thatch from which a few curls of smoke still rose. Some of the blackened areas were already cold, which encouragingly suggested that the attack was not recent and that the culprits could be quite far away. Even so, I was tense with fear as we passed the first silent houses and my fear intensified when I caught sight of the first body. It was a woman in bright cotton clothes lying sprawled on the ground as if she'd been running hard when she fell. There was no obvious wound and Leandro and Sven were surveying her without touching, discussing in low voices what had killed her and how long ago, noting that there were only a few flies buzzing round her and no vultures had arrived. As I looked at the body, fear pulsed around my body, spreading a chill that defied the sun and producing an odd, detached feeling as if I was starting to float away. It crossed my mind that I might be about to faint and realised in a hazy way that this would be acutely embarrassing. I took a couple of deep breaths and leant on the doorframe of the nearest house until my body settled down. Mathew, who was standing next to me, came up and asked if I was all right. I made no pretence but answered shakily, 'I think so.'

'You look pale,' he said, kindly. 'You might want to sit down. Is this the first time you've seen a dead person – in real life that is?'

I admitted that it was. When my grandfather was dying it was just before my GCSEs and Mum went alone to Calcutta.

Leandro suggested most of the party should go on beyond the village clearing and wait in the woods out of sight of the path until he and Reece had finished their investigation. As he spoke, two vultures wheeled into view and circled above us, while the flies around the bodies were becoming a small cloud. The other body, also that of a brightly-dressed woman, was lying in the doorway of a house. The only normal village sight was one chicken scratching about in the dust, perhaps the one that squawked when Reece was reconnoitring.

'Shouldn't we do something?' said Sven

'Like what?' said Reece.

'Report it?' suggested Sven. 'At least let the authorities know.'

'If there are any authorities that still have any authority,' Zak added.

Dieter remarked, 'The only "authority" round here is probably the thugs who did this.'

'Has anyone got a signal?' asked Jalal.

Those whose phones had some power left, got them out but none had a signal.

'This was a shit idea, wasn't it?' Dieter growled looking hard at Leandro. 'We've been walking towards the danger, not away from it.'

'We don't know what happened or who did it,' Jalal pointed out.

'That's right,' agreed Nyezi. 'It may be a local conflict, or bandits or anything, not to do with the coup.'

' Whatever – we've walked slap into the path of killers,' Dieter retorted.

'Talking like that won't fucking help,' Reece hissed back in a way that rang with suppressed violence, and then, to Leandro, he said more calmly, 'Come on. Let's get on with it, Leo,' and to Mathew, 'Why don't you take everyone off to somewhere less exposed.'

'Do you think we should bury them or anything?' Radhika asked tentatively.

'It will take too long,' Leandro answered briskly, 'and will confuse the police if they ever get here.'

We were about to follow Mathew out of the village when we heard a little cry, rapidly rising to a wail, and a bundle of cloth beside the woman in the doorway was pushed back by a small hand to show the face of a howling infant. We stopped instantly and stared for a moment before Zehra ran forward and knelt down by the child who was pulling at the dead woman's clothes pathetically.

'How did I miss him?' breathed Reece critically to himself.

Radhika and I followed Zehra, stopping a few paces away, where "he" was revealed to be a little girl, between a baby and toddler; nearly but not quite able to walk.

'Poor thing!' whispered Radhika with feeling. Zehra talked to the child soothingly in Swahili and coaxed her into her arms where the child continued to howl and stretched out her little arms towards the dead woman before Zehra carried her away into a patch of shade at the side of a house.

'She must be hungry,' said Radhika, 'and thirsty. At least we can give her some water. '

I got out my water bottle and Zehra carefully started putting drops in the child's mouth. She didn't stop crying but between sobs started to swallow the water. Radhika dug out one of the cups and handed it to Zehra.

'Is she hurt at all?' asked Sven, who had joined us.

'There's a bit of a graze here,' said Zehra, making a stroking motion over the child's arm without touching the raw patches. 'You could examine her in a bit but let's try to get her to calm down and drink.'

'Yes, drinking's most important.' Sven agreed. 'And there's not much I can do for her if she is hurt.'

'But you are a doctor at least.' Zehra looked at him hopefully.

Sven shrugged. 'I will try, of course. But I'm not that sort of doctor now and, even if I was, we have no supplies. You are doing the best thing without anyone telling you.'

Zehra looked down at the child and said, 'She must be hungry. It's a pity we don't have any milk.'

'Shall I go and look in all the houses to see if there's a tin anywhere?' I asked, although I didn't like the prospect of rummaging through other people's possessions in abandoned, half-burnt houses.

To my relief Sven said, 'No, better not in case there's anything unpleasant. I'll go. Is that alright?' he asked Leandro who had told us to stay together and not wander round in order to minimise messing up possible clues about the attack. Leandro asked him to wait until they'd done their investigation. Leandro carefully photographed the two bodies and some of the damaged houses and then joined Reece examining tracks in the dust. The rest of us joined Zehra in her patch of shade and sat down. The baby soon started drinking enthusiastically, even trying to hold the cup, and her screaming died away into intermittent unhappy sobs. Zehra carefully wiped away the dust, snot and tears from the child's face and cautiously began cleaning her body before handing her to Sven who gently examined her, concluded that she was unharmed apart from some bruising and the grazing to her arm which probably happened because the mother – he supposed the dead woman in the doorway to be her mother – had her tied to her back when she fell. He put some disinfectant on the graze and suggested crushing up a couple of cashew nuts and giving her a little sugar as the only food we had that could be eaten raw. The baby was not at all sure about either offering, spat out some but also swallowed a little.

Time passed. Leandro and Reece moved away slowly and disappeared behind a half-burnt house. The vultures flapped away from their tree and perched on the roof of the house where the woman lay dead. When one of them dropped down by the body Zak threw a stick at it, cursing in Russian. The bird only grudgingly retreated to the roof again. Zak fanned himself and muttered something about it being horrible leaving them to be eaten. He asked Mathew why he didn't say prayers for them, seeing that he was a priest, but I was unsure whether this was rhetoric or a real question. Mathew answered that he was indeed praying but to say prayers formally over the dead might not be appropriate if they weren't Christian. Zak thwarted another attempt by the vulture to start its lunch and said, as he sat down again, 'Where do you think they are?' which might have referred to the women's souls, to the murderers, to the other villagers or to Reece and Leandro. No one answered.

When Reece and Leandro came back they reported that the women had been shot and there was a fair amount of spent ammunition lying around; they couldn't tell how many attackers there were but they must be fairly well armed and some of them, at least, were wearing combat boots. It appeared that they had come along the path we were about to take and had left along a path at a tangent to the one we arrived from, a route which suggested they were trying to keep to thinly populated, relatively inaccessible areas where they were unlikely to encounter police or army. Dieter snorted at the idea that the police or army might be in the least functional. The attackers had clearly taken what they could carry and done their best to damage what was left. They had probably taken whatever tinned food or drink was there but a fair amount of dried produce had escaped the looters.

'What are we going to do now?' asked Radhika.

'The child is a complication,' said Vernon.

'Why?' I asked. 'Surely we'll take her with us?'

'We certainly can't leave her here alone,' Vernon continued, 'but perhaps the villagers are hiding somewhere quite near. You don't think we should wait and see if they return?'

'If they do, it would be best for her,' agreed Zehra. 'We have nothing to feed her. These people probably breast feed for at least a year, often two or more. She needs her mother's milk.'

'Her mother's dead, isn't she?' Reece objected.

'We don't know if that is her mother,' said Zehra. 'She might just have been the person nearest to the child when the attack happened. And anyway, someone else might have milk.'

Sven got up and said that he was now going on his search to see if there might be any tinned milk.

Leandro proposed that we leave the village at once in case the marauders returned, but stay nearby for the next two or three hours which would give the villagers a chance to return. Dieter was against any delay and for heading back as fast as possible, given that it had been an idiotic blunder to leave the relative safety of the airport and a nearby city. Others reminded him that the airport had seemed far from safe and the city had been out of reach. An angry tension was building which Mathew managed to calm by urging us to head at once to a hiding place and then discuss the next steps there. While this was going on Sven returned unsuccessful and said the best thing would be to make maize pudding and water some down to a thin gruel for the baby. Leandro raised the problem that if we were to cook in our hiding place the smoke from the fire would give us away. The tension between us mounted again.

'We can go without food but the child needs something,' said Sven. 'She's hungry and we don't know how long she's been hungry.' There was an awkward silence until Leandro said, 'We could cook here as the smoke will merge with the smouldering roofs. Two of us could stay and bring the food to the rest later. I'll stay.'

'Don't be silly,' said Vernon, 'we can't risk you as you are the one who knows the way – well you and Nyezi and Reece. I'll stay. And I'll use one of the village pots. You don't want to risk our only means of cooking.'

After a brief argument, Vernon stayed with Mama Ulemu who bossily insisted she would cook when Tom, under pressure, had translated for her the gist of what was going on. The rest of us withdrew some way away to a miniature gulley with a dry streambed at the bottom. We sat in silence listening for any sounds from the direction of the village, but nothing disturbed the quiet of midday. Zehra was kept busy rocking and bouncing the baby in an effort to dissuade her from bawling again. I offered to take a turn and the small warm body next to me, with the little toes wriggling on my lap, provided an element of comfort in the overall darkness. I rocked us both backwards and forwards trying not to think of the bodies and the vultures or imagine what the dead women saw and felt in their last moments. I looked round our group, wondering what the others were thinking. Leandro and Reece had positioned themselves just under the edge of the gulley where they could see out without being seen. Dieter was irritably scratching the soil with a stick. Frieda had calmly taken out a journal and was reading. Zehra, who had been keeping an eye on the baby, suddenly smiled and pointed. Following her gesture I looked down at the baby and saw she had fallen asleep.

18

A Name

Nothing interrupted the cooking in the deserted village, so that Vernon and Mama Ulemu soon returned safely with the food. As we ate we began talking again, cautiously, in low voices.

We speculated some more about the attack until Radhika turned our attention to the baby by asking, 'What shall we call her? We'll have to give her a name for now. We can't go on calling her "her".'

'None of us know what girls might be called here,' objected Nyezi.

'It doesn't matter,' said Radhika. 'We aren't going to guess her real name so we might as well chose anything we like. Only I think it should be one of those names that crop up in many places, not too tied to one place or language.'

'It must be an African name,' announced Magome with an attention-seeking noise that I think would be written in a 19th century novel as "hurrumph". 'An African girl must have an African name.'

'Nadia, call her Nadia,' said Zak. 'I've met a lot of girls in Africa called Nadia but it's a Russian name as well. She'll be able to go anywhere.'

'Amina is a very popular name,' said Jalal.

Radhika queried "Amina". 'Doesn't that pin down her religion? We shouldn't impose a religion on her.'

'Call her Massassi,' said Nyezi. 'The name of the first woman in the world.'

Sven raised the objection Radhika had made to Amina, which caused a brief skirmish about the relationship between myth, religion and archetypes, but I unintentionally cut across this by objecting that if she went to an English speaking school "Massassi" might get turned into Miss Arsey or Messy Arsey.

Radhika, who had introduced the archetypes, dropped them and said, 'I think she's a Tara. That's an easy name to say and has enough different meanings not to tie her down. Tara means star in Sanskrit, which is lovely, and in Ireland it's the home of kings.'

Magome pre-empted a possible discussion of Tara by declaring. "Kibibi", that's the name. Kibibi, Little Lady. Very nice.'

After several more suggestions a consensus was eventually reached for Lulu, which fitted the criteria of being easy to say and having multiple meanings and origins including an African one. That was the agreement but for some reason no one adhered to it and the name that stuck was Tara despite its weaker credentials. Perhaps it was because Tara woke up just after Radhika suggested the name and I tried it out on her, liked it and everyone heard me calling her by it. For whatever reason, we all referred to her as Tara and never as Lulu, all except Magome who determinedly called her Kibibi.

The naming was a good diversion but afterwards we reverted to speculating about what had happened in the village and what it meant for us. As Leandro and Reece had told us, the murderers, whoever they were, had come, but not left, by the path we needed to take. That meant that, if they were an isolated band, the path should be safe, but if they were part of something larger, then it was all too likely we could run into another group taking the same route. Again, those of us whose phones had any charge left searched in vain for a signal. Everything would have been simpler if we could find out what was happening beyond our forest. It was possible that going back would be safer than going on but we had no way of knowing. When we originally set off from the airstrip we had calculated that there was a good chance we could reach the border by the end of the third day of walking, but that had already started to look unrealistic long before we found the abandoned village. Now, we agreed, it was certain we would have to spend another night sleeping out.

'We were probably a bit unrealistic about the distance,' Mathew speculated. 'But we couldn't really know.'

'We'll manage,' Jalal asserted, tossing a little stone up and catching it as he had a habit of doing.

Mama Ulemu and Zehra were quietly discussing the practicalities of transporting Tara. Mama Ulemu volunteered a cloth to tie her to someone's back and Zehra decided to sacrifice one of her cloths to make improvised nappies by tearing it into strips.

Magome was talking to Tom in their language. Tom only murmured monosyllabic replies.

'I said it was unrealistic, if you remember,' Dieter reminded us. 'We could still always turn back.'

'That's what we've been saying,' Magome, now speaking in English, backed him up, indicating that "we" included Tom and, in a vague way, Mama Ulemu. 'We don't know what is ahead and it's still a long way. And maybe more bandits will come this way. The bandits didn't take the path we came on. So we can go back that way. That will be safer.'

Tom looked uncomfortable and I thought he hadn't agreed with Magome but wouldn't take a stand against him.

Leandro watched for more comments but said nothing himself.

Vernon was next to speak. 'In our situation it doesn't help to keep going back over decisions. Back at the airfield we decided that it was unsafe to stay and we have no evidence we were wrong. No one was compelled to come and those who were doubtful but came anyway should accept that decision.'

'Well said,' added Reece. 'They can shut up.'

'What if we've all changed our minds?' Dieter insisted.

'We haven't,' said Leandro. 'Going back at this

stage is not an option. But, if it will make you more comfortable, let's see what everyone thinks. It won't be a vote. We will hear from everyone. That's clearer.'

As he predicted, almost everyone was for going on. Mathew, Frieda and Radhika said they didn't know enough to take a position themselves but trusted Leandro's advice. Tom said it was difficult when the people who might know said different things. Leandro came last to Magome and Dieter, and even they modified their position. Magome, in a roundabout way, withdrew his objection because, he said, we should all agree, and Dieter accepted that at this stage going on might be best but wanted it on record that he was right that we should never have started. So, we turned to working out the next move.

The plan was for Leandro to walk far ahead while Nyezi would follow at a distance leaving another long gap between him and the rest of us. If Leandro saw anything sinister he would indicate to Nyezi who would run back to us, and we would all vanish into the trees. Reece would bring up the rear and it was tacitly understood that if we had to scatter and Leandro did not come back he would take over Leandro's informal role of leader.

Before we put the plan into practice someone needed to go back to the village to check whether anyone had returned. Tom, surprisingly, as he had previously taken little part in anything, offered to go. Reece, who evidently didn't think much of Tom's competence, suggested they would go together. The two of them went and came back reporting that there was still no sign of life. The fate of the absent villagers must remain a mystery.

When we set off in the line decided, we began with a little practice run of our emergency procedure. It was a shambles with us scattering chaotically into the forest, some throwing themselves flat well before they were properly out of sight of the path. Not encouraging, but probably better than not practicing at all.

The next hours of walking were quite different from the last two carefree days that to me had felt so much like a jaunt in Epping Forest, except for the much missed tea room. One change was purely physical: I had volunteered to take the first turn carrying Tara and was finding it harder than I'd expected, not only because of the extra weight but the cloth tying her on to me pulled my shoulders, while her little body against mine, though pleasant to feel, was making me hot and sweaty. The main difference, though, was the sense of threat. The forest now no longer existed just for itself, for the patterns in its sunlit leaves and the varying grain of its tree trunks, but for its role in our drama, a role which was deeply contradictory: on the one hand a protective cover; on the other a treacherous obstacle, concealing the danger. Our limited field of vision, which previously just made the journey seem a little monotonous, was now frightening and frustrating. On we went, hour after hour, acutely aware that any moment the quiet of the forest might be turned into a mayhem of violence.

We stopped for a short break after about two hours, turning off along another dry streambed which took us out of sight of the path. I found myself next to Leandro while I was struggling to get Tara out of the cloth. He helped me and then sat down with us, letting Tara play with one of his fingers, wrapping and unwrapping her miniature hand around it. I felt a flicker of excitement from Leandro's nearness and wanted him to speak to me.

'Do you get used to it?' I asked. 'I mean as a journalist. I suppose those women were nothing compared to what you've seen?' How often must reporters be asked this sort of question? I sounded inane even to myself but Leandro amiably gave the answer I expect he was always giving. 'I haven't got used to violence and death but the difference between just knowing about it and seeing it gets less.'

'You mean the shock is less?'

'There are different kinds of shock. There is anger or outrage about human brutality – that kind of shock shouldn't get less. It does with some people but I hope it won't with me – but there's shock as in the shaky feeling you get after a fright or if you see something like a damaged body, whatever the cause of the damage – people can feel that sort of shock watching a surgeon cut open someone's stomach, even when they know it's to help the patient. That kind of shock gets less as you see more of the things that at first brought it on.'

'It's difficult to imagine quite how that happens but it must or people would never be able to survive wars, earthquakes, famines; the sight of other people dying around them.'

'You mean if seeing a hundred murdered people had a hundred times the affect on you that seeing those two did?'

I nodded. I didn't speak because I was trying to supress tears, although why I should cry for complete strangers I couldn't understand. I just managed to ask, 'Did it take you long?' Another inane question!

'You shouldn't think I'm a war correspondent,' he said. 'I write on politics and development, and here wars are quite a big part of it, of course, but it's not like living on a front line. Remember, I've just come from a conference on sustainable building, not a war zone.'

'I'm sorry,' I said, not as an apology for my stupidity but for failing to hide my tears.

'Don't be embarrassed. Let go. It's good to react.'

I couldn't stop myself but sunk my head on my hands, shaking with sobs, although I couldn't make out if I was weeping for little orphaned Tara, for the dead strangers or from fear that I might too end up as putrefying vulture food. As soon as I could I diverted Leandro's attention to Tara who served as a convenient excuse.

'Poor thing! I can't stop wondering how long she was lying beside her dead mother.'

'Let's hope she's too young to remember,' he said, and playfully took his finger away from her and gave it back, causing almost a giggle.

We sat in silence while I recovered myself and decided to ask something that had been puzzling me. It was difficult to formulate so I started obliquely.

'You seem to have known Vernon for a long time.'

Leandro laughed, 'Everyone knows Vernon. He's what I think you call in England "a national treasure", although perhaps we should say "continental treasure" as he works in several countries.'

'You also seem to know Reece rather well.'

'No. Why do you think that?'

'You always seem to be deep in discussion with him…'

'Why not?' He was looking amused.

'No, no reason. Only you seem to be very different sorts of people…'

'You mean even though I'm from a poor country and he's from a rich one. I'm higher class? I'm bourgeois and he's proletarian?' Leandro said this in a teasing way but I was embarrassed that he had picked on something that was true, although I denied it.

'No, I meant that, I mean, as a sort of person – your ideas, you seem very different.' I floundered. 'His story for instance…'

Leandro laughed again. 'So, because people who disagree usually don't talk to each other, you wonder why we do? I think you haven't taken in what his business is?'

'He didn't say exactly, I don't think.'

'No, not surprisingly. But he did mention an earlier career didn't he?'

'I don't know about a career but he said he'd been in the army.'

'Yes, and you may not approve of your army but it has a good reputation for training. I spent time in our army and I know that training counts… '

Leandro could see I was beginning to get his point and pressed on. 'Yes, and it's a long time since I did my service, so it's an extra bonus that he isn't so out of practice.'

'I got the impression his business might be a bit dodgy but are you saying he's a…" I paused, '…a mercenary?'

'"Strategic advisor" or "security consultant" is perhaps more the term he'd use. I'm surprised you didn't realise.'

I must have sounded judgmental because Leandro added: 'All part of the global market place! And, you know, it's not men like Reece who pull the strings and make the big money. As you have discerned he's not – what's your nice English phrase? – "out of the top drawer"? Probably had limited career choices. He doesn't give away much but it's clear he didn't have a great start in life.'

Leandro spoke mildly but made me feel ashamed of my casual disapproval when Leandro could be so relaxed about a man in a trade that had helped to bring havoc to his country. I was wondering what I could say to redeem myself when Leandro got up and called an end to the break. I started to arrange Tara ready to load her but Leandro said I'd done my turn. Sven came forward and Leandro helped him organise the cloth while the sight of the tall blond man carrying a woman's burden sent Mama Ulemu into a fit of laughter.

The next stage of walking was easier for me with only my little rucksack to carry, but there was no escape from fear.

That evening, we chose a sleeping place well off the path and, to avoid being given away by smoke, waited until dark to light our cooking fire, sitting for the most part in silence. When the fire was lit and the maize pot put on Zehra spoke up tentatively.

'I know it may not seem right after what's happened but... could we go on with the stories?'

At first no one answered. Then a few people commented, also slightly guiltily, that it would be a good distraction, something to take our minds off the danger. So it was decided that we would start at once without waiting for the food to be ready. The draw went to Frieda who at once quietly rummaged in her bag and produced a bit of paper.

19

Frieda's Story

'I make a rule to never talk without notes,' she said waving the paper, 'but I can reassure you they're minimal and this doesn't mean I will be long.

'I feel distinctly underqualified for this game. Fiction is not my favourite reading and I'm disinclined to theorise on the basis of next to no information. That maybe why, when I tried to focus on Jalal's bison, I found that, instead, I began to see Franz Marc's *Blauen Pferde* – blue horses. Some of you may know the paintings and I'm afraid if you don't, with no internet, I can't show them to you. But, in case it helps, Marc was a German painter, killed on active service in 1916 and known for intensely coloured paintings of animals, especially a series of blue horses. As a child I first found these pictures when idly leafing through my mother's art books and I was immediately drawn to them. Unlike many of the other pictures, which had no recognisable subjects, these horses were unmistakably horses, very special and striking ones. The animals fill, or almost fill the picture, and are both powerful and graceful, their necks arched and their rumps echoing the curve. As a child I used to imagine putting my arm around the neck of one of these creatures and walking with it through the bright rounded hills that appear in the painting's background. My mother saw how I liked the pictures and in one of her caring phases obtained a print of the Large Blue Horses and put it on the wall of my room. So, I came to know the image really well. I would lie in bed and will one of the horses to leap out of the frame to be with me. If you know the pictures you will understand why Jalal's red bison evoked them – the chunky solidity and the clarity of outline that in the cave paintings is free of any background at all, in Marc's, stands out against a rather sketchy background. By the time Marc was painting, cave art was known and known to be ancient and I think it had already made a stir in the art world – long before Picasso made his remark about everything afterwards in art being decadence. So, it is possible that it was an influence on Marc, but I don't know. The superficial resemblance could be mere chance. Unfortunately, my early fascination with his horses did not mutate into a mature interest. In fact, I did learn a little about Marc as a teenager but what I learnt was a disappointment and caused me to consign my blue horses along with dolls to the dustbin of childhood. What disgusted me most was Marc's colour theory – blue being masculine, spiritual, strong; yellow being feminine, soft and sensuous – although even while I resented the allocation of spirituality to men, it was also the whole gamut of spiritual and religious references that saddened me, since by then I was a committed atheist.

'Looking back, my reaction against the paintings seems petulant, a product of teenage bigotry, but what I want to draw attention to is how we know – or critics think they know – so much about meanings encoded in those paintings. Still, I think critics may argue and puzzle over them but some aspects like the colour symbolism seem to be widely accepted and the reason they are accepted is because the artist told us. It isn't to me obvious at all from looking. Yes, there is perhaps a crude association of blue with cold and yellow with warmth, and in a lot of European languages there is a corresponding sexual connotation, chaste as opposed to sexy, so that the Virgin wears blue and prostitutes wear yellow; but on the other hand yellow can stand for light, happiness, clarity, hope while blue can also stand for hope. There's so much variation in colour symbolism that I find it difficult to see much that is "natural" about it. If Marc hadn't written about his work and talked to friends who in turn wrote about what he said, I doubt if I'd ever have thought those beautiful blue horses were associated with masculinity and spirituality or that the choice of animal subjects expressed the painter's ideas about the superiority of animal spirituality to that of humans. Not only did Marc write about his ideas but he lived in a world in which artists generally theorised about their work, wrote manifestos, and formed groups with other artists who shared their ideas, which all provides more context for reading the paintings. We know about his training, who he worked with, which contemporary artists he particularly admired… If even with that mass of evidence a degree of uncertainty remains, how could we ever expect to "read" the cave paintings?

'Yes, I know it's a game and the idea is to put them in a story not to read them but there's not much difference is there? That's one difficulty. The next difficulty, as Mathew and Nita also complained, is to imagine life in a world in which not only your own people but all humans are hunter-gatherers. It's particularly hard if the idea has no attraction for you and for me it has very little, irrespective of whether the culture was one of harmonious equality as in Nyezi's story or strict hierarchy as in Dieter's. Either way, it would lack the things that give me most pleasure: books, universities, laboratories, gardens, the theatre and pavement cafés. A wilderness may be pleasant for a brief excursion, but to live in it always? To have no concept of a city? I can't help but see the life as being either boring, if food is plentiful, or ghastly if it is scarce. Learning that art and material culture hardly changed for around 15,000 years deepens my prejudice. What does that suggest? Two possibilities occur: either people were extraordinarily contented or they lived under terrible oppression. I'd like to think the former as it's painful to imagine that the centuries of oppression we know of were preceded by millennia of misery. (And of course the former also holds out the hope that oppression is not an intrinsic condition of society.) But even if the reason was contentment, what kind of contentment discourages all innovation or experiment?

'This has been a long preamble and I wonder if I should leave it here – a non-story? I have a story of sorts I could tell. Against my inclination I forced myself to make one up, but even I don't approve of it. I'd like to think the paintings are inspired only by the natural world but, in that context, I've not quite been able to invent a convincing reason for painting them in caves. One of the awkward fragments of information Vernon has given us is that the painted caves were not lived in. So, the pictures were not done to enhance daily life. They might, of course, have had no purpose in the sense we are looking for but were simply an expression of *joie de vivre*. But if that was so, why not paint them by the light of day on the nearest suitable surface, as Leandro has his Neanderthals do? Why go to the extreme inconvenience of painting in the dark?

'I have probably now talked as long as I would to tell a short story which is a way of taking my turn. So, shall I spare you the unoriginal story and give way to the next person?'

There were cries of, 'No. Tell it!' 'Of course you must tell it.'

Frieda sighed and began.

'At that time people were haunted by the fear that when the sun retreated for winter she would not return. They had a story about this which was that, in the distant past, the days were all long and the world enjoyed perpetual summer. There were no seasons and no years. At that time, the sun and the moon lived together in harmony and produced a host of children; the stars. (Incidentally, if anyone objects to the genders, remember in German the sun is feminine and the moon masculine – *die Sonne, der Mond.* Also I'm sorry there are echoes here of Dieter's story but I'm fairly sure I'd planned this before he told his.)

'The moon used to go away every month and the sun never asked him where he went but believed that he was hunting. She did not know that in those far away hunting grounds he had a second wife, the Dark Woman, and every time he went away he visited her. The Dark Woman knew about the sun and pretended to accept the moon's regular departure but in secret was bitterly jealous and one time followed him all the way back to the home of the sun, where she waited until he came outside. Then she leapt on him and smothered him with her desire. The sun saw him suddenly disappear into darkness and ran out in great anxiety to find out what was happening. At first the sun could see nothing, but when the couple started to separate she caught sight of the Dark Woman and realized how the moon had been lying to her. She hid her anger but retaliated by taking a human lover by whom she became pregnant. The moon then flew into a terrible rage, killed the sun's lover and was going to tear the foetus from her womb, when the sun fled. As she got further and further away the world began to freeze and everyone started begging her to come back. She refused to return unless the moon agreed to let her bear the child. When he agreed she was encouraged to make another demand – that her lover would be restored to life and keep her company whenever the moon went to visit the Dark Woman. The moon resisted but after a great deal of bargaining they reached a compromise: her lover would return to life and visit her; not every time the moon went away, but only once for every twelve of his departures. Then, if the man made her pregnant during his visit, the child they already had would age and die before the next was born. At first the sun was happy and after some months brought forth a child who was neither like a man nor like the sun but a beautiful bison with a coat that echoed his mother's golden light. He was fully-grown after only six months when it was time for the sun's lover to return. The sun was overjoyed to see her lover but, fearful of the threat to their bison son, at first resisted his advances until her desire for him reached such a pitch that it melted her resolve and she again became pregnant. When she felt the new child move within her she saw that the bison was beginning to age, which grieved her so much that she crept away, preparing to abort the new baby to save her first born. Again the world started to cool and people were afraid and tried to persuade her to give birth and return. They sent to her a clever midwife who divined that the new baby would be in the form of an exquisite horse. So they set about singing the praises of the baby yet to be born and painted a picture of him to tempt her to relent and allow him to be born. They waited anxiously as the world grew dark and cold, but their efforts worked because the sun allowed the horse to be born and, slowly recovering from the grief of the bison's death, brought back warmth to the world.

So, this is how it came about that time is ordered by the departure and return of the sun following the life of each of her children. That is why, at the midway between the longest and the shortest day, people would celebrate the coming child with paintings and song, to convince the sun to abandon her last child to give birth to the next, each one adopting the form of an animal.

'When each year died the painting made for it remained and this proved to be a danger because people who went near the image might start to relive anything or everything that happened in that year. Past grief had to be suffered over again, past quarrels were reignited and even the reliving of a happy event caused pain through the knowledge that it was past. To solve this difficulty it became the custom to clean away the painting of the old year, but even when the physical signs of the dead year were gone, people found that the year itself still lingered in the place where the image had been. What is more, the invisible presence was more dangerous because it was harder to avoid. People might pass it by accident; even sit down casually beside it not knowing that they would come under its power.

'All kinds of difficulties were caused by the influence of these unseen images: old hatreds would be stirred up, old loves rekindled long after the lovers had settled and born children with other partners. Then came a particularly horrible incident, a massacre that seemed to have no cause until people remembered a feud long past, which the perpetrators must have been made to relive by the influence of one of these invisible years. Then everyone in the region gathered to discuss what to do, and at this gathering the idea was put forward that the years would be painted where they could not normally be seen and where no one would come on them by chance. After that people only ever painted the image of the new year in the depth of a cave and, when people entered the cave for any of the associated ceremonies, they were well aware they would be in the presence of past years and would take precautions against harmful influences. Over time, the parade of past years became a site for deliberate commemorations, mourning and exorcism as well as for the bringing on of the next year.'

Frieda sat back and put away the scrap of paper which she had held to the ready but hardly referred to.

'There it is, to my shame. I should have been able to think of something less derivative.'

'Derivative?' queried Radhika.

'Yes, I'm sure you can see it's a mélange of half remembered myths from sanitised school books and the like. I recognized what was happening as I formulated the story. I tried to change course but the myths proved hard to eradicate.'

'Perhaps because they're universal?'

'A doubtful notion! What business do characters linked to an agricultural cycle have seeping into the minds of hunter-gatherers?'

'You mean Persephone and Adonis?' Radhika asked with a casual ease as if she was talking about mutual friends. 'But don't you think those stories could have evolved from earlier ones? You don't need to be a farmer to notice that in the north there is a growing season and a dead season.'

Leandro turned to something else: 'You may have done a bit of borrowing for your seasons myth but there was another theme less familiar to me, about the power of an image surviving the image's destruction. Where did that came from?'

'It's hardly original' replied Frieda. 'Holy images or images of gods are treated with respect, aren't they? Some images, like we talked of earlier, must not be seen at all or only seen by certain people.'

'Yes, but do they survive destruction?'

'I'm sure there are examples.'

'Possibly, but apparently they aren't in your head just now, which means something else must have made you think of it.'

Frieda looked angry but after a hesitation decided to allow herself to be drawn.

'Yes, Leandro, you do like to dig and dig, don't you? Alright, if you insist the "something else" was my mother's concentration camp number.'

There was an embarrassed silence before she went on. 'She spent her life deciding to have it removed and then deciding not to, because for her it would always be there and would be worse when no one else could see it.'

There was another silence before Radhika asked cautiously, 'She must have been very young when she was in the camp?'

Frieda turned to Radhika as she answered quietly, 'Yes, she was young. But wasn't sent until very late. What happened is that at the time of the Anschluss the parents of a close school friend offered to take her in and pass her off as a distant cousin.'

She stopped and said, 'But that's nothing to do with this.'

'Please go on,' Leandro urged.

'Did she go to them?' Radhika asked. 'And where was this?'

Frieda reluctantly continued. 'It was Vienna. So her friend's parents thought they could get away with it because they had recently moved to an outlying suburb where they were not known. Accepting the offer was a difficult decision for my grandparents because at that time people did not know quite what was coming and they had to break off all contact with mother who was only ten. One of mother's sources of guilt was that she never said goodbye properly to her parents. The decision saved her life because the rest of the family all perished.

'My mother and her adoptive family were eventually betrayed by neighbours, but not until near the end of the war. Mother was sent to Theresienstadt and I've speculated that perhaps she won extra privileges because of her drawing and painting skills – she had a distinct talent and was already hoping to go to art school. It's only speculation as she would never talk about the camp or how she survived, but she did, and aged sixteen wound up in one of the rehabilitation camps.'

'And what happened next? Did she go back to Vienna? Was there anyone to go back to?'

'What happened next set the scene for a string of more serious indecisions than her dilemma over the tattoo. Although her immediate family was dead there was a large extended family who had got out before the Anschluss. The important people were an uncle in South Africa, a distant cousin who had returned to Vienna, and another cousin in Israel, and all three pressed my mother to move in with them. For some reason my mother decided soon against Israel but dithered between Vienna and South Africa. Initially, she went to live with her adoptive parents who had survived their imprisonment and still lived in the suburban house that had last been her home. The Vienna cousin put pressure on my mother to live with her and reclaim my grandparents' former apartment, but this was not going to happen quickly. Compensating Jewish survivors was a low priority for the post-war government and relevant papers silted up in dusty files. Eventually, Mother left for Johannesburg. According to her it was a terrible mistake. The South African police with their cold blue eyes, fair hair and tidy uniforms reminded her of the concentration camp guards, while the prevalence of barbed wire, guard dogs and *niet blankes* signs also encouraged flashbacks. The uncle, my great uncle Solly, lived with his wife, Jessica, and three sons in a spacious house surrounded by a large garden and were very solicitous, but she did not feel at home. The family, although not strict, were practicing Jews whereas her parents had been entirely secular and her adoptive parents, nominal Catholics, had little to do with the church.

'Solly only had the three sons and no daughters. Soon Mother found herself being eased into the role of good Jewish daughter, for which none of her previous life had prepared her. From the start there were conflicts over her education. The uncle wanted her to make up the academic education she had missed whereas she only wanted to go to art school. When the time came she enrolled herself, and was soon part of an artistic bohemian circle in which the Communist Party was a strong influence and many people were, to a greater or lesser extent, dissidents. She was, I can see from photographs, very beautiful, and with her romantic past as a holocaust survivor she became something of a star in that little circle – at least that is was what my father said of that period in her life when he knew her only very slightly as the foreign cousin of a student friend, the eldest of uncle Solly's sons. Mother began to achieve some recognition as an artist, had her work accepted in one or two group exhibitions and sold a few paintings. That all came to the end with her first mental breakdown, precipitated by a brush with the police when she was arrested, imprisoned briefly for questioning but soon released.

'After a spell in hospital she returned to Uncle Solly's where she slowly recovered. That was when my father fell in love with her. He was just the sort of young man Uncle Solly and Aunt Jessica could have dreamed of for my mother: a young doctor, steady, charming, from a good Jewish family. No doubt Solly encouraged the match and my mother perhaps imagined it would cure her restlessness. If so, she was deluded. Not long after they were married she picked up her political activities and tried to involve my father who, although firmly against apartheid, disagreed with illegal action. Afraid that his fragile wife might be arrested again, he proposed that they leave South Africa, at least temporarily, for London where he obtained a training post. But I don't know why I'm telling you all this…'

'Except that now we're waiting for you to arrive,' said Radhika. 'I thought you told me before you were born in South Africa, but now the stage seems set for London.'

Frieda shrugged dismissively but continued. 'London didn't last and nor did the marriage. I don't have much idea of the circumstances but they were in the process of separating when Mother found that she was pregnant. By this time the cousin in Vienna, my Auntie Lou, had managed to get back the old family flat and wanted mother to go and occupy it with my father, whom she imagined could just set up practice in Vienna. It was another tug of war because, when Solly and Jessica got to hear about the separation and pregnancy, they urged Mother to go back to stay with them. They won, and that is how I was born in South Africa. Some of my earliest memories are playing in Solly's big garden with a black nanny employed to look after me while mother tried to re-establish herself as an artist.

'It was also in that garden that I first became aware of the offending tattoo, although I must have seen it before without registering it. My mother was sitting on the terrace with me on her lap and we were playing tickling games when I noticed the number and poked it curiously. Mother's reaction instantly told me that there was something special about it, some kind of dark secret, because her mood change was like a cloud passing over the sun. She pushed my hand away, heaved me off her lap, abruptly got up and said we should go and play on the lawn.

'My father moved back to South Africa and there were attempts to patch up the marriage, but it was never going to work and eventually they divorced. Not long after I started kindergarten, Mother suddenly decided that we should move to Vienna – whether because something came up to do with the flat or because she thought the solution to her life lay there, I don't know.

'Although I missed the garden, I settled quite easily into my Austrian preschool but for Mother the move was not a success. She had to let part of the flat and give English tuition to live. She was trying to paint and used one room as a studio where she would vanish periodically and only allowed me in if I was very, very quiet doing my schoolwork or drawing on my own. She later told me conflicting stories about her art. In one version there were critics who thought it innovative and important but it did not sell; in another her work also attracted favourable comment but between housework and teaching she could never produce enough to build a reputation; in another she could not bring herself to exhibit at all because she thought the work was not good enough. I am afraid I resented her moods and did my best to ignore what was going on in her life.

'There were times when I was sent away, either because Mother was having a painting blitz or was with a lover – she had a number of affairs – or because of another breakdown – she had at least two more. Sometimes I went to Great Aunt Lou's but I preferred to stay with Bergitte, Mother's old school friend whose parents had taken her in during the war. Bergitte was married by then, with children around my age, and her house was full of music, sweet cooking smells and laughter. Twice I was sent to my father in South Africa. The first time I must have been about eight and enjoyed it but the second, when I was a teenager, was a disappointment. By then I was used to travelling around Vienna on my own and I found it suffocating being stuck in a formless suburb unable to go anywhere unless someone took you by car, in a world where there seemed nowhere much to go, even in a car, except to barbecues at similar houses in similar suburbs. I even began to dislike the sun that shone so reliably and persistently on the rows of detached houses with their green lawns and bright flower beds, watered, as it seemed continuously, by black men. I missed my freedom, I missed my friends, and I missed my books.

'I had found science in secondary school and it was into science that I retreated from mother's dithering dissatisfactions. I realise now how little I really know about her. It's ironic that I didn't probe more when I was so inquisitive about almost everything else. I might perhaps have made the effort when I was older but she died rather suddenly, of a brain tumour, when I was twenty one.'

Tara, who was on my lap, had been whimpering a little and now started to yell. I got up and walked around trying to comfort her so I missed what happened next and, when I returned, people had decided to settle to sleep without any more stories. It was not a good night. Tara woke and cried several times and the rustling sounds this time did not evoke cockroaches but creeping terrorists.

20

Morning

Zehra and I were up before dawn because something was wrong with Tara. Her crying had woken us and Zehra tried to comfort her while I looked on ineffectively. Seeing that I was awake too, Zehra whispered to me to get some water for her but Tara pushed the cup away and cried louder. To avoid waking everyone else Zehra carried her some distance down the track shushing and soothing her as she went while I followed with the rejected water and a dry cloth ready to change her soiled one. None of our efforts relieved her apparent misery and we spent what seemed a long time pacing up and down with her until her cry tailed off into a miserable whimper. We slowly returned to the camp where Zak, who had the last watch of the night, was making tea and maize porridge, anticipating the dawn when the fire would be smothered. We thinned down some porridge for Tara but she turned her head away when I tried to feed her some. She felt hot and we decided she probably had a fever. Zehra commented on this quite calmly but I was terrified that she was becoming seriously ill.

By this time most people were stirring and I tried to pick out Sven among the shadowy figures who were coming or going into the forest to relieve themselves. Sven, when I found him, confirmed that she had a fever but thought it was not worryingly high – possibly a passing reaction to the strangeness of everything and especially the change of diet, which might be upsetting her system. He looked at her grazes, judged them to be satisfactory but smeared more antiseptic on them anyway and otherwise only suggested that we kept on trying to persuade her to take some water.

While we were fussing around Tara I raised a question that had been bothering me. 'What will happen to her if her family is all dead or can't be found?'

'I suppose she'll end up in an orphanage,' said Sven, 'but first we all have to get to safety and then we'll see. There will probably be someone from the family.'

'I don't suppose an orphanage here would be a very happy place,' I said.

'I'd been thinking of that,' said Zehra. 'I'd take her home with me but it would be too difficult. We already have one of my little sister's sons with us so he can go to a good school. Another may come next year but it's more that my husband has such a big family with a lot – really a lot – of children and there are cousins of his who have been asking why we don't adopt one or two of their children. So what would they say if, instead, we took in a complete stranger? And a girl – another girl?'

'We only have to take her to safety,' said Sven. 'There must be hundreds of orphan children here that all need homes. Just because we found her that doesn't mean there's more reason why one of us should take her in.'

The little group gathered around us included Nyezi and Radhika, neither of whom seemed convinced.

'There may not be a reason,' said Nyezi, 'but we feel differently because she's here with us. I should do something but I'm in trouble with my parents for not being married yet and I don't think they'd be pleased if I arrive with a strange baby girl but no wife.'

'I could manage one more child,' said Radhika. 'And we have talked of adopting rather than having another of our own but I wouldn't impose India on Tara. The fetish about lightness makes it bad enough being a dark Indian, especially if you're a girl, but being African would be really hard.'

'I wonder if I could adopt her,' I said timidly. I was feeling desolate about abandoning her to some dubious institution.

Leandro, who was on the edge of the group said, 'It would be a nightmare of bureaucracy.'

I thought for a moment and then said, 'But not impossible?'

Leandro gave me a hard look before answering, 'Probably not quite impossible, but do you really want to be on your own with a child at your stage of life?'

I stared back at him and tried to answer truthfully, 'I would not have planned to have a child but now she's here the choice is different. She isn't "a child", she's this child.'

That was where things were left, as we were about to set off and Leandro had to go on ahead. I was going to take Tara again, but Sven said better that he carry her and I go behind where I could see her and watch for signs of worsening sickness. We had previously decided that the fittest of us would take turns with Tara. As Leandro, Reece and Nyezi were engaged in security duties, that left Sven, Tom, Jalal, Zak, possibly Vernon, and me. The day before Mama Ulemu had tried to step in, insisting, or so I deduced from the nature of the short argument that took place, that she was tougher than all us city wimps. That was fair comment to the extent that despite her age she was not visibly finding the walking hard but we declined her offer because she was not only old but also smaller and thinner than anyone else. Frieda and Dieter were also excluded on grounds of age, and Vernon should have been but argued that he was perfectly robust. Zehra and Mathew were struggling with very bad blisters; Radhika had started to have trouble with one of her sandals, while Magome was barely coping, suffering from conspicuous foot problems and constantly out of breath.

Soon after we left, Tara fell deeply asleep, so deeply that I was frightened for her; but I moved up behind Sven and felt her forehead which did not seem hotter than before. I would have liked to stop and get Sven's view but Sven thought it could wait until we had a break, as we usually stopped for a short rest every two hours or so. The going that morning was mainly level except for a few dried watercourses which had carved out steep shallow valleys, forcing our path to plunge down and up again. At the second of these we ran into a troop of baboons but otherwise saw nothing much of interest before we paused for our first rest. I helped Sven off with Tara and sat with her cradled in my lap, which I thought would be less likely to wake her than putting her flat on the hard ground. Responding to my anxiety, Sven felt her forehead and listened to her pulse and breathing, after which he gave the view that she seemed slightly better.

My thoughts switched again to the future, a future in which I imagined her, a two or three year old in a little cotton frock, holding my hand as we stroll beside the grassy verge near my parents' house. I returned to the present and whispered to her as she slept, 'You'll come home with me, won't you? We'll live near my mummy and daddy on the street with the wide, grassy verge. We'll go to the park where you'll go roly-poly down the bank. You'll tell the time by a dandelion clock. The sun will shine through the grass making it glow the brightest of greens…'

Leandro overheard and said to me, 'Nita, there are other havens. Listen.' He bent down and talked softly to Tara, 'You hear the kchuk, kchuk, kchuk of your mother's panga as she digs. She has brought you to the fields and, for a while, you poke a stick in the soil to copy her until you tire and wander off to hide in the cassava patch. You breathe the smell of the damp red earth and listen to the kchuk, kchuk, kchuk of safety. You wander again and suddenly you lose the way. There is silence and all you can see is cassava and its thick stems and feathered leaves. You panic, but then you hear again the kchuk, kchuk, kchuk and hurry towards the sound until you see your mother in the space beyond the leaves. You run and hide your head against her capulana as she bends to hold you. Strong black arms wrap around you and you drink in her smell of smoke, cotton and young woman. Years later when you study in some bleak town, struggling with your future, you will remember the kchuk, kchuk, kchuk and the smell of the damp red earth and of your mother.'

Leandro turned back to me and said, 'We don't know she doesn't have a family hunting for her.'

I answered a little sharply, 'I know, Leandro, the first thing we must do is look for her family. No one is thinking anything else.'

'We'd better get going again,' Leandro said, and got up to resume his place ahead of the line.

Jalal approached to say rather shyly that it must be his turn to carry Tara and I helped him on with the cloth, an arrangement he evidently found embarrassing.

We stopped for a lunch break – cold maize porridge because we had banned ourselves from cooking by daylight – and continued the stories. Zak drew the bent straw.

21

Zak's Story

'I'm going to tell you about a strange experience,' he began. 'It happened in Moscow but you will see it has something to do with the caves. Anyway, I think it does.'

'At last I was able to take my family on a visit home. It was our first trip back after years of struggling with our business in Namibia. I think I told you that I'd gone there first as part of the Soviet aid team. I was there with my family for the short time between Namibia's independence and the disintegration of the Soviet Union. I said "short" as it was just a couple of years but looking back it seems much longer because we arrived in one world and left in another. We saw the birth of someone else's country and returned to witness the death of our own. The state we had represented was gone.

'My wife and I had suspected then that my job had no future and before we left Africa we'd hurriedly looked at commercial openings, talked to our contacts… It wasn't our first time in Africa as I'd served in Zambia before and it wasn't our first contact with Namibians as I'd met SWAPO leaders during the long war with South Africa, men who were now in government and remembered me. Back in Moscow I found, as expected, that jobs were being cut or downgraded and everyone was looking for openings in the private sector. We ran back to Namibia to launch our first little business, but to begin with things went badly. There was no possibility to go home. I couldn't leave anyone else in charge. But we got through the bad times and at last could take a holiday.

'The new Russia had also been through very bad times but by then life had started to settle down. It felt strange being back in Moscow – so familiar and so changed. It wasn't just the neon lights, the advertisements, the signs of outlandish wealth or even the presence of almost African poverty that struck me, but the things people talked about. Of course I shouldn't have been surprised. We'd been in touch with friends and family; we'd followed the Russian news. But being there was different.

'You may think this doesn't have much to do with caves, but it's hard to separate one thing from another. The night before the day I'm coming to I spent a drunken evening with an old friend from student days who talked in a way I'd never have expected about the "soul" of Russia and whether the church was a good thing or not. He wasn't quite a convert. One minute he'd grumble about ignorant, reactionary priests and the next he'd talk about the church being the soul of Russia. Of course, I'd heard about the rebuilding of churches but in the time I'd been back I'd not heard much about religion, and certainly not much in favour. My parents were war veterans; they'd been loyal Soviet citizens and felt betrayed. To them the oligarchs, the church and the corruption, all went together. For myself,' Zak added, as a polite aside directed especially towards Mathew and Jalal, 'I have no idea if there's a God or not, but if there is and if He is good, then I'd be sure our Russian priests are not his agents.

'My friend didn't turn me into a believer but he made me curious. I'd promised to take the children sightseeing the next day and because of our conversation I decided to take them to the Kremlin churches, an essential tourist visit that I'd so far put off because of the queues, and perhaps other reasons.

'We went from one dark, gilded interior to another. The children were quite interested at first as we tried, between us, to identify the people and events in the icons, but nothing began to stir in me the kind of feelings my friend had talked of. It's true I felt the weight of history, but who would want to linger over that bloody history? Or return to it? All that gold glowing in the dark reminded me of the film, *Ivan the Terrible*. It's such an old film I guess none of you have seen it, but it has Tsar Ivan as a small boy in some of those grand buildings, surrounded by the aristocrats plotting against him.

'Nothing really surprised me until we came to the Cathedral of the Annunciation where the iconostasis had a gap at the far end on the left. Perhaps an icon had been taken for renovation. Perhaps there had never been one there. Instead, you looked through a gold frame at a section of wall. Expecting every rectangle to contain a picture, I completely misread what I was looking at. The wall was of uneven stone and included a large crack. It was grey-pink in parts with greenish patches of lichen. At first I thought it was an abstract painting and was shocked at seeing something so modern there, so different from the icons. Before I said anything stupid to the children I saw what it really was, but even when I had worked out that the "painting" was just a piece of rock I still went on staring at it. Somehow the frame made it seem like an icon, something to worship. I left the church feeling that what I had seen meant something.

'Of course that was years ago and I don't know why your stories have brought back that memory. There must be a reason, and one reason I can think of is that the rock was a piece of the Earth and it was framed as something to worship. Could that be the point of the cave paintings, to honour the rocks on which they stand? A sort of offering to the Earth?'

He fell silent and that appeared to be all he was planning to say.

'Well, Vernon, could it be?' Nyezi asked.

Vernon was evasive as usual. 'Well, yes, it's possible. They could have something to do with Earth worship. Some of my colleagues have a theory that the rock features around them are significant. And yes, if the purpose is to honour the Earth that would be a reason to put them underground, wouldn't it?'

'Those people – our forgotten ancestors – were right,' said Zak, now sounding slightly manic, 'and that's where everything went wrong; it was when we stopped honouring our Earth, when we started to rape her, strip off her forests, rip out her treasures. That's what I felt in front of the iconostasis. It was a message. It must have been. But I didn't listen. I walked away. I just walked away…'

He put his hands to his face in a ravaged-by-guilt gesture but I wondered how he squared this revelation with his business. Had he not said something about extraction?

Radhika was more sympathetic. 'You're not the only person to walk away,' she said gently. 'There have been so many messages: the trees dying, birds vanishing, floods and drought, epidemics… What will it take for us to stop walking away? '

Further contributions were forestalled by Dieter sighing, 'Cue the violins!' and asking, 'What about the last three stories. Are we going to have them or do the lucky ones get off?'

'Perhaps not now,' Leandro answered. 'We're further from the border than I would like and I think we'd better get going.'

22

Afternoon

The next stretch proved harder than anything we'd done since the climb on the first day of walking. The ground began to rise again and, at the top when it levelled off, the terrain became rockier, forcing the path to wriggle about up and down and side to side. The surface underfoot became uneven, scattered with treacherous loose stones and instead of continuous woodland there was only scrub, patches of grass and occasional massive baobab trees, unfortunately leafless at that time of year. Early afternoon was a bad time to be crossing such an exposed area and we were all suffering from the heat. When Vernon, who was taking a turn carrying Tara, stumbled and nearly fell, Sven insisted he would manage better with the child, which meant we had to stop while the change was made. Leandro, out in front, did not know we had stopped and got so far ahead that Nyezi was no longer in contact with him.

We only caught up with him, eventually, at a junction where he had stopped to wait. Here we all bunched up, completely disregarding our security plan, and some cross words were exchanged. Leandro and Reece took time to decide which was the right fork to take and while they debated we stood exposed to the sun's glare.

We continued in discomfort. Magome kept stumbling but managed to save himself from falling. Then, suddenly, Dieter slithered on one of the path's downward twists and fell spread-eagled, grazing his hands so badly that they bled. Nyezi ran forward to alert Leandro and when they re-joined us we decided, as it was nearly time for the two-hourly break, to retreat to a small area of shade provided by the partly hollowed trunk of an ancient baobab. Water by now was running low, but Sven damped a corner of cloth to clean Dieter's hands as best he could and put antiseptic on them. He then checked on Tara who was strangely subdued, for some time neither sleeping nor crying. He thought she was still running a temperature but less than before. Most of us would have liked to stay huddled in the shade for longer but Leandro, evidently bothered about our fitful progress, said all too soon that we should go on.

We had not scrambled and plodded far when Radhika, whose sandals were not coping well with the terrain, twisted her foot, leaving her in such pain that we were forced to stop again, this time edging into a couple of even smaller bits of shade cast parsimoniously by some jutting rocks. Sven's long unused professional skills were called on yet again and, after careful examination, he pronounced there was no sign of a break but that left the question of how bad the sprain was. The ever well-equipped Sven produced a bandage and strapped the ankle firmly, regretting there was no ice to apply. Mathew and Zak went over to some scrubby bushes to prospect for walking sticks, returning with a few rather bent samples just long and strong enough to be of some use to those most in danger of slipping. Radhika got up, took a few cautious steps and reassured us that her ankle would do and that the damage was not nearly as bad as the initial pain promised. We set off again, adopting an even less ambitious pace than before. Those small accidents, happening one after the other, had a demoralising affect. I think we all had a feeling that they were a prelude to something much worse.

At last, quite suddenly, at the top of a rise we saw the sight we were longing for. There below us, at the bottom of a wooded slope, a significant river snaked through much greener grassland. That was the border; our destination. It is hard to convey the ripple of elation that ran through the party as each one in turn arrived at the viewpoint and stood in silent delight. Our excitement, however, was damped when Leandro said, 'That's it, that's the border. But I'm afraid we can't make it today.'

He pointed out that there were less than two hours of daylight left and he did not want to attempt to ford the river in the dark. In our condition it could take us nearly an hour to descend the valley side and, once down, there was at least another twenty-minute's walk to the bank and no guarantee we would not have to walk further to find a place to cross. In any case, there were no settlements on the flood plain so we would have to walk a few more miles to anywhere we might find food or lodging. He indicated, in the very far distance, a few huts that might be the edge of the small town we were aiming for. We had to accept the sense of what he said and reluctantly agreed that we would camp again somewhere on the way down into the valley. Unfortunately, the forest cover on the valley side was denser than almost any we had passed through before so that most of the way down the path was hedged in by undergrowth, much of it woody and some also prickly. We were nearly down when the vegetation thinned, as forest mingled with grassland, and we were able to leave the path to find a place to stop.

When our fire was ready and we were waiting for the orange glow of sunset to fade before lighting it, we drew the straws again – now only three. Sven was left with the bent one and readied himself without fuss, seeming neither pleased nor nervous. I imagined his offering would be more seminar paper than story and at first it sounded as if this was right.

23

Sven's Story

'The events which follow happened among people who were living in a large band made up of several families. They cooperated in practical matters, shared rituals and had systems for managing their connected lives. Every few years, men would elect some of their number to take offices of responsibility under a Leader. The Leader was chosen from those who had previously held some of the offices but, unlike them, he was appointed for life – unless he became feeble or was impeached for wrongdoing or misrule, which happened from time to time. The election of the Leader was a complicated affair involving offerings to ancestors, speech-making and formal and informal meetings, mostly for men, but some for women, and some for everyone. The outcome had to be a consensus so that the ballot had to be run over and over again until the vote was unanimous. It was a huge performance even though the practical powers of the Leader were quite limited – at least in theory.

'One day the people chose as Leader a man called Bonebreaker. Names generally reflected something about a person's appearance or personality and were given in early adulthood, replacing childhood names. Bonebreaker got his name because he was powerfully built, large, strong and a fearless hunter, qualities that many people thought made for a good leader. At the time he was chosen people thought of the bones broken as those of the big game animals he brought down and butchered. Bonebreaker was the head of his close family which included seven brothers, also large and strong and yet completely under his thumb. He had three wives, which was a lot at the time, and several sons. He was known to control his wives and children with a hard hand, but most people were not worried because sometimes heads of families behaved like that towards their own family members, which didn't mean they lacked due respect for everyone else.

'Things at first went on quite normally. Bonebreaker behaved as a Leader was supposed to, did more or less the right things and exercised authority with an even hand. But little by little, people began to notice his behaviour changing. He started to act in a bossy way towards people who weren't from his close family and often over matters that weren't the Leader's business. Then, little by little, he began to favour his own close family above others. If anyone objected he beat them up, often with support from the seven large and strong brothers. His name then began to acquire a new meaning.

‘There were mutterings but no one did anything; some because they were close to his family and got the benefits; some because they were trying to get close by marrying a daughter or niece to one of his sons or nephews; some because they were afraid; some because they were lazy and could see it would be trouble confronting him; and some because they couldn’t see anyone opposing him and they always just did what everyone else did.

‘Things went on very slowly getting worse until there came a time when the Leader’s wives stopped getting pregnant. We would say now he had become infertile but he blamed his wives and started to take new ones. In doing this he bullied and pressurised people so that he was able to take the best girls for himself. This was not considered good behaviour from anyone and certainly not from the Leader.

‘The muttering got worse but most people thought, “Well, he’s getting on. He can’t last much longer.” But he wasn’t that old and did not show any signs of nearing the end of life, perhaps because he gave himself the best camping spots, the best furs, the best food and had a large family round him, which meant he didn’t do any work except for a bit of hunting, and then only if he felt like hunting.

‘I guess some of you people will complain later on that this is unrealistic because why didn’t people just walk off. All right, I have listened. I know it’s been pointed out that hunter-gatherers aren’t tied to a place in the way peasants are. If someone starts to behave like a tyrant the people he tries to oppress can simply walk away. But do they always? Would it always be so easy? Back to the story:

'Well, a few people did leave, and more talked about leaving but failed to do more than talk. It was only easy to leave in the summer months when they were travelling around. In the winter they stayed in one place and before the weather got very severe they stockpiled food which, because the other officials had been forcibly sidelined, Bonebreaker and his brothers controlled. Anyone leaving then would have gone into extremely harsh conditions without stores to see them through. Often people talked about leaving but went on just talking until it was too late. Then when spring came somehow everything would seem better. And so it went on. Perhaps they did not really want to leave. Everyone was interrelated and they were all used to living more or less together. And Bonebreaker was a very good hunter and, as many people said, a fine man. Perhaps living with him was not so bad after all.

'That depended on who you were, but for some young people there came a time when things started to get much, much worse. At first, when Bonebreaker started collecting new wives, he only went for girls who were not yet promised to anyone. But fairly soon he started to go after girls who had other plans, or whose parents had plans for them.

'One year things went very badly for one particular young woman called Never-Gives-Up and a young man called Clever Hands. Never-Gives-Up was, as her name suggests, strong minded and Clever Hands was very good looking and known for his skill at making tools and decorating them. These two were planning to get married during the next marriage season and they were deeply in love – not a condition people thought necessary for marriage but one that did, from time to time, lead to a marriage. Now, Bonebreaker had his eye on Never-Gives-Up and, although she refused, he threw his weight about and leant on her parents, demanding to have her. Her parents were quite willing because of the benefits which would flow to them as a result of the alliance. Never-Gives-Up strongly resisted the match but her parents eventually talked her into it, persuading her that love is transient, Clever Hands would soon forget her and they would all benefit from joining the family of the Great Leader.

'The young couple did not, however, forget each other. This may be due to the power of love, but love may have been assisted a little by circumstances. For Never-Gives-Up was far from happy in her marriage. Not only was Bonebreaker old enough to be her father but also he was demanding and rough, lustful but unaffectionate. As for Clever Hands, he had limited opportunities to settle for an alternative match because Bonebreaker's predations had caused a shortage of brides.

'The young lovers contrived occasionally to meet but it was hard to find an opportunity to be alone together for any length of time in a place where they could be sure none of Bonebreaker's close family or toady friends would see them. So, their meetings were brief and unsatisfying. The situation became worse in the autumn when the band moved to their winter home, some shallow caves in a sheltered valley. There the women had more work to do around the camp and it was not so easy for Never-Gives-Up to slip off alone on the pretext of foraging. When the severe cold set in they knew it would become even harder to leave the camp inconspicuously. Clever Hands cast around for a hiding place and remembered that he'd seen caves up the valley, away from any frequented paths. He went to look and found some that were deep enough to provide good shelter and quite free of bears or lions or other dangerous inhabitants.

'For him it would be easy enough to visit the caves secretly because there were still hunting opportunities in winter and, although men usually went in groups, it was not unknown for them to go out alone. But Never-Gives-Up had to think of a good reason why she might disappear into the snowy waste alone. At last she had a plan. She went to one of her aunts who was known to have supernatural powers as a healer and was also very fond of her. Never-Gives-Up explained the situation to the aunt who thought for a time and then worked out what to do. Never-Gives-Up was to ask Bonebreaker, meekly, if she could consult the aunt about why she was not yet pregnant. This she did and although Bonebreaker at first raged a bit because some of his other wives had tried all kinds of remedies which hadn't worked, eventually he told her to go and see what the aunt would say. So, the aunt made sure that everyone knew that she was retiring into the wild for a day to make contact with powers who would advise. When she came back she told Bonebreaker that she knew what Never-Gives-Up must do but it was so very hard she did not want to say what it was. Bonebreaker, of course, pressed her to speak up and eventually she said that Never-Gives-Up must make up some ochre paste and prepare special food as a sacrifice. Then she must go into the forest completely by herself, climb up to a sheltered place under a certain crag and there she must make secret signs on her body with the ochre, offer the sacrifice, and spend the rest of the day and the entire night alone reciting a formula of words the aunt would give her. She was to do that once every seven days until she became pregnant. Bonebreaker at first complained that it was too hard and she might freeze to death, but eventually his wish for another child overcame his desire not to lose his youngest wife and he sent Never-Gives-Up out into the cold.

'Off she went, well wrapped in furs and carrying the ochre paste and the food for the sacrifice. She walked up to the crag, but instead of stopping there, scrambled on up to the cave that she and Clever Hands had chosen as their meeting place. There she found Clever Hands waiting for her just inside with a lamp already lit. They took the lamp and went together much deeper into the cave until they came to a space where the walls were not very damp, the floor was flat, and the air was definitely warmer than outside. There, at last, they made love, as they had desired to do for so long. Afterwards they ate the sacrificial food and then slept for a while, woke to make love again and held each other close until it was time for Never-Gives-Up to return. Before they parted Never-Gives-Up stripped and rolled in the snow to remove the smell of Clever Hands in case her husband noticed. The lovemaking and the cold snow left her glowing as if on fire.

'After seven days passed they met in the cave again and then again after another seven. On the following seventh day, however, Never-Gives-Up arrived to find Clever Hands was not there. She waited and he did not come. It was cold in the cave mouth and she could not go to their usual resting place, their "nest" as they called it, because she had no materials to make a lamp or to light one. She moved as far back in the cave as she could see, to the farthest place that the daylight penetrated. There she sat on a rock waiting uneasily. She felt nervous alone and close to the dark passage they had previously taken together. On their second visit they had explored some way beyond their nest to check that there were no natural or supernatural dangers lurking there, but the cave went on and on showing no signs of coming to an end so that they could not be sure that there was nothing down there to be afraid of.

'Never-gives-Up distracted herself by examining all the area she could see, looking at every crack and fold of the rock, and as she stared she thought she started to see all kinds of things in the rock face: hills and valleys, a tree trunk, but also people or bits of people, a face here, a kneeling figure there, and also animals or parts of animals, the head and shoulders of bison here, the face of deer there, the paw prints of a lion somewhere else. She was both delighted and frightened by what she saw. After a while she got up and felt some of the shapes, running her hand over them. Then it came into her head to use the ochre she had brought with her to make the shapes appear more clearly. She decided against anything to do with a lion or a bear, as she did not want to think about fierce animals that might really be in a cave. She felt like that even though she knew perfectly well that if such animals were using her cave there would be droppings or paw marks and that they would not go deep inside, not beyond where she and her lover had been. That was clear enough if they were really lions and bears, but suppose they were something else borrowing the form of those animals, something that belonged to darkness and left no trace when it walked? She shuddered but had a feeling of reassurance when she looked at the great bison head. It has a friendly look about it and began to appear even more encouraging when she started to smear the warm coloured ochre over it.

'She was working away trying to make the outline look right when a voice just behind her made her leap so violently that she grazed her arm on a jutting piece of rock. To her immense relief she saw that the owner of the voice was Clever Hands. After recovering herself she fell into his arms and they held each other closely. He told her he had been delayed because his father asked him to help collect fire-wood and he did not want to refuse for fear of raising questions about why he was suddenly so anxious to go off into the forest.

'Clever Hands liked the beginnings of the bison picture and helped her finish it before they went to their nest. This time, after lovemaking, he suggested they bring out some of the other hidden animal forms in the rock faces around them. She agreed enthusiastically,and they set to work.

'During their next meetings they gradually created a pageant of animals around them, which made their retreat seem more friendly and special. Because he was already skilled at carving animals on ivory ornaments or the handles of bone implements, Clever Hands was very good at the work of creating animals on the cave walls. But when Never-Gives-Up suggested they paint some of the human faces half-hidden in the stone he reacted very strongly against this. He told her that it was a rule he had been told by his grandfather never, ever to represent a person because it would bring bad luck. He was unable to explain why but he was very sure they should restrict their creations to animals and only to those animals they respected. Never-Gives-Up did not question this because, above all, she wanted their hiding place to contain nothing that could bring bad luck.

'After several more meetings the aunt's magic worked and Never-Gives-Up fell pregnant. Bonebreaker was delighted and showered the aunt and Never-Gives-Up with presents. But the sad result for the lovers was that the reason for solitary trips into the forest was removed. For the months of her pregnancy they were parted and suffered deeply, although at least now Bonebreaker was less hard on Never-Gives-Up and her life became a little easier.

'After the band left for the summer hunting grounds a baby boy was born, healthy and strong, and when he had grown a few months, the aunt, who was extremely fond of her niece, told Bonebreaker that the child's health would be at risk if the rituals were not resumed as soon as the band returned to their winter home.

'So, every winter Clever Hands and Never-Gives-Up continued their lovemaking in the cave, and two more children were born. Never-Gives-Up was quite content with her double life but Clever Hands became more and more troubled that his children were alienated from him and would grow up not knowing their true father. He became ambitious to overthrow Bonebreaker and tried to guide those who still muttered against the Leader to join him in a plot. There were young men who complained that they were deprived of wives, not only by the Leader himself but also by the Leader's brothers and a few other favoured old men who had started to follow Bonebreaker's example. Then there were the other old men, not so favoured, who railed against the disregard for tradition. Clever Hands talked cautiously to them but, as before, people were afraid, and the plot had gone no further than some secret discussions when circumstances brought things to a head.

'Because Never-Gives-Up was the only one of Bonebreaker's wives now producing children she become by far his favourite. The other wives resented his attentions to her and were jealous of her continued pregnancies. Some of them approached Never-Gives-Up's aunt and asked her to use her powers to help them too. The aunt found herself in a difficult situation and at first excused herself by telling them that she had been granted the boon once, for one person only, and could not repeat it. But they went on pestering her to try until, eventually, she provided them with the advice that she had given to Never-Gives-Up except for designating different sites for vigil, all far away from the lovers' cave. So, the wives went out to spend freezing nights in lonely places, but did not get pregnant. Some said that the aunt spoke the truth when she told them she could not work the wonder a second time, but others began to suspect that she had deliberately withheld key details. One day, the most suspicious of the wives decided to follow Never-Gives-Up when she went for her vigil. Of course the suspicious wife soon discovered that there was indeed an element missing from the rites prescribed by the aunt to the other wives.

'She was furious to think that she and her co-wives had all been made fools of and her first reaction was to rush down to the camp to spread the news. Half way down, however, she hesitated. She knew Never-Gives-Up had not wanted to marry Bonebreaker and remembered how she too had shrunk from being mated with the greedy old bully when there were plenty of smooth-skinned, radiant young men needing wives. Indeed, she had once had her eye on one or two of them before Bonebreaker's summons cut short such hopes. She began to think that perhaps Never-Gives-Up was acting fairly. After all, many people secretly complained against Bonebreaker, accused him of grabbing too many women, misusing power and trampling on tradition. Perhaps his wives would not be violating tradition if they withdrew their loyalty. It even occurred to her that some of them might improve their lives by following the example of Never-Gives-Up.

'This is why the news of the love affair did not immediately break. The wife who made the discovery first whispered it to the co-wives she was closest to and they whispered it to some of the young men they were attracted to and, because some of those young men were involved in the never materialising plot, they whispered to other plotters and someone warned Clever Hands that his secret was starting to leak out. They all knew that a secret being shared among so many would not remain a secret, which meant that Clever Hands and Never-Gives-Up were in danger. Now, at last, Never-Gives-Up agreed that they should try to overthrow Bonebreaker but both were aware that it would not be easy. Bonebreaker's close family was large, with a mass of connections through his many wives and through his seven formidable brothers. Of course there were tensions, especially with some of the parents and siblings of his unfortunate wives, but the seven brothers would certainly stand by him and would intimidate everyone else.

'The biggest danger was that Bonebreaker would suddenly learn of the love affair when the lovers were in the camp, where he could certainly kill Never-Gives-Up and possibly Clever Hands as well before anyone could move to oppose him. So, the lovers and their allies agreed a plan and made preparations. The plan required recruiting the co-wife who had discovered the lovers. It was a risk, but they needed someone Bonebreaker would not suspect. They had to rely on the rumour coming back from people she'd been whispering to, that she approved of their affair and wanted to be rid of Bonebreaker herself. If the rumours were wrong, or she changed her mind, it would almost certainly result in the death of the lovers and many of their supporters.

'Next time Never-Gives-Up went to meet Clever Hands in the cave they were joined by her big brother and two of Clever Hands's closest friends. There was no lovemaking this time. One of the friends remained outside to watch while the others prepared. Then they waited tensely to see if the co-wife would do as she promised and whether it would have the result they hoped.

'Down in the camp the co-wife carefully picked an argument with Bonebreaker which, as she knew was likely, led him to abuse her and soon to insult her for failing to produce a child. At that she said, as if to herself but just loud enough for him to hear, that even the buzzards knew it was not her fault. Then, of course, he wanted to know what she meant and she led him on for some time saying she hadn't said anything, he'd not heard right, it was nothing, until he shook her violently and threatened to beat her. Then she ran some way away and shouted so that many people around could hear, that since he forced her to tell him, then the obvious reason Never-Gives-Up was the only wife now bearing children was that she had another man. Then she taunted him. How had he not seen it? What did he think happened during her solitary vigils that so reliably got her pregnant? Did he really think Never-Gives-Up shivered all night under a bleak crag when there was a warm, cave near by?

'As she intended, he flew into a blind rage. First he came after her with murderous intent, but she had already put some distance between them before she spoke and now ran off at great speed while another of his wives, who was not in the plot but was fond of the young woman, demanded why he was threatening a wife who was not the one who had done wrong. The other wives muttered agreement. By now the commotion had attracted the attention of many people and others were gathering to see what it was all about. Bonebreaker's fury was driven as much by the pain of public humiliation as by jealousy. Realising he would only lose more respect by punishing the messenger, he let her go, seized his weapons, a lamp and some smouldering branches from the nearest fire, and set off at once for the cave she had mentioned. He did not pause to organise support, but casually called on his brothers and friends to follow as witnesses to the offence and to the vengeance he was about to wreak.

'At the cave, the man on guard saw Bonebreaker approach from far away and warned those in the cave before hiding himself near the entrance. Bonebreaker stormed up and into the cave but, as far as the light penetrated, he saw that it seemed deserted. He moved cautiously on to the limits of the light, and then lit the lamp and went on, followed by some of his brothers who had now caught up with him. He signalled to them to be silent, as he wanted to catch the couple in flagrante and kill them locked in each other's arms. They edged on until they reached an open area where they paused, astounded and disconcerted because here a little lamp was burning under a dramatic painting of a bull. They had seen nothing like this before and the sight was extremely unsettling. Some of the brothers were for going back. While they lingered there for the first time they heard the sounds of human presence. Never-Gives-Up could be heard singing softly an explicit love song, which echoed strangely in the cave. The confirmation that she and her lover were really there drove Bonebreaker into a new fit of rage. But still he signalled to his followers to be silent and crept on to a point where the cave narrowed into a passage that allowed only one person to crawl through. In the darkness ahead, however, he could see a faint light and now hear endearments faintly echoing. Incensed, he crawled silently forward, sure that his prey was waiting unawares. Indeed, when he reached the tight entrance to the little area where the light and voices came from, he could now see the two figures entwined. To reach them he had to wriggle the last few feet on his belly. But the lovers seemed so totally absorbed with each other that he was not disconcerted, quite sure he could creep through and then pounce.

'The moment he poked his head out of the narrow passage Never-Gives-Up's brother and Clever Hands's friend, who were waiting by the opening, set on him, jammed his mouth closed and slit his throat. He died almost instantly without being able to scream. They dragged the body aside and waited.

'His brothers following him were mystified and stopped at the beginning of the passageway. Their leader had apparently gone through and nothing had happened. No challenge. No execution. The soft sounds of the lovers' endearments could still be heard. They did not want to call out as they had been bound to silence. They retreated and, after a whispered consultation, decided that Bonebreaker must have gone through unseen and found a hiding place where he was waiting for them to join him and witness the crime before he struck. So, the next brother quietly began to wriggle though and was despatched in the same way. One after another the brothers were killed and laid aside until the last one was dead. Then their followers hesitated. Surely seven witnesses were enough, and now the transgressors would be confronted and punished. But nothing happened. They waited and waited but still nothing happened except that the lamp that had illuminated the distant chamber was extinguished and the soft sounds of love making ceased. All was darkness and silence. It was so odd that no one wanted to wriggle through the passage to investigate. Then suddenly, out of the darkness came an appalling noise amplified by a thousand echoes, a crashing of rock on rock and a roaring voice that told them they were trespassing and the earth would swallow them up. Instantly, they fled for the cave entrance, stumbling and scrabbling in their terror. When they had gone, Clever Hands put down the horn he had used to disguise his voice and softly laughed.

'At the cave mouth Bonebreaker's supporters were surprised by the scene that greeted them. They could not know that while they were in the cave most of the population of the camp had arrived outside and that the friend of Clever Hands who had hidden near by had emerged from his hiding place to confront the crowd. The young man had launched into a fine speech in which he carefully avoided, as yet, denouncing Bonebreaker, but just kept asking rhetorical questions: why had so many customary rules been broken under his leadership, why had food been unevenly distributed, why were there so many young men without brides? In this way he kept the crowd at bay until the remnants of Bonebreaker's vengeance party came out of the cave in disarray, to tell a vague story of dark forces at work and of the strange disappearance of Bonebreaker and his brothers. They had just finished their account when Clever Hands emerged with an air of triumph carrying high Bonebreaker's head and followed by his two comrades and Never-Gives-Up.

'The mood of the crowd, until then indecisive, began to change, as people took in that Bonebreaker and his most brutal enforcers were all dead. The secret plotters, now liberated from fear, roared support for Clever Hands. Now many others who had suffered under Bonebreaker but had not dared even to discuss opposing him, joined those denouncing the autocrat. The remaining men with close ties to Bonebreaker were completely outnumbered and fell silent. Clever Hands and the other tyrant killers were greeted as heroes and some of the plotters hastily urged Clever Hands to take the position of Leader. Then Clever Hands endeared himself even further to the crowd by declining, firstly, on the grounds that the band should return to the proper methods of choosing its Leader, and secondly, that, however necessary and justified the killing had been, he and his comrades were polluted by the blood and should take no part in public life until they had performed the necessary acts of expiation. This pleased the traditionalists and many more who feared the killings would simply mark a further departure from rules of governance already eroded by Bonebreaker. Clever Hands went on to say that the first step in the process of expiation was to ensure a proper funeral for the dead men. Whatever their misdeeds, he said, they were members of the community and in death should receive the usual rights. It was another far-sighted move which released the dead men's relatives from the absolute obligation to extract vengeance. In the end most remained peacefully in the band, while those who could not be reconciled with the killers were too few to impose their will. Instead of causing dissension, once summer came, they simply left and went their own way.

'With the first part of his speech Clever Hands appealed especially to older people who remembered the time before Bonebreaker's time as Leader. With the second part he knew he risked losing them again, but he was not going to waste the opportunity provided by his moment of victory. While the people were in shock from the dramatic end of their Leader he wanted to seed an idea for quite radical change, especially in the relations between young and old. He led up to it carefully. First of all he talked about his personal situation, the wrong that Bonebreaker had done to him and his family by stealing his betrothed. (Never mind that he and Never-Gives-Up had not been formally betrothed. Few people would remember.) He spoke first about his father, how his father had been deprived of a daughter-in-law and grandchildren. He introduced a touch of pathos, reminding them that his father had died without ever knowing the children of his son. As a theatrical gesture he asked Never-Gives-Up to approach and in front of his widowed mother confirmed her as the mother of his children. Only then did he talk about the hardships suffered by Never-Gives-Up, although he was careful because everyone probably knew that her parents had been complicit in handing her over to Bonebreaker. He passed quickly over the parents' role to concentrate on the brave aunt. He moved on soon to talk about all the other young men cheated out of their brides and about young girls unwillingly made to become extra wives to old men. How much better, he reminded the people, were the customs observed before Bonebreaker, when men rarely took more than one or at most two wives and when young people often chose their partner. (This was a slight exaggeration but no one seemed to notice). He then suggested that things had been better still even earlier and he recited an obscure passage from a legend which appears to refer to young men and girls looking about to chose their partners in a place away from everyone else. Clearly, he said, that is what happened in the days before people were corrupted. When he and Never-Gives-Up retreated to the cave they were only following a time-hallowed precedent. He urged his listeners to go in and see how he and Never-Gives-Up had made their cave a place of harmony until violated by Bonebreaker and his men.

'Clever Hands finished and gestured to the people to go into the cave. This they did, and when they saw the space where the animals were painted they stood amazed.

'After his speech at the cave entrance, Clever Hands did as he had promised and took no official part in public life until properly cleansed of the blood letting. But his influence was strong and the Leader who replaced Bonebreaker used to consult him on everything. When the Leader died, Clever Hands, by then properly eligible for the position, was chosen Leader by the quickest election ever known.

'After these events it became the custom during winters for young people from puberty until marriage to retreat at certain times from their elders and to stay in a cave, where they would paint, tell stories, sing and dance. The cave that Clever Hands and Never-Gives-Up had occupied was not used because of the killings that had taken place there. But it was visited as a kind of shrine, especially by lovers whose choice of partner was for any reason thwarted, and by couples who seemed unable to have children.

'I cannot say if the new customs – or revived customs – meant that young people "lived happily ever afterwards", but the community grew and divided to form other bands that went their way and found new winter homes where the young people also painted other caves in which they gathered. Always, in these gatherings, the story of Bonebreaker, Clever Hands and Never-Gives-Up was told over and again until everyone knew it by heart.'

Sven made it clear that this was the end and, after the usual applause, Radhika complained half-jokingly, 'You should have allowed them to be "happy ever after". We are in need of completely happy endings.'

She was right that the atmosphere was sombre. Exhaustion, and the prospect of yet another night in the bush, had dampened the spirit of argument and no one rushed to speak.

Eventually Zehra said, 'At least he let the lovers live.'

'I suppose,' Radhika added 'it's a cheerful idea to suppose the caves were a kind of teenage club, a place to socialise and have fun rather than somewhere intended to awe and frighten people.'

'What are we going to do now?' asked Zak. 'There's only two left. Are we going to go to bed or are we going to hear them?'

Again no one was in a hurry to answer. Jalal threw more wood on the fire and Nyezi said, 'Looks like Jalal thinks we're going to hear them.'

'I'm easy,' said Mathew and one or two others muttered that they felt the same.

'If we are going to have them we should get on with it,' said Reece, which seemed to settle it. No one had thought to ask Vernon for his comment on Sven's story and he did not volunteer one.

This time, the last draw, the straws selected Radhika.

24

Radhika's Story

'I'm fortunate, because the night when we were all so cold the Serpent Spirit came to me in a dream. As I'm sure you know, the Serpent Spirit encircles the world and knows everything that happens and has ever happened. There are so many things I should have asked her, so many things really useful to me and my future, but I had gone to sleep worrying about what my story would be and all I could think of in the dream was the mystery of your painted caves. That is typical of spirits. They offer to open doors to everything but there's always a catch – at least there is always a catch if what you want is wealth, power or esteem in this world. Perhaps I was lucky that I didn't think of a getting-on-in-the-world kind of question for which I might have been punished – although, to think that way, I wonder if I'm giving in to a rather Western and punitive idea that knowledge is dangerous and humans have to pay a bitter price for it. But I must get on with telling you the answer to the question I did ask. Of course, the Serpent is devious so I can't guarantee either that she was telling the truth or that I correctly interpreted what she said. I leave that to you to decide.

'Long before the time of painted caves, people were making images, scratching, drawing, whittling, carving, painting… That came with having hands because hands will do those kinds of things. And when they were scratching, drawing, whittling, carving or painting, mostly, they made their marks look as much like animals as they could because animals interested them above everything else in the world, even other people because people are just there, around all the time. It wasn't that the people needed animals as food. They did eat some animals, but those weren't the only ones that interested them or even the ones that interested them most. Animals weren't just interesting for practical reasons because some were dangerous and some were useful; they were interesting because they live and move; they are like humans and not like humans; they are flesh and blood, they eat, drink and sleep; they show fear and anger; they mate, have babies, grow up and die as humans do. They are not human but they can seem to be. They sometimes seem to think and plan, show cunning, behave with cruelty or bravery; and many animals appear to grieve when one of their kind, especially a young one, dies. They are also mysterious. The humans who lived among them knew a lot about them; about the characteristics of each species and even the personality of some individuals that they had the opportunity to see often, but there was so much more that they did not know. When birds sit together twittering, are they talking? When the sleeping lion's tale twitches, is he dreaming? People did not know any animals in the way that thousands of years later they would come to know those they domesticated and lived with. When all creatures ran wild they were only to be seen now and then. So, who could know what they get up to when no human is watching? Perhaps they are humans in another shape? Or spirits? Perhaps when no one is watching they change into humans. Perhaps some humans are secretly lions or wildebeest. Why do some animals graze and others prey on them? The behaviours of different species were a way of talking about human traits: gentle like deer, vain like a stag, slippery as a fish, aggressive like a lion. Humans were constantly thinking and talking about animals, sometimes imitating them, making up stories, singing songs about them. So it was natural that they also made animals with their scratching, drawing, whittling, carving, painting.

'Now many of those animal shapes were integrated in things for personal use or gifts, like the handle of tools or weapons, or small things like jewellery and charms to ward off danger; most people did that kind of work from time to time and it was done to please, to adorn, to protect particular humans. But large-scale animal figures on rocks or trees were different in that they were made by specialists on behalf of all the people. I say "on behalf of" rather than "for" because people moved from place to place while the paintings remained where they were, living their own life, there for all to see and yet not needing to be seen; an offering to whatever power it is that gives the shared quality of life to animals and humans. The specialists who made them – let's call them artists for convenience although all our words are tainted by our modern lives – had to develop not only technical skills but the ability to see beyond what the eye shows us, to see something essential hidden within appearances.

'Artists were highly respected for these abilities and because their work reaffirmed both the sameness of humans and animals and their difference; the making of each painting helped to guarantee a state of harmony between humans and other forms of life. Artists might be moved to paint at any time but always they made new paintings for seasonal festivals and ceremonies for coming of age and marriage.

'Artists, who might be women or men, were chosen by divinations and trials when young. Once chosen they would pass through a period of apprenticeship, learning from an older artist how to prepare surfaces, make and apply colours and, more importantly, how to watch and read the different animals. People lived in quite small wandering groups and each one would have one or more artists among them, and the artists from different groups far and wide were bonded together in an association.

'The artists all aspired to greater perfection and there were always some whose work was admired above others and who gained a special reputation, which would bring artists from far away places to visit and spend time trying to learn from them.

‘Now there came a time in one generation when a particular artist gained a reputation above all others and earned the nickname of “The Seeing One” because when she painted (it happened she was a woman), the spirit of an animal leapt from her hand as if she was in its presence. There was an irony in her nickname because she began to lose her sight very early although for a long time no one realised because by then her family had taken on most of her domestic tasks and her painting continued to be so brilliant that people assumed her tendency to grope around and trip over must be to do with increasing clumsiness rather than loss of sight. Eventually, however, her daughter could no longer dismiss the evidence and asked her, “What has happened to your eyes that suddenly you seem to be blind.”

‘“All that has happened is old age,” she answered. “It is not sudden. My darkness has been gathering slowly for two or three years now.”

‘“But only last month you created a lion which was the nearest to perfection that you have ever done.”

‘“Yes,” came the answer, “I can still see the inner being. In fact I have found that it becomes clearer as this world fades.”

‘“That, I think I understand, but how can you paint the image on the stone if you can’t see your hand or the stone?”

‘The Seeing One shrugged.

‘“How can I know? If I succeed then my hand must be guided.”

‘When the news of the woman’s blindness reached other artists most were amazed and declared that this near miracle required a very special celebration, but some were sceptical, perhaps jealous, and made out the woman was a fraud, that her eyesight was only slightly weak, or even that it was a plot on the part of The Seeing One to enhance her prestige. There had always been a certain tension about women artists; some men questioned whether a woman could acquire the detachment needed to achieve true inner vision, and such questions helped stir up ripples of envy about The Seeing One's reputation.

'Gradually, the story of a blind artist spread far and wide attracting increasingly heated arguments which threatened to turn violent. When The Seeing One became aware of this she was disturbed and asked her followers to call everyone together so that she could speak to them. So, her followers called everyone to a place where meetings were held and when everyone had come they led The Seeing One into the centre where she began to speak. Unexpectedly, for an audience accustomed to long, elaborate speeches she was very brief.

'"Some of you accuse me of deceit. Others defend me and now you are close to fighting. Why? Are there not better ways to resolve disputes? Why not put this question to a simple test? Only I know what I can and cannot see, but tonight I will paint in the dark and then you will know. You may put guards nearby to be sure that no one smuggles a lamp to me."

'After some grumbling most people were moving to agree, until someone pointed out that the sky was clear that day and even before the moon rose the stars would give enough light to make the test doubtful. The arguments started up again until one of the artists who completely believed in The Seeing One got up and reminded the company that there were caves not far away that went back and back to places where no daylight ever penetrated. He suggested that the assembly go to the caves and that some of the doubters would take The Seeing One to a chamber beyond the reach of daylight, leave her alone there for whatever time she asked for and then return with lamps to see what she had done.

'His idea was greeted with enthusiasm and The Seeing One agreed, asking only time to arrange and prepare her colours. Some were afraid for her because a cave is a strange place where few people would want to be alone, but she assured them that she was now often alone in darkness and was not afraid. So, she was led into the cave and left there for a day, and in the evening everyone returned with flaming torches. They advanced slowly into the first chamber and then on through a narrow section and down into the chamber where The Seeing One had been left to work. As the first people entered there was a startled cry which, as others began to gather, turned to a ululation of joy. There, stretched across a suitable rock surface, the people saw an elegant reindeer, which seemed all the more impressive lit by the torches and surrounded by darkness. The Seeing One was sitting silently on the floor.

'Word of this remarkable feat soon spread around the whole territory and became a legend that long outlived anyone who had been present in the cave; a legend that inspired other artists to strive for new standards of perfection. Gradually, through the influence of the legend, there developed a new custom; the test of darkness, when the most highly reputed artists from the whole region would attempt to prove their inner vision and skill by painting in the dark. It became a great event when everyone would gather outside the cave to dance and sing in honour of the participants – "competitors" is not quite the right word because, although there was an element of rivalry, our notion of a numbered ranking was unknown. The climax was the moment when, at an agreed time, everyone crowded into the cave bearing a mass of lamps and torches that lit up for the first time the works of inner vision which had just been completed. It was in every sense a revelation.'

Radhika gave a little bow to indicate she was finished.

'I was convinced,' Sven said, 'until you got to the blind part. Painting in the dark! Would it be possible?'

'The idea of a blind artist reminds me of something…' Frieda said, but after a little thought had to admit she could not identify what it reminded her of.

Dieter suggested: 'Wasn't there someone who struck blind an artist so that no rival could commission him?'

'Not an artist, but an architect.' Zak corrected. 'It was the architect of St Basil's Cathedral. Ivan the Terrible so much admired it that he ordered the architect to be blinded to prevent him from making a similar masterpiece anywhere else.'

'But Radhika's story has it the other way round,' Mathew objected. 'Someone manages to create despite being blind. Is it possible? What do you think, Vernon?'

'I'm pretty sure I couldn't draw with my eyes shut,' Vernon answered promptly. And then added thoughtfully, 'But the idea has an element of the unlikely that could be right.'

'It's getting late,' Leandro said, 'and we have only one more story. Should we ask Magome to speak?'

Magome seemed prepared. He sat up, shuffled about to adopt an authoritative, story-telling pose and signalled that he was about to begin.

25

Magome's Story

'One day Buffalo and Lion had an argument about who was the most beautiful. As they couldn't agree they decided to ask the next animal that passed to settle the matter. It happened that the next animal was a mouse and the buffalo called out "Mouse, Mouse, I need you to do something for me." Mouse was very surprised that he could do anything for a buffalo but he stopped to listen and Buffalo said to him, "Mouse, you have to look at Lion and at me and tell us which you think the most beautiful." Now, as soon as Mouse heard the word "lion" and saw that Buffalo was accompanied by a lion he was terrified and squeaked, "No, no. I'm far too small. I can't see you properly to judge. You must ask a bigger animal…" and he disappeared under the root of a nearby tree.

'"It's true," said Lion in a haughty tone. "A mouse would hardly be able to judge. I see Gazelle coming this way. Lets ask him." But as soon as Gazelle caught sight of Lion he ran away, terrified.

'"There, you see," said Buffalo, "Gazelle took one look at you and ran away which proves he must think you are horrid-looking. I win."

'"Don't talk nonsense," said Lion. "You never told him what we wanted and as I usually eat gazelles it's not surprising he ran away. Now, I'll hide behind this bush and next time an animal comes along you talk to him."

'The next animal was Giraffe who listened patiently to Buffalo but he didn't like at all the idea of having to look a lion in the face so he said, "I'm terribly sorry, but I won't do. You need someone who can look from all angles but I have a dreadfully stiff neck today and just can't lower my head. So, I'd only be able to look at you from above and that wouldn't be fair." And he stalked off stiffly, pretending he couldn't move his neck.

'After a while they saw Jackal approaching, and Buffalo said to Lion, "You'd better talk to him as he's probably more afraid of me." Jackal knew Lion quite well but kept a bit of distance between them while they talked. When he had heard what Lion wanted he thought to himself, "Whichever one loses the contest will be very cross with me. This job sounds like an opportunity to either be gored by Buffalo or torn apart by Lion. I must find a way out quickly." He slunk back a bit and bowed his head saying, "Oh, Lion, this is a very great honour but, truly, I'm not worthy of it. I don't know anything about beauty. I must be very ignorant about these kind of things because I hear other animals saying that a wart hog is an ugly thing but it looks quite handsome to me. So, I'm really not your best choice. Why don't you ask Monkey? He's a clever animal. His opinion will be much better than mine."

'Lion was quite convinced as he anyway didn't have a good opinion of Jackal. So he said to Buffalo, "Jackal's idea was very good. Let's go over to the trees and find Monkey."

'They walked over to a big tree where they knew Monkey lived and they explained to him how Jackal had reminded them that Monkey was very, clever. Now Monkey was a bit flattered but he also knew that Jackal was cunning. He said to himself, "There's something odd here. Jackal's not usually one to flatter me. He likes to tell people he's cleverer than me. So why would he pass on to me the chance to play judge?"

'To gain time, he said, "Oh, Lion, oh, Buffalo, you are asking me to perform a very difficult task. I must think for a little about whether I am capable of it." He sat scratching his head in deep thought for a few minutes while Lion flicked his tail impatiently and Buffalo pawed the ground. That reminded him how both animals had awful tempers when roused and he realised why Jackal had suddenly become so modest. He jumped up and said, "I would like to help you but this isn't the best way to resolve your dispute. You are so much cleverer than I am. Your only problem is that you can't both see both of you. You can only each see the other one. Now you could judge very well for yourselves if only you could see both of you side by side as I see you. I have a much better idea than asking some other animal who isn't as clever as you. Why don't you go to Human? Human is always making pictures of animals that look just like the animals themselves. Go and ask him to make a picture of the two of you and you can use your very good judgment to answer your question yourselves."

'They were both vain enough to think secretly that they were cleverer than all the other animals, and so they thought Monkey's idea was very good. They went off to looked for a human and asked the first man they met to do a portrait of them standing side by side. They didn't tell him why they wanted this and the man didn't see any reason why he wouldn't grant their request. It would be a good opportunity to draw better pictures, he thought, because for once the animals would be cooperating instead of changing their position all the time and walking away when the picture was half done. So he said, "Yes, I'll do your picture as long as you agree to stand still just as long as I need you to."

'The man finished the picture and told Buffalo and Lion that they could move. They hurried to see what he had done and Buffalo quite liked what he saw, but, after staring at the picture, Lion started to roar furiously and looked round for the man who saw that he was dangerously angry and quickly climbed up a very tall tree.

'"You have made a fool of me," roared Lion, "What is this creature with small eyes and silly little ears and fluffy stuff all round its face? That thing isn't me. I am very grand and very fierce." Lion tried to climb the tree but it was too high and the branches too thin.

‘Buffalo was pleased at this and said, “It’s quite obvious now that I am the winner since now you yourself are upset to see what you look like. You must admit that I am the winner.”

‘“It’s a cheat and a lie,” roared Lion. “I don’t look like that.”

‘“You look just like that,” said Buffalo, “which makes me very happy, since if he’s got you just right then he must have me just right and look how strong and how beautiful I am!”

‘Lion had an idea. “But you aren’t like that picture at all. You can’t see yourself so you just don’t know. But look how thin he’s made your legs at the bottom and how huge your shoulders are. Now, if you were really like that your legs would just snap wouldn’t they? So, Human has cheated us.”

‘Buffalo looked again and saw that what Lion said was true. The thin legs looked very fine but wouldn’t be able to carry such a powerful body. The picture couldn’t be quite right. Then he too was angry and said, “Wait till I catch Human. I will toss him on my horns and ground him into the earth.”

‘The man shivering up the tree then saw that Monkey was up there too laughing his head off at them all, and the man grabbed his tail and said, “This is all your fault. If you don’t find a way to sort it out I’m going to pull your tail off so you and your children will never be able to climb trees again or mock us from up in the branches.”

‘Monkey was frightened and saw that he had to get rid of Buffalo and Lion quickly before Human pulled his tail off. So, he called down and said, "You are both cross-eyed. It is a very good picture of both of you and Lion doesn't look silly at all but very fine, as he always looks, of course. Now, if you don't agree why don't you call some other animals to judge whether the picture is any good?"

'Lion and Buffalo didn't really believe Monkey, because everyone knows he is not a reliable animal, but they decided to give his suggestion a try and went to call the other animals to come and look at the picture. While they were doing this, the man climbed down the tree, ran away as fast as he could and hid. But he wanted to know what the animals would say about his picture. So, he asked White Stork, who was a friend of his, to watch what went on and tell him. When the animals gathered to see what Lion and Buffalo wanted they were afraid to agree too much with one or the other and, instead, they said, "If these pictures are wrong maybe the ones this human makes of us are wrong too. Before we give our opinion of these ones, shall we go and look at some of the other paintings that are scattered around, which we never before bothered to look at?"

'They all went off to some rocks where they had seen men making pictures. Now, some of the animals found pictures of themselves and liked the way they looked; others found pictures of themselves and thought they did not look smart or grand enough; others didn't find any pictures of themselves at all and were cross about being left out. The ones who were dissatisfied talked louder and longer than the ones who were happy and, in the end, got all the others to agree that the reason these humans make pictures is to mock the other animals. Then they all got cross and decided look for Human and punish him. "I'll kick him," said a zebra. "I'll maul him," said a leopard. "I'll nip his nose," squeaked a mouse. "I'll gore him," bellowed Buffalo. "And I'll tear him limb from limb," roared Lion, who had quite forgotten the competition.

'White Stork flew off and told his friend what had happened and the man thanked him and ran far away, all the way back to his village where the animals wouldn't follow. When he got there, panting and dusty, everyone asked what the matter was and he told the whole story of how the animals had got in a rage about the pictures. His words worried the other people who liked to paint and, after they had discussed the matter carefully for a long time, they decided that they should never again let an animal see their pictures. That is why, after this, no one ever made animal paintings in the open where they might be seen but always hid them in the depths of a cave.'

Everyone laughed at this ending and Radhika remarked, 'I have a painter friend who'd love this. It's just how he thinks of critics.'

It was remarkable how our previous gloom had dispersed, but after a bit of lighthearted banter we remembered that it was late and we faced another night of shivering and listening to the little noises that might be cockroaches or the feet of terrorists.

26

The Border

It was good judgment to delay our crossing until the morning. We walked down to the river easily enough but found that it was too deep for us to wade across safely. Why the path led to that point was a puzzle until we saw on the other side an object that might be a raft, parked on the edge of the water, half hidden by reeds. The sight raised hopes that it might be the kind of basic ferry that consists of a raft attached to a loop of rope that allows travellers to pull the raft to their side and then pull themselves across. We searched along the bank and in the water for our end of a rope but could find none. Either there never was one or it had been removed.

While some of us were looking for the rope the rest unilaterally decided that it was time for a rest. It had been Tom's turn to carry Tara, and now Zehra took her from him, sat down and encouraged her to take some water. Mama Ulemu sat beside her approvingly and

Radhika joined them, lowering herself with a sigh of relief as she got off her painful ankle. I was one of the last to give up searching for the rope, convinced it had to be somewhere but, when I finally admitted defeat, I flopped down with the other three women. Since our swim in the little river on the second day I noticed that the women had tended to gravitate together and after Tara joined us we became quite a tight little group, except for Frieda who came and went and was often with Vernon. As we sat now on the river bank, I looked around and reflected that we had shuffled ourselves quite a bit since the first day when people were grouped more or less by whom they already knew.

As we now sat gazing across to the far bank there was a chilly atmosphere of demoralisation.

'Oh lend us your wings,' murmured Radhika, looking up at a kite soaring overhead.

'What a mess!" Dieter complained.

'Yes, you see the crossing is not possible,' announced Magome, as if no one had noticed. 'And we have come all this way.'

'Two days longer than we bargained for and now stuck!' Dieter continued. 'What do we do now. Go back? Fours days walking? With terrorists on the paths? Where's our leader?'

Leandro did not hear as he was still standing by the river conferring with Reece. Instead it was Frieda who spoke a little sharply: 'That is stupid talk, Dieter.'

'Okay, we have a problem,' Mathew intervened trying to sound calming, 'but Frieda's right that it's better to stay cool.'

‘And do what? Pray?’

‘Naturally I’m praying,’ replied Mathew mildly. ‘Maybe some of the rest of us are praying too.’

‘For a bridge to appear?’ Dieter mocked.

‘Dieter, couldn’t you just let us enjoy our rest?’ Vernon cut in with a kind of weary finality which seemed to end the conversation.’

For a while the only sounds were cicadas and occasional chirping birds.

Soon Leandro re-joined the group and suggested that we walk upstream hoping to find a better place to cross. There was a faint path along the bank so the going was easy, but our quest proved frustrating. Twice we came to a stretch where the water ran fast and shallow interrupted by numerous pebble bars so that it looked easy to ford. Each time, Leandro, testing it, got a good way across but was then stopped by much deeper channels. After the second of these places we stopped and discussed our options. One was to go back to our starting point where a couple of the best swimmers could swim over to investigate the raft, if it was a raft, and see if they could make it serve to ferry us across. The drawback was that if it was not a raft we would have wasted two hours walking there and back. Alternatively, we could walk on upstream in the hope of finding a better place or we could research the present spot for the least difficult route and tie cloths together like rope to help people past the bad bits. We decided on a combination. Leandro and Reece would research the present spot while Sven and Tom would walk on very fast for no more than twenty minutes to see if there was a better place. The rest of us settled down to wait.

As we sat idly it occurred to me then that if this really was the border, it was a big disappointment. Whenever the border had been mentioned, I had vaguely pictured a striped barrier, a flag, neat border guards, perhaps a little tea stall and people waiting impatiently to welcome us. Of course, if I'd spelt it out to myself, I would have realised that it would not be quite like that but I would still have expected some sort of reception, something to mark our passage from danger to safety, the end of our walk in the wilderness. And I certainly imagined we must be regarded as missing persons by now and the focus of international concern.

As the river got no shallower upstream we prepared to cross where we were by a zigzag route involving only two difficult channels. We managed these somehow, with the stronger people making a chain to pass across our bags and baby Tara and then stretching tight between them a rope of twisted cloth to provide something for others to hang onto. The worst bit was the last deep channel just before the far bank. We all got soaking wet and there were some tense moments, but eventually we were all across.

There was still no sign of people or habitation, which was not surprising as we had seen from above that there was a wide flood plain. We followed the riverbank back downstream, as we assumed that the place we had seen the possible raft was the usual crossing and so hoped to find a continuation of our original path. It took a long time, as the bank was a muddle of shingle, half-dried pools and patches of scrub. So, it was with considerable relief that the guess about the path proved right and we were able to re-join it and continue at a better pace.

Sometime in the early afternoon our path disgorged onto a real road and very soon afterwards we reached the huts we had seen from the far hilltop, which turned out to be, as we hoped, on the edge of the town. Soon, we were walking past a development of little brick houses and then through a more salubrious area of bungalows with gardens, where we attracted rather embarrassing attention from passers by. Our party of, by now, bedraggled strangers, many of them white, arriving on foot, must have been an unusual sight. We brazened out the stares and found our way to the town's only or main hotel, an unprepossessing, stained and cracked concrete block which promised, at least, a level of comfort somewhat above what we had become accustomed to. We were fortunate that our arrival did not coincide with any official delegation or major wedding so that there were just enough rooms to go round if most of us shared. We booked into them, as we had little idea what the onward travel opportunities would be, and then went to a rather rundown bar and restaurant for a late lunch. While we waited to be served almost everyone rushed off to find somewhere to plug in a phone charger. The man who had eventually, and rather reluctantly, checked us in assured us that there was a signal here and Wi-Fi.

27

Dispersal

After the meal there was a busy scattering of people in different directions as everyone was intent on making phone calls and reinserting themselves into normal life. It was a sudden change in behaviour that reminded me of a passage from *Alice Through the Looking Glass:* Alice has been walking through the forest of forgetfulness with her arms round the neck of a fawn, neither of them knowing or caring who or what they are. When they emerge from the forest Alice instantly recognises that she is walking with a charming fawn, but the fawn gives her one look and bounds away, alarmed to see a human child. It was a passage that always drew a tear from me.

Knowing I ought to follow the stampede for communication, I picked up my newly-charged phone and dialled my parents' number. It rang a long time before my mother picked up. When she heard my voice

I was expecting squeals of relieved delight but she only said, quite casually and even with a slightly peevish tone, 'Oh Nita, at last! I've been trying to get you for two days. Do you never turn on your phone?'

'Well, Mum, you know I don't always have a signal.'

'And I tried Skyping and emailing…'

'Okay, but we're in touch now. Was there a special reason you were calling?'

'Does your mother need a reason to talk to her daughter? It's over a week since we spoke.'

'I'm sorry, but actually, I've been away…'

'What, in term time? You never mentioned there was a holiday coming up. Anyway, I hope it was fun. Where did you go?'

I was beginning to realise that a coup attempt doesn't count as news in Britain, or at least not if the country affected is poor, African and not significant either as a perpetrator or target of jihad. Evidently, neither the coup nor the disappearance of a planeload of would-be passengers had been reported anywhere where my parents, who take the *Guardian* and are avid Radio 4 listeners, would have heard about it. My guilt about their supposed anxiety had been quite unnecessary. I hesitated and decided I didn't feel like recounting everything just then. So, I answered, 'Oh, just a forest area, for a bit of walking. Sort of place you'd love, Mum.'

'That sounds nice. Any swimming?'

'A bit. There were a couple of rivers. Not everyone could swim.' I pictured the morning's river and our struggle to cross the last of the channels.

'Are you sure that was wise? What about bilharzia?'

'They were fast flowing rivers, Mum. Anyway, how are you? How's Dad?'

She started telling me a convoluted story about some neighbours down the road who keep bees and how some of their bees had swarmed and it was a big drama. Then Tara, who had been sitting on my bed contently playing with my hairbrush, started to bawl.

'Oh, I can hear a baby,' said Mum. 'Whose is it?'

'It's just someone's baby I'm looking after for a bit,' I said, 'but I'd better go and see to her. Talk soon?'

'I'll ring you tomorrow.'

We said our goodbyes and rang off. I was left with a pang of loneliness. It was the first time I had deliberately misled my mother about anything of significance.

The police showed up a little later just after Zehra and I had been out to the nearby shops to buy Tara a few items of proper clothing and some nappies. Word of suspicious arrivals had evidently reached the authorities. The police were extremely officious and unpleasant at first, but Leandro and Vernon tamed them with an excellent double act of well-connected journalist and elderly celebrity. Soon they were sitting over beer with the officer in charge while the rest of us, after our papers had been scrutinised, were encouraged by gentle hints to leave them to it. Before retreating we had learnt two important pieces of news. The coup had failed and the rebels had been repelled from anywhere near Mufalenge. That meant it was safe to return, and also that our cross-country expedition might have been unnecessary. This last was not clear since there had been clashes between army and rebels somewhere near Mufalenge but, clear or not, the news was a cue for Dieter to complain.

The mood was friendlier later when we assembled in the bar to hear what had been arranged over beer. The police had ended up being very helpful. Those with valid visas or no need of them, that is Vernon, Leandro, Nyezi, Zehra, Jalal and Reece, could travel on the next day to the airport of the capital where they would have their passports stamped both in and out and from where they could all make their way home, or in the case of Reece, to his intended destination. Reece, in fact, had already gone. Once the passport stamping had been solved he had made his own mysterious arrangements and ordered a taxi. The others would leave the following morning. For those not equipped with the right papers the police and Leandro had cooked up a solution that would be convenient for us and trouble-saving for the police. It was fixed that we had never entered the country. The police would drive us to the nearest border crossing on a bus route from where a car ferry took traffic across the river. The guards on both sides were tipped off to let us through to a bus stand where we could get a bus back to Mufalenge.

'What about Tara?' I asked.

'You'll have to take her with you to Mufalenge,' said Leandro. 'Mathew, you must have contacts in the church who'd know the best way to find out about her family. Or Nita, your NGO might help.'

'Of course,' said Mathew, 'and there's an orphanage that could take her in the meantime – unless, Nita, you really want to look after her. You might find the school will object.'

'We'll see,' I said.

That night there was a celebratory meal. Tom and his mother had been reluctant to join but Leandro talked them round. Sven had done what he could for various blisters, cuts, and sprains and we all sat down freshly showered. Tara, looking splendid in her new finery, tottered from one to another of us clutching our knees and accepting little mouthfuls of chicken and chips.

After we had talked for a while about our journey, its discomforts, dangers and the destroyed village, the conversation reverted briefly to our stories and which of our inventions were more plausible. During a moment's lull Mathew, who had been poised to say something for some time, asked Vernon, 'Do you and Nyezi have to be so doubtful about everything? You keep on saying things like, "It might have been… We have so little to go on." Aren't there some finds that tell you something definite? Like, if you find a burial where the dead person has been buried with his possessions, isn't that clear proof that the people believed in an afterlife?'

'Not necessarily,' Vernon replied enigmatically.

'Why not? What other reason could there be?'

'What about a kind of extreme death pollution?' suggested Radhika. 'A belief that death somehow attaches to a dead person's things?'

'Indeed, that could be a reason,' Vernon agreed, enthusiastically acknowledging a new idea. 'Or it could be that personal possessions have no meaning or value except for their owner. In that case it's logical to bury or burn them with the owner's body. That could be likely in a world where people have few possessions and ones that are easy to acquire, things that people make for themselves or for those near them. It could be part of a ritual acknowledgment that a person no longer exists, no longer needs possessions either here or anywhere else.'

Vernon let this sink in a moment before continuing.

'The burials you're probably thinking of, Mathew, where we know or assume grave goods are for an afterlife, are from long after people took to farming. The shift to farming must have changed the meaning of possessions as people started to own, or claim to own, the sources of life: land and water. It wouldn't be sensible to project ideas backwards from then to the time before agriculture when the idea of a person owning the sources of life might have been unthinkable.'

Mathew did not look convinced but made no comment. It was Frieda who spoke next.

"I do think your profession is a little strange," she said to Vernon with a smile. 'You spend your lives scratching away hunting for small clues and compiling vast amounts of data, even though you admit it tells you very little and there is every reason to think you will never know anything important about the people who left you those little clues."

'Hang on!' exclaimed Vernon. 'That's a big claim – we'll never know anything important!'

Nyezi laughed but said nothing.

Dieter looked hard at Vernon and said, 'It's more or less what you keep telling us yourself. If you don't agree when someone else says it, tell us what important things you know.'

Vernon shrugged. 'To me hundreds of small things are important; like how many people lived together, what they ate, that they knew how to make a needle and presumably had a use for one...'

'But even there you are guessing,' objected Frieda. 'You find a needle but are left saying, "presumably" they could sew. I've heard historians say they envy anthropologists who can ask the people they study direct questions, but at least the historians' people almost speak to them though their letters and diaries, ledgers, chronicles and, of course, literature. Isn't it a little perverse to pick a topic where the evidence is quite so thin?'

'Some people might think you made an odd choice with your bugs,' he retorted.

'Indeed, they do. People are prejudiced against bugs. Especially my kind of bugs. Pretty butterflies or friendly honey bees would be more acceptable.'

Leandro challenged Vernon: 'Frieda's work's a diversion. And anyway it has obvious uses. But yours?'

It was Nyezi who promptly counter-attacked: 'You know quite well what Vernon could say and you agree really, don't you? That's why you've had us all telling these stories. You know the questions matter even if we can't answer them. To know what we can become we need to know who we are, and our long past must hold clues – if only we could read them.'

Vernon thanked Nyezi for defending him and added with a shrug, 'Or maybe we just happen to have found this way of making a living and we like it. Now, I'm noticing empty glasses. More beer anyone?'

Frieda said she would pass, as she was tired and thinking of going to bed. That prompted one or two others to say they might do the same. The party was evidently about to break up and there was a sudden quietness round the table. Perhaps we were all thinking, as I was, that this was the moment of goodbye. In the morning those of us returning to Mufalenge were leaving early when not everyone would be up. We had become strangely close in our few days together and parting felt sad. In the short term, Leandro, Mathew and I would be in touch over the fate of Tara, and the others had asked to be emailed about the outcome. Over dinner there had been talk of an online reunion sometime, but I thought it unlikely that everyone would be there.

About the Author

D M Dickinson is a documentary filmmaker and writer. Her previous books are nonfiction and include two on film and politics. *Rogue Reels and Cinema and State.* She lives in London and has worked for extended periods in Africa and India.

Matador